# THE MAGIC SHELL

## A SEVEN KINGDOMS TALE 6

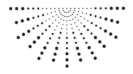

## S.E. SMITH

# ACKNOWLEDGMENTS

I would like to thank my husband Steve for believing in me and being proud enough of me to give me the courage to follow my dream. I would also like to give a special thank you to my sister and best friend, Linda, who not only encouraged me to write, but who also read the manuscript. Also to my other friends who believe in me: Julie, Jackie, Christel, Sally, Jolanda, Lisa, Laurelle, Debbie, and Narelle. The girls that keep me going!

And a special thanks to Paul Heitsch, David Brenin, Samantha Cook, Suzanne Elise Freeman, and PJ Ochlan – the awesome voices behind my audiobooks!

– S. E. Smith

Paranormal Romance
THE MAGIC SHELL: SEVEN KINGDOMS TALE 6
Copyright © 2019 by S. E. Smith
First E-Book Published December 2019
Cover Design by Melody Simmons

Summary: A fisherman makes the discovery of a lifetime only to be transported to a magical world where he joins forces with a powerful princess to save not only her kingdom, but the entire Seven Kingdoms.

ISBN: (Paperback): 9781944125950
ISBN: (eBook): 9781944125943

{Romance (love, explicit sexual content) | Action/Adventure | Fantasy (Urban) | Fantasy Dragons & Mythical Creatures | Contemporary | Paranormal

Published by Montana Publishing, LLC
& SE Smith of Florida Inc. www.sesmithfl.com

# CONTENTS

# CAST OF CHARACTERS

**Isle of the Elementals:**

King Ruger and Queen Adrina LaBreeze
Gem Aurora LaBreeze – Princess of the Elementals
Wayman – High Chancellor to the King and Queen and Gem's Cousin
Samuel – the King's Personal Guard

**Isle of the Monsters:**
Empress Nali

**Isle of the Pirates:**
The Pirate King Ashure Waves

**Isle of the Giants:**
King Koorgan – Presiding King of the Giants
Gant – half Giant/half wizard, Koorgan's friend and Second-in-Command
King Samui and Queen Malay of the Isle of the Giants: Koorgan's parents and the original rulers of the Giants

**Isle of the Dragons:**
Drago – King of the Dragons

**Isle of the Sea Serpent:**
Orion – King of the Isle of the Sea Serpent
Magna – The Sea Witch

# SYNOPSIS

Ross Galloway is more than ready for a new life away from Yachats, Oregon. All he needs for his plans to fall into place is a little money and a lot of luck. He gets his break when he discovers something out of this world on one of his dives – a real-life mermaid.

His plans to cash in on his discovery don't work out quite the way he'd planned when the mermaid gives him an unexpected gift – a magic shell. Swept overboard by the spell contained within the shell, Ross surfaces in a strange, bizarre world.

Princess Gem LaBreeze is an Elemental, a powerful species that can control the elements. Transformed to stone to protect her from the evil threatening the Isle of the Elementals, she is awakened by a man from another world – a stranger who is as arrogant and uncouth as he is unpredictable.

Gem and Ross, forced together in a desperate race against time, learn that opposites can attract and that sometimes the roughest surface hides the tenderest of hearts. Can an unlikely hero and a lone woman survive the traps set to stop a destructive alien creature that has been unleashed, or will the Isle of the Elementals fall back into the ocean and disappear beneath the waves forever?

# PROLOGUE

**Isle of the Elementals:**

**Three years ago**

The corridors of the Crystal Palace were alive with the residents' early morning activities, but Princess Gem Aurora LaBreeze was only mildly aware of the hustle and bustle as she strode down the magnificent corridor. Her mind was preoccupied with what had happened at the meeting that she had attended the night before. She was still trying to process everything that she had seen and learned before she presented it to her parents.

The most shocking part of the meeting had been seeing the Dragon King! The last she'd heard, Drago had cloaked the entire Isle of the Dragons in a deadly fog after the Sea Witch turned his family and all of his subjects into stone. In the years since, he had never reappeared – until last night when he had attended the meeting of rulers and representatives – all because a woman from another world had come and changed everything.

Nali, the Empress of the Monsters, had claimed that this woman, Carly

Tate, had initiated a chain of events that would bring the kingdoms together to destroy 'the alien creature'. That's what they were calling the evil entity who had taken over Magna the Sea Witch and forced her to terrorize the Seven Kingdoms.

Given that her free will had been enslaved for centuries, the others attending the meeting had voted to spare the Sea Witch's life if possible. Gem had been the lone dissenter. She did not yet know why her parents had been so adamant that she must vote for Magna's death no matter the circumstances, but she was sure they would not be happy when she informed them of the decision made.

Gem's expression softened when she saw the old guard standing protectively outside a set of splendid double doors. The guard bowed his head in respect and opened the door to the conference room as she approached. The beautifully carved doors told the tale of the Elementals. Reaching out, she lovingly glided her fingers along the surface of one door.

"Your parents are expecting you, Princess. A word of warning, though, the High Chancellor is with them," the guard murmured.

"Thank you for the warning, Samuel," Gem replied with a rueful smile.

"My pleasure, Lady Gem, I'll also have a word with the young guards about their manners – again. I think you've broken more than one heart with your arrival this morning alone without even realizing it," Samuel replied with twinkling eyes.

She glanced over her shoulder and saw several young guards staring at her with crooked grins. She chuckled and shook her head when one of the young men flushed and smiled broadly at her. With a stern glare from Samuel, the group quickly retreated in different directions. She returned her attention to the old guard.

"New recruits – I swear I go through this every time. This is their first time in the palace. I wanted to give them an opportunity to see the daily workings. You'll be all they talk about the rest of the day!" he said as he shook his head in rueful amusement.

"I do it just to keep you happy. It gives you something to chastise them about," she teased.

Gem was still smiling when she entered the conference room. Samuel had been her parents' personal guard for as long as she could remember. She had spent countless hours quizzing him about the different scenes depicted on the doors, and he had spent the same number of hours enthralling her with the history of the Isle of the Elementals. He had also taught her how to use a sword.

The smile on her lips faded when she saw the High Chancellor talking with her parents. She didn't care if the man was her distant cousin, she didn't like or trust him. Ever since they were children, she had avoided Wayman whenever she could. She did not understand why her parents had chosen to promote him to such a powerful position after his parents' untimely deaths.

As she crossed the room, Gem pulled her attention away from Wayman and focused on the flash of amusement in her mother's eyes. Queen Adrina LaBreeze raised an eyebrow and Gem forced a smile in response, nodding politely to the High Chancellor as his calculating gaze swept over her. She nonchalantly locked eyes with the distasteful man, her serene smile never wavering, and as usual, a spark of anger flared in her cousin's eyes before he looked away. The bastard had a long way to go before he would ever intimidate her.

"Welcome home, darling," her mother warmly greeted.

Gem stopped in front of her mother, and lightly kissed her on both cheeks before she did the same with her father. Her father held her arms a fraction longer before he released her. She ignored Wayman. If there was one way to get under her cousin's skin, it was to deny him the attention and power he craved.

"Did you have a good journey?" her father quietly enquired.

Gem bowed her head in agreement. "It was interesting," she casually hedged.

She glanced at Wayman. She would speak to her parents about the meeting later. Her gut was telling her to be extremely cautious about sharing information in front of her cousin. If her parents decided to inform Wayman about where she had gone and what was discussed, that would be their decision.

"I was not aware that you had left the Isle, Gem. I believe there is still a decree in place that severely restricts all travel," Wayman commented pointedly.

Gem shrugged. "My travel was sanctioned by the King and Queen, Wayman. I saw no reason to share my movements with you," she retorted.

Wayman's eyes narrowed and he pursed his lips before he softly said, "As our Majesties wish, of course. " He inclined his head deferentially toward King Ruger and Queen Adrina.

Gem looked at her mother when she felt a touch on her arm. It was only then that she realized that she was clutching the hilt of her sword. Her cousin always pulled a desire out of her to see if his blood ran red or black.

"Wayman, we will meet with you later. We would like time alone with our daughter," her mother graciously stated.

Wayman stiffened at the dismissal. He gave her mother and father a curt bow and shot her a speculative look. Gem casually turned and watched as he silently walked toward an exit concealed behind a large tapestry on the left side of the room.

She waited until she heard the door open and close before she turned back to her mother. Her father chuckled and Gem huffed.

"I don't know why you put up with that worthless piece of—" she muttered with a disdainful sniff.

"Sometimes it is better to keep those you don't trust close to you," King Ruger replied with a sigh.

Gem looked at her father with surprise. "I didn't realize you felt the same way," she said.

"He has always been very much his father's son, I'm afraid," her father replied.

Her mother released an inelegant snort before she changed the subject. "What did you discover?" her mother asked.

Gem looked at her parents with deep concern. "The others are going to try to capture Magna. Nali warned against killing her. Drago—"

"Drago!" both of her parents exclaimed at the same time.

"The Dragon King has returned?" her father demanded.

Gem nodded. "Yes. There was a woman with him. She is not from our world," she expounded.

"Not…" her mother began, tilting her head with sudden interest.

"Tell us about her," her father urged.

Gem thought about Carly Tate. "She is so sweet and gentle, and she looks a great deal like someone of our world might, though she seems to have no magic of her own. Nali said her presence has initiated a series of events that will save our world – as long as Drago does not kill Magna," she said.

Her mother's brow creased. "Nali has the Goddess's Mirror. She would know," she acknowledged.

"But why would she tell them not to kill Magna? Surely if the Sea Witch is dead, the kingdoms will be safe once more," her father argued.

Gem shook her head. "Nali said that it is not actually Magna doing these things, but an alien that has taken over her body. Nali thinks Magna is fighting against the creature," she shared.

"A creature like—" her mother murmured, looking at Ruger with a worried expression.

"What is it?" Gem asked.

"What does this alien creature look like?" her father quietly enquired.

Gem frowned. "I don't know. Nali said it fell from the sky, and she saw a black shadow moving over Magna. Why? Do you know what it is?" she asked.

Her parents looked at each other before they turned their attention to her again. Her father reached for her mother's hand and squeezed it.

"Come with us," her father quietly instructed.

Gem nodded and silently followed her parents out of the conference room. She was surprised when they exited through the door that led outside. She paused and looked behind her. She had a nagging feeling that they were being watched.

"Where are we going?" she asked as she turned back to her parents who were descending the steps out into the central gardens.

Her mother paused on the steps. "It would be better if we showed you," she softly answered.

Gem, intrigued by her parents' behavior, followed them down the steps and onto the path. The interior gardens consisted of numerous smaller, themed gardens contained within a larger one. Set within a vast maze were individual walled gardens covered in ivy, each with a theme of its own.

Her mother loved the rose garden while her father preferred the desert cacti. Her favorite was the night-blooming garden. She followed them through the maze. The tall hedges that lined the paths continuously changed. The only constants were the eight walled gardens.

It had taken her years to learn the minute nuances in the energy field that would guide her through the maze to any of the gardens that she wanted to visit. She looked down at her hands. A rueful smile lit her face when she realized that she had unconsciously lifted her palms to feel the pulses of energy.

She slowed her steps when she felt an unfamiliar pulse leading to the left. Looking up, she saw her mother pause and give her a sad smile.

"What is it? It feels almost like…," She shook her head, unable to pinpoint the emotion.

"Grief, pain…," her mother stated.

Gem looked at her mother in confusion. "Yes," she replied.

Her mother held out her hand. Gem walked forward, slid her hand into her mother's, and they rounded the corner of the maze. Her breath caught in stunned disbelief when she saw her mother's favorite garden crawling with wild, thrashing vines covered with sharp thorns.

"What happened?" Gem asked in a barely audible voice.

"It is best if we are inside the garden before we speak of this," her father replied.

Adrina reached out and murmured to the vines. She lifted her hand and one of the runners wrapped around the tip of her finger. The sharp edge of a thorn brushed across the pad and drew blood. Only when the vine recognized her mother did they retreat far enough to create an opening to the door.

Ruger stepped forward and waved his hand in the air. A crystal key appeared. He reached up, took the key, and fitted it into the door. Gem couldn't help but wonder what was hidden behind the door that was so important to protect.

She paused and looked at her father in concern before she followed her mother into the garden. Her eyes swept over the interior. She had not been inside this garden since she was a child.

Gem stepped forward, her mouth agape at the beauty of the twin trees wrapped around each other in the center of the garden. She had never seen trees like this before. They looked like two bodies embracing each other. The larger tree was wrapped protectively around the slightly smaller one. Wild climbing roses grew around the thick trunks, but there was only one rose blooming. The rose was a dark red with veins of black running through it, and it was larger than a dinner plate. She stepped forward to touch one of the petals. A low gasp slipped from her when her father grabbed her wrist to stop her.

"Don't touch it," he warned.

"Why? I don't understand. Why is it so cold in here?" she asked, pulling her hands back to rub her arms.

"It is the dark shadow that Nali mentioned," her mother replied in a soft voice.

"The dark shadow...," Gem looked at her mother, then her father before she returned her attention to the rose. "Are you saying the alien creature that has taken over Magna is here? How? When? Why didn't you tell me sooner?"

Gem watched as her parents exchanged glances, their expressions filled with a wealth of conflicting emotions. "Yes, the alien creature is here, but it is not the same one that has taken over Magna," Queen Adrina began. "Not long after the end of the Great War, King Samui and Queen Malay of the Isle of the Giants came to us, seeking help. They had been sailing near the Isle of the Sea Serpent when an object fell from the sky. The meteorite damaged their ship, and it took several days to repair. While they were stationary near the crash site, Samui found a piece of the meteorite – and it was alive. It slid under his skin and began consuming him. Malay immediately sought our help," her mother explained.

"But... why? Why not return to their kingdom?" she asked, looking up at the entwined trees.

"Malay is my sister – your aunt. Giants must marry outside of their kingdom. Malay fell in love with Samui when they met as teenagers," her mother shared.

Gem looked at her mother in surprise. "Why did you never tell me about her?" she demanded.

"You were very young when Malay and Samui arrived. The alien creature was growing rapidly, spreading throughout Samui's body. Nothing we did could stop it. In a matter of days, we realized that it was taking over his mind," her mother quavered, her voice filled with anguish.

Ruger stepped up to Adrina and wrapped his arm around her waist. "We were in this garden, trying different forms of magic to pull the creature from Samui, but the creature was too powerful. Samui started to fight us. Malay tried to stop him. When she touched him, a portion of the creature spread to her. Your mother and I knew that if we did not stop them, they would cause devastating damage and loss of life – not to mention the possible spread of the alien infestation to other Isles. I invoked an ancient spell of the Elders and turned them into trees," he explained.

Her mother waved a hand at the rose. "Recently, the vines began growing and we noticed the spread of darkness through the petals of the rose. We believe the creature has grown strong enough to seek an escape – into a new host," she said.

Gem looked at the flower. The black had almost overtaken the red in the short time they had been talking. The movement of the soft petals was almost hypnotic. She had to curl her fingers into a fist to resist the temptation to reach out and caress it.

"Why hasn't it spread from Magna?" she asked in a distracted voice.

"Magna is a very powerful witch. The creature uses the power of the people it occupies. I think Magna sensed the danger and was able to bind the creature to herself so that it could not spread, very similar to what Malay and Samui did when they used their combined magic to seal the creature within themselves when they transformed into the trees. If we could find a way to pull the creature out and contain it, we may be able to save Malay and Samui, but we need to do it soon. If not – if not – we may be forced to end their lives in order to kill it because we cannot let it spread," her mother explained in a slightly uneven voice.

"If such a creature is as powerful as you say, perhaps it would be better to allow it to live." Wayman's deep voice caused all of them to turn to face him directly.

"What are you doing here?" Ruger demanded.

Wayman's lips twisted into a sardonic smile. "What I should be doing, your Majesty, acting as your advisor," he replied.

Gem watched with growing unease as Wayman stepped into the garden. His eyes were not on them, but on the transformed figures of Samui and Malay. She stepped in front of him, stopping him in his tracks.

"You were not asked to be here," she snapped.

Wayman looked at her. "I can think of no other place that I should be but here," he stated with such grim certainty that Gem wondered if this was about more than a determination not to be left behind. A movement near the door of the garden pulled her attention away from Wayman for a moment.

"I apologize, your Majesties, I tried to stop him from following you, but I lost him in the maze," Samuel said in a breathless voice.

"I will handle this, Samuel," Ruger reassured the old guard.

"Wayman, don't!" Adrina cried in alarm.

In the space of an instant, disaster unfolded before Gem's eyes. Wayman reached out with both hands and grabbed the now completely black rose. His body stiffened, and his eyes widened. Black tentacles wrapped around his arms and rapidly engulfed his body.

Ruger quickly pulled Gem and Adrina away from Wayman. He pushed them behind himself.

Adrina grabbed his arm. "Change him, Ruger," she advised.

Wayman turned and looked at them. His face was hard and his eyes were now the color of a moonless night. A snarl curled his lips, and he lifted his hands towards them.

"I am free!" Wayman's lips moved, but the sound coming from him was rough, hoarse, cold, and odd.

Her father started to respond, but before he could, long, sharp spears of black shot out from Wayman's palms. Samuel, quick as lightning, jumped in front of her father. The spears pierced the beloved guard's body, lifting him off the ground where he dangled for a moment before the alien in Wayman's body tossed him aside like a child's discarded toy.

Gem reached out to her friend as her horrified cry filled the air, "No! Samuel!"

"Run!" her father yelled.

Gem stumbled when her father turned and pushed her and Adrina through the doorway of the garden. He wasn't far behind, and once through the doorway, he slammed the door and muttered a hoarse command. Stepping back, they watched as the vines that had protected the garden began to transform.

"It is spreading," her mother said in a grief-filled voice.

Gem grabbed her mother's hand and began pulling her back along the path. The creature *was* spreading – and the vines were greedily reaching for them. She turned to look at her father when she realized that he wasn't beside them.

"Father?" she cried.

Ruger stepped back. Adrina held out her hand to him. His eyes were focused on the growing black mass. Gem hissed when the walls around the garden suddenly crumbled and Wayman stepped through the tangle of vines – a contemptuous sneer on his lips.

"This is what true power feels like, Ruger. You should have embraced it instead of trying to lock it away," Wayman hissed.

*"Water freeze, hold him still,"* Ruger ordered.

Gem watched as water droplets formed around Wayman's body before turning to ice. Inside the ice, she could see the black tentacles wriggling. Her hand tightened on her mother's arm when the vines reaching for them began to retreat. Hope swelled inside her until she caught the malicious gleam in Wayman's eyes.

"Father, watch out!" Gem shouted.

She pushed her mother to the side and jumped forward. Her arms wrapped around her father's waist knocking him off of his feet as the ice shattered, sending shards of sharp ice crystals flying toward them. Rolling to her knees, Gem pulled a blade from her boot, and threw it. The blade went deep into Wayman's shoulder, knocking him back several steps.

Rising to her feet, she helped her father up before turning to her mother. They needed to get out of here. The creature screeched with rage and reached to pull the blade out of Wayman's shoulder.

"Mother!" Gem cried in alarm.

Adrina was lying on the ground, a long shard of ice protruding from her side. A dark stain of blood spread outward from the wound, turning the light green material of her gown to a deep red. Gem knelt and cupped her mother's cheek.

"Ruger, you must – we must – the Elders' spell. It is the only chance to save our kingdom now," Adrina whispered.

Ruger wrapped his hand around his wife's and nodded. "Gem, you must seek help from the other kingdoms. If they can kill the creature in Magna, they may be able to do the same here. If nothing else, warn them about what is to come," her father ordered.

With a frown, Gem looked from her mother's pale face to her father's. "I won't leave you! Samuel...," she began.

Her father reached out and grabbed her arm. "You are our only hope now, Gem. I will place traps along the way to slow the creature down if it should break free, but you must not let the creature touch you. Go!" her father ordered in a stern voice.

Gem wanted to protest but her father was already chanting the spell. She rose to her feet when she saw the mist forming around him. The creature – and Wayman – shot a tentacle toward her parents. Gem instinctively lifted her hands and closed the maze in front of them. As she backed away, she saw her father help her mother to her feet. Her mother's voice blended with her father's as they recited the enchant-ment together.

Fear and grief engulfed her. The black vines broke through the hedges, ripping them from the ground and tossing them aside as they hungrily reached for more hosts to inhabit. Wayman's features were shifting from wood, to stone, and back to flesh.

She continued to back away – afraid to turn her back lest the creature attack her. Her eyes widened with horror when her parents' voices faded as the mist enveloped them and their bodies melted away. The silencing of their voices did not stop the magic they had unleashed, however. The rolling fog grew thicker and began to expand.

"Join me, Gem, and accept your destiny," Wayman called.

Gem shook her head in denial, her voice frozen with fear. Backing up toward the edge of the first turn in the maze, she spun on her heel and fled when the dark grey mist of the Elders' magic continued to spread, rolling in a thick wave over the ground. Behind her, she heard Wayman's howl of rage, and she knew that the creature was fighting the magical power that was slowly overtaking the Isle.

Fear spiked inside Gem as she ran up the path leading to the towering cliffs of the Isle of the Elementals. Her cries of warning remained mostly unheard. Whatever spell her parents had released was closing in from three sides of the Isle.

The creature's shrieks grew louder and more frustrated, but Gem couldn't stop to turn around and see what was happening. Using the power of the wind, she created a tunnel ahead of her and let it sweep her along just before the mist cascaded over her former position.

All she could hear now was the wind whipping past her ears, her hair swirling so wildly that she could hardly see. The magic required a lot of her energy. She wouldn't be able to keep it up for long.

The tunnel was barely wide enough for her to pass through, but it created a vortex that would open a portal and send her from one side of the Isle to the other. At one point, her elbow brushed along the mist. Her arm tingled and began to fade. She tucked her arms close to her side and away from the mist.

One by one, the people around her disappeared as if they had never existed. The black shadow tried to capture the residents, but its long tentacles passed through empty air. The rolling cloud of the ancient spell was erasing everyone that she had ever known, loved, and fought beside, but Gem was not afraid of the spell sweeping over her home. Her father knew what he was doing – and whatever the consequences of this powerful magic, they were far better than the alternative.

A part of the creature slipped into the vortex, she could sense it, a hungry dark force concentrated in a black tentacle. Gem ran faster, refusing to be overwhelmed by her terror. She needed to be smart if she was to save her people. Her muscles were protesting, and her lungs were straining painfully. She couldn't run forever.

Ahead of the mist now, she released the power of the wind, huffing a ragged breath of relief as the spell stopped draining her energy. A giant fallen tree blocked her path up ahead and she raised a trembling arm, palm facing outward, and focused.

The tree dissolved into millions of particles. Gem ran through the glittering pieces. Once she was past the spot, she closed her fist and the particles reformed.

Breathing heavily, she glanced over her shoulder when she heard the sound of shattering wood. The dark talons of the creature cut through the dead tree, ripping it in two. Gem turned around and continued toward her destination.

Up ahead, she could see an opening in the trees and the unmistakable shape of etched stone. Hope blossomed inside her – just a few more yards and she could escape. The sound of her breathing echoed in her ears, and she could see her breath in the suddenly chilled air. Out of her peripheral vision, she saw the mist of magic closing in on her. Time was quickly running out.

Once she reached the edge of the cliffs, she would transform. It was too dangerous to do so yet. If the ancient magic caught her, she might never be able to reform again.

"Mine. Come to me," the icy form behind her demanded.

Gem ignored the command and pushed herself harder – running as fast as she could. Around her, the trees bent to give her passage before straightening in an attempt to slow the malevolent creature chasing her. The black tentacles greedily grasped for her, but she stayed a few steps ahead.

Several yards ahead, she could see the stone gazebo standing like a silent sentinel above the cliffs. The stones of the Elders would give her some protection from the creature. She cried in relief when her foot touched the first intricately carved stepping stone.

The stones glowed under her feet. She was almost free. She grasped the stone pillar and stepped into the safe haven of the gazebo, gasping for air. Her heart thundered in her chest as she turned and took several steps back from the black tentacles that curled around the outside of the gazebo.

"You cannot touch me here, creature! Nothing is powerful enough to break the spells of the Elders," Gem declared, hoping that what she was saying was true.

"Your magic cannot stop us. It will give us power. With the power of your kind and the magic of the Sea Witch, we can take over many worlds," the entity said in a hypnotic tone.

Gem turned around as the black shape encircled the gazebo, cutting off her only means of escape. A wave of intense sorrow washed over her. There was no one to help her. Her father had hidden the Isle of the Elementals from the world long ago to keep the other kingdoms safe, but it had also isolated them. If she couldn't get off this Isle, no one would ever come to save them.

"You will never use me," Gem proclaimed with growing determination.

The creature continued to encircle the gazebo before forming into a shape that was heart-wrenchingly familiar: her mother. Overwhelming grief filled her, but so did another emotion – rage. She pulled the short sword at her waist free of its sheath and took a step forward.

"So much power. You can undo what the others have done. I can sense the power inside you. Power you do not even know you possess," the entity that looked so like her mother said in a whispery voice.

"Power that you will never control," Gem passionately vowed.

"But I will," the creature replied.

Gem watched with growing horror and fear as the creature slowly advanced. The stones under the alien's feet began to glow. Streams of color rose up to wind around its body. The outer skin of the alien bubbled and sizzled as if it were being cooked until a thin crust formed. The crust turned to ash and fell away, but the alien appeared unfazed by the damage being wrought and continued moving closer to her. Raising the short sword, she sliced through a tentacle when it reached for her. The creature screeched in outrage but didn't back away from her.

One tentacle after another greedily shot forward trying to capture her within its evil grasp. Behind the creature, Gem could see the magical mist her parents had invoked rolling ever closer to them. She stumbled backwards when the magic reached the gazebo.

Gem knew it was too late for her to escape from her Isle. She and her people were doomed. Her only hope was that the battle against the Sea Witch was successful. If it was, there was a chance that Drago, Orion, and the others would know how to defeat the entity that Nali had seen in her mirror.

*Please, Goddess, if you hear my plea, send someone to help save my people and the Seven Kingdoms,* she silently begged – and miraculously, a voice responded.

"You cannot disappear, Elemental, you are needed," the Sea Witch vowed.

Gem's eyes widened in shock, and she stared at Magna's ethereal form as it suddenly appeared behind the black shadow. Then she watched in horror as the Sea Witch opened her hand and directed her magic toward Gem. Over the thunderous pounding in her head, Gem heard the alien's howl of rage as Magna's spell rapidly spread through her body, turning her flesh to stone.

*All is lost,* she thought in despair before the world faded around her.

# CHAPTER ONE

**Off the coast of Yachats, Oregon:**

**Present Day**

Ross Galloway steered his trawler out of the marina and through the narrow inlet. Once out of the no-wake zone, he pushed the throttle forward. Even at full speed, it would take him an hour or more to get out to a good fishing spot.

He looked toward the shoreline and noticed a woman sitting on the beach. She raised her hand. He didn't know if she was waving or just shielding her eyes from the glare of the sun. He recognized her as Mike Hallbrook's sister, Ruth. For six months, she had been plastering the town with Missing Person flyers, looking for her brother.

Mike's disappearance had almost sealed Ross's fate as a suspected serial killer. It was only Mike's bizarre reappearance, his assertion that Ross wasn't a killer, and some photos that had saved Ross from ending up on death row. Just because he had a history of having problems with authority and he knew everyone who was missing didn't mean he was some kind of ax murderer. Still, once a rumor was started, it was hard to end it.

"She probably thinks I'm out dumping another body," he muttered as he turned and stared out at the sea through the salt-crusted windshield.

He needed time to think. Ross hated to admit it, but lately he'd just felt lost. It was a feeling that didn't sit well with him, especially since he wasn't the type who usually took shit too seriously.

He patted his pocket for his cigarettes before he softly cursed. He'd sure picked a hell of a time to quit smoking. If he hadn't been on his old fishing trawler alone, he might have considered downing a couple of bottles of beer, but that luxury would have to wait until he got back to shore.

And it would only be a couple of beers – he was too afraid of ending up like his old man to drink more than two. Alcohol did strange things to certain people. Some could drink it and never feel a thing. Others could have one beer and be under the table. Then there were those who became more affectionate when they were drunk. Those kinds of people Ross could deal with, but fuck if he'd ever hang around another mean drunk like his dad. He shook his head and pushed the thought of his old man out of his mind. The son-of-a-bitch hadn't died soon enough as far as he was concerned. Let the Devil deal with him now.

A little over an hour later, he carefully picked his way to the back of his fishing trawler. He kept the uneven outline of the rocky coast on his starboard and the beautiful Pacific ocean to the port side. He didn't bother to set out an anchor since he planned to do some drift fishing. The first thing that he needed to do, though, was to check the nets to make sure they weren't tangled. He looked up at the rigging and decided it wouldn't hurt to climb up to double check the top lines as well.

It had looked like one of the lines was twisted from below. The last thing he wanted to do was to risk the line getting caught when he pulled the nets back in. It would be a bitch to fix, especially if the sea became rough as it tended to do at the most inopportune moments.

Half an hour later, he finally saw what the problem was, fixed the roller, and untwisted the line. Holding onto the rope, he stared out at the shimmering water. It wouldn't stay clear and sunny like this for long. By mid-afternoon, the cold, moist air coming in off the water would hit the warmer surface of the land, and a fog would roll across, a thick blanket of it that would be almost impossible to see through.

He drew in a deep breath, held it for several seconds, and released it. It was no wonder he was restless, given the recent events. There had been a rash of disappearances over the last couple of years and most eyes had turned to him as the most likely cause. People assumed he was like his old man – or even worse.

Ross had known Mike Hallbrook, the Yachats Detective that had disappeared a good six months back. They had played pool and drank beer down at the local pub on occasion. There wasn't much else to do around the area except fishing and hiking.

Hell, he had even known Carly Tate and Jenny Ackerly. It was kind of hard not to know everyone around when you lived in a town the size of Yachats your whole life. He had even dated Carly a couple of times.

*Man, that was a mistake,* he thought with a shake of his head.

Carly had to have been the clumsiest woman on the face of the Earth. She damn near burnt his boat down and emasculated him – all in the same day. He felt sorry for any guy who got mixed up with her. She was nice – and cute – but she needed to come with a death and dismemberment insurance policy.

Ross snorted. Funny how being accused of murdering three people paled in comparison to everything else going on. His mother had died a month ago. Her death had left him feeling like he was in a vacuum as he tried to deal with his grief and all of the paperwork and details involved with her estate. Taking care of all the bills, meeting with the lawyer, and arranging her burial had left little time for him to do much of anything else, including fish.

And if the death of his last living relative hadn't been enough to make him question his life, seeing a real-life mermaid had. For a moment, he let his mind drift to that strange day just a few short months ago, smirking to himself at the irony of it all. He'd never believed in fairy tales as a kid, and here he was now, thirty years old, and he'd gotten to meet a mythical creature from another world. Hell, it was like something out of an old Twilight Zone episode, only this one didn't look like half a fish. Magna the mermaid had been one exotic woman – one with gills.

Shaking his head, he reached into his pocket, out of habit, looking for a piece of candy to help curb his desire for a cigarette. He frowned when he felt something besides the change he had shoved into his pocket. Wrapping his fingers around the object, he pulled it out and looked at it.

He chuckled. Ross doubted the mermaid liked him very much, but she'd given him this gift the other day at the restaurant. It was a shell she'd found right there on the table, same as all the others, but the look on her face when she'd handed it to him…

*"Good luck on your journey,"* she'd told him, and god, her voice was haunting, like she'd had the pain, trials, and tribulations of a hundred lives. Yeah, it was just a stupid shell, but she had given it to him, and it made him think of her and the mysteries surrounding her. He wondered what her world was like.

The thought had no sooner formed in his head than the world suddenly shifted around him. Ross shook his head to clear the ringing in his ears, and the rope he was holding suddenly vanished. With wide eyes, he swayed unsteadily, and desperately reached for something to hold onto when the trawler rocked as if a rogue wave had battered it from underneath. For a brief instant, his body was weightless as he was tossed through the air and over the side. His loud curse was cut off when he hit the icy cold water and sank as if he had his weighted dive belt strapped around his waist.

The weight of his water-soaked clothes pulled him even deeper. He struggled, kicking upward, but no matter how hard he tried, it felt as if his feet were embedded in concrete. Above him, he could see the hull of his boat. He stretched his arm out and splayed his fingers, hoping that by some miracle, a tow line had fallen overboard. As he stared up at his boat's hull, the brief thought that he needed to clean and paint it flashed through his mind. Then the inane thought was replaced by a more sobering realization – he was about to join the list of missing people.

*Only there won't be anyone who gives a damn when I don't come back. Ah, hell, I don't want to die like this,* Ross thought as he sank, struggling, into the inky blackness.

# CHAPTER TWO

**Isle of the Giants: Seven Kingdoms**

**Present Day**

"Are you sure you want to travel alone?" King Koorgan asked for the third time.

His Second-in-Command, Gant, looked up from where he was securing his bag and raised an eyebrow. "Don't you have someone else to bother? What about Lady Ruth, isn't she missing you? You've only been married a day. Shouldn't you still be locked away in your bedroom enjoying marital bliss?" he dryly asked.

"I told him that you were a big boy and could handle this without his help," Ruth commented from the doorway of Koorgan's office.

Gant stood up straight and smiled. "Considering he is usually the one that gets lost and needs rescuing, I think that is an accurate observation," he chuckled.

Koorgan glanced back and forth between Gant and Ruth with an exaggerated scowl. "You are both aware that I can hear you, right?" he dryly retorted.

"Of course," Ruth teased, sliding her arm around Koorgan's waist.

"I will do everything in my power to find your parents, Koorgan," Gant promised.

Koorgan soberly nodded. "I know you will. The mirror did not show anything the last time we tried, but it might not hurt to try to retrieve it," he suggested.

Gant grinned. "If given a chance, I'd do it just to teach Ashure that pirates aren't the only ones who can steal," he said.

Ruth shook her head. "Just be careful, Gant. Koorgan told me what happened to LaBluff," she reminded them.

Koorgan's expression turned grim. "Yes. He is so irritating that it's easy to forget... but perhaps it would be better to give Ashure some space, my friend," he cautioned.

"I promise to be careful," Gant vowed.

"I should go with you," Koorgan said.

"No, you should not. The kingdom needs you, and Ruth needs you. Plus, I am a better tracker than you are – and far more charming when it comes to retrieving information," Gant retorted.

"Oh yeah? Marina is still tickled pink about your use of those golden collars," Ruth mockingly reminded Gant.

Gant blanched at the not-so-subtle sarcasm. "I did what I had to do to return you to normal. I would do it again to protect you, my Queen, and Koorgan and the kingdom," he stubbornly declared.

"And we both thank you for your help despite the method you used to achieve it," she acknowledged.

Ruth stepped up to him and pressed her hand against his cheek, then lightly kissed his other cheek. Humor swept through him when he heard Koorgan growl in disapproval. He grinned at his King.

"You can kiss the other side if it makes you feel better," Gant jested.

Koorgan chuckled and wrapped his arm around Ruth's waist. "Get on with you. Let me know the moment you discover anything," he requested.

"I will," Gant responded, lifting his bag to his shoulder.

Gant bowed his head before striding for the door. The knowledge that King Samui and Queen Malay of the Giants were still out there filled him with hope. Now all he needed to do was find the hidden Isle of the Elementals and discover what was going on.

*Whatever it is, surely it can't be any more difficult than keeping Koorgan out of trouble,* he thought with a chuckle.

～

Ross desperately struggled to break free from whatever was pulling him down. An image of the warning signs at the beach popped into his mind – rip currents. All the experts said not to fight the current, instead swim parallel until you are out of it.

Forcing himself to relax, he began swimming parallel with the current, ignoring the weight of his clothes and boots. He would need them to help retain as much heat as he could. The last thing he wanted to do was to freeze to death before he got to shore. In the back of his mind though, he thought it strange when he realized that the cold wasn't bothering him as much as it should have. Hell, he felt almost warm! The only thing he could think of was that he was already slipping into hypothermia and just didn't register it.

Finally he felt the current's pull ease enough that he could break free. He watched the small air bubbles escaping his lungs float upward. His chest was burning, and he knew that if he didn't surface soon, he was going to drown. Kicking his feet, he swam upward, following the bubbles. He was thankful that he had kept fit over the years, even if he did smoke. Fishing was hard on the body if you weren't in shape. He had learned that valuable lesson from watching his father struggle to do some of the simplest things before dropping dead of a heart attack at forty-nine.

He saw a glimmer of light on the ocean's surface and it renewed his adrenaline-fueled determination to continue.

*I'm going to live, damn it,* he thought as he rapidly rose toward the surface.

He broke through the surface of the water, gasping fragrant air into his burning lungs. Frowning, he turned in a slow circle, looking for his trawler. How had it gotten so blasted late? He glanced up and was stunned to see a myriad of stars shining above him.

"What the fuck? There's no way I could have been under water that long," he gasped, still trying to catch his breath.

Ross kicked his legs to keep his body afloat as he glanced around again for his boat. All he saw was endless ocean. Fear swept through him and the soundtrack from Jaws began playing to a rhythm that matched his pounding pulse. What the hell was going on? Swallowing, he searched the star-filled sky again and felt pure terror.

"This isn't right," he muttered, staring up at the unfamiliar configurations of stars that looked so large he felt like he could almost reach up and touch them. "What the hell is going on?"

He stared in amazement as not one but two moons rose on the horizon. He began to pant when he saw a land mass about a quarter of a mile ahead of him slowly come into view from the light of the moons. Glancing around him one more time, in the futile hope of seeing his trawler in the moonlight, Ross finally gave up and started the long, grueling swim toward the only hope for survival that he could see.

"This better not be a mirage," he muttered as he did the breast stroke.

The vague thought that he was dead and had finally made his way to Hell didn't sit well with him. Neither did the fact that if there were a

Hell, he would probably be stuck with his dad for the rest of his immortal existence in a never-ending purgatory.

All sorts of thoughts came to him as one minute stretched to two, then ten, then half an hour, then an hour. He continued to swim toward the land that was his only salvation. Exhaustion pulled at him, making his arms and legs feel like jelly. At times, he flipped onto his back and floated to conserve his energy before striking out again.

Ross grimaced when his life flashed before his eyes. He was honest enough to admit that he wasn't very impressed with it. He hadn't been all that bad, but he hadn't been all that good either.

A near-death experience was a hell of a way to be forced into reflecting on some of the less than stellar choices that he had made. He thought about his life from the first time he'd gotten into trouble with the law at the age of eight for shoplifting to the countless women he had been with simply to relieve the emptiness of his life.

"One good thing about kicking my smoking habit is that I can, at least, do this," he reflected in a tired voice.

Tears of relief actually burned his eyes when the waves pushed him closer to the beach. "Finally!"

Striking out with his last surge of energy, he kicked until his left foot hit the sandy bottom. Putting his feet down, he stumbled forward on trembling legs. He fell several times before he was able to stand up.

He lifted a trembling hand and wiped off his face. Brushing the moisture out of his eyes to clear his vision, he pushed through the thigh-deep water. His legs finally gave out on him when he had taken almost a dozen steps onto the beach. Sinking down to his knees, he rolled until he was lying on his back and panting, staring up at the brilliant night sky

"If this is hell, it has to be the most beautiful place I've ever seen," he whispered.

The gentle breeze was warm, as was the beach of tiny pebbles under him. He'd thought it was sand at first, but it was slightly coarser. The moons were higher now. One was slightly behind the other, making it appear as if one was full while the other was a waxing gibbous.

He spread his arms out, grabbed a handful of the pebble-sand, and rubbed it between his fingers. The feel of the warm grains helped him truly register that he was alive – in a strange world – but alive. His eyelids suddenly felt like someone was pressing their fingers against them. He tried to blink away the fatigue, but it was too much and his body relaxed against the beach as it molded around him.

"Just for a few minutes," he murmured as his eyes closed with a will of their own. "I'll just close them for a few minutes. "

He smiled. This might not be Hawaii, but it was balmy. A sigh slipped from him as he released his hold on consciousness. The thought that maybe he'd ended up in Heaven instead of Hell passed through his mind before the empty void of exhausted sleep overtook him.

The bright sunlight felt like someone was shoving a dozen needles through his retinas. A low, hoarse groan sounded in his ears. His throat was dry, and his mouth felt like he had been licking a salt block.

*Oh yeah, that light is definitely about to burn a hole through my eyelids and directly into my brain. Must have had some lousy beer because I know I didn't drink enough to have a hangover,* he silently groaned before he remembered he had wanted a beer, but he hadn't actually drank one.

Rolling onto his side, he froze when he heard the soft crunch under him. Cracking his eyes open, he stared in disbelief at the long beach. He groaned again and allowed his head to fall back to the ground as he realized he wasn't having a bad nightmare.

"Shit," he muttered under his breath and opened his eyes again.

Pushing himself up onto his knees, he wiped his hands on his damp jeans and stared at the landscape around him. He rose unsteadily to his feet and turned in a slow circle until he was once again facing the sea.

A sea that looked suspiciously as if the water was falling off the edge of the world. A humongous infinity pool.

He lost his balance and staggered when he shook his head too quickly. Staring down at the multi-colored beach to steady his swimming head, he swallowed. A sudden feeling of suffocation rushed through him, making him feel warm – very warm.

Shrugging out of his jacket, he dropped it to the ground and grabbed the hem of the beige knit sweater he was wearing under it. He ripped the knitted wool over his head and dropped it on top of his coat. Now clad in his plain black short-sleeve t-shirt, he tilted his head back and enjoyed the cool early morning breeze coming in from the water.

He ran a hand over his forearm. His arms were muscled from years of hard physical work. A long tattoo ran up one arm, a reminder of a moment of weakness. It was a sea dragon that curled around his arm from his wrist and up until its head came from his back and stared out from his shoulder. He had been sixteen and mad as hell at the world – especially his father.

Ross took a long breath and shook his head. Reaching down, he grabbed his sweater and jacket and turned back to look up at the cliff. His clothes were already drying in the warm breeze.

Rotating his head to pop his neck, he stared at the tall rock face. There was a staircase cut into it. Striding toward the steps, he decided it was best to find out where he was and how he was going to get back home. He shrugged away any misgivings as he began the long climb. After all, it wasn't like he was the type to run from trouble.

*Not that it'd matter if I was the type to run, trouble always seems to find me wherever I go,* he thought as he looked up at the long line of steps to the top of the cliff.

# CHAPTER THREE

Twenty minutes later, Ross was cussing up a storm again, this time very loudly. He was hot, unbearably thirsty, and his thighs and calves were killing him. This cliff was like a Stairmaster from hell. He looked up and released a long wheezing hiss. A low groan slipped from him when he realized he was only about half way up and still had a long way to go before he reached the top.

*Maybe I'll be lucky and there will be a water fountain at the top of the cliff, or better yet, a beer kiosk,* he thought with a bitter sigh of frustration.

Turning and pressing his back against the rough rock, he gazed out at the ocean again. His eyes widened in trepidation, and he forgot about everything when he suddenly realized that he really wasn't on Earth – at least not any Earth that he recognized. The evidence was so overwhelming he could barely speak.

"Aw hell, Ross. You really are in deep shit this time. The question is – how deep a pile will it be?" he murmured to himself as he studied the edge of this world.

From this vantage point he could see the water from the ocean as it poured over the edge like Niagara Falls, not that he had ever seen the

Falls in person, but it's what he imagined it would look like. Beyond the well-defined edge was sky – blue, radiant sky filled with large, white fluffy clouds. Wiping a hand down his face, he clutched his jacket and sweater against his side as his legs gave out and he slid down the rough wall. He sat on the stone steps and took in the mesmerizing scene for a moment as his mind grappled with what he was seeing. The one thing that he kept coming back to was that what he was looking at was stunningly beautiful.

"Maybe this *is* Hawaii. They've got waterfalls and cliffs. That's it!" He snapped his fingers. "I had some kind of meltdown, developed amnesia, thought I was on my boat, and went for a swim. I'll get to the top of the cliff and discover I'm really on Waikiki. Bars, babes, and palm trees will surround me, and I'll be living the dream. Yeah, and maybe I'm not really having this conversation with myself," he muttered before he looked at the edge of the world again.

He didn't want to think about the fact that he knew he wasn't really having a mental holiday from reality, that he'd seen two moons last night, that he could feel the hard stone under his ass, or that he knew damn well that he had been off the coast of Oregon in the middle of the day.

He looked back up to the top of the cliff. If he was going to find answers, he needed to start somewhere, and at the moment, going up was the best solution. With a shake of his head, he wearily rose to his feet and began climbing the staircase again, thinking that this had better be a one-way trip because he sure as hell didn't ever want to see these stairs again, much less climb them!

Three-quarters of the way up to the top, he stopped for a moment, rested his hand on the rock face, and moved his right leg to work out the cramp in his calf. Rubbing his hand on his jeans, he suddenly remembered the shell that Magna had given him. He'd been holding it when the world had turned crazy. Maybe there was a link between the shell and his unexpected trip. Reaching into his pocket, he pulled out the contents. There was no shell, only a pocketful of change.

Returning the change to his pocket, he patted his other pockets to see if the shell was inside one of them. He looked out at the water with a growing sense of dread when he didn't feel it.

"Shit a gold brick," he cursed, knowing that he must have dropped the shell when he fell overboard.

He clenched his jaw in determination. If there was one witchy-mermaid who could give him a magic shell, then there had to be another one somewhere. That is – if he wasn't dead and in one of Dante's levels of purgatory. The only other explanation he could come up with was that he must have been transported to Magna's world.

"Ha ha ha. When I find my way home, I'll let that Sea Witch know that her little joke wasn't very amusing," he muttered with a bit of snark.

He ignored his protesting leg muscles and returned his focus to the last section of steps. If there were stairs, there had to be people, he reasoned. Someone was sure to know where he was and how he could get back. He just hoped they didn't turn him into a frog or some other disgusting creature before he had a chance to ask them.

It took Ross another ten minutes to get to the top. He leaned over and placed his hands on his knees, breathing heavily. He stiffly straightened and wiped a hand across his sweaty brow.

*God, I hate stairs,* he thought.

Placing his hands on his lower back, he looked around. There was a path that led into the trees. He winced when he turned, his aching muscles protesting all of his recent physical activity. From the view at the top, he could see that beyond the water falling off the edge of the world, it looked like the whole damn world was floating on a cloud.

"Where the hell did she send me – the top of the beanstalk?" he muttered.

This was crazy! He ground his teeth together and adjusted his sweater and jacket. He scanned the path ahead of him. He would follow it, but he sure as hell wouldn't do any singing and dancing. There would definitely be no skipping.

"I swear if I run into a tin man, a scarecrow, and a cowardly lion, I'll use the tin man as a stove, stuff the scarecrow inside him, and cook the damn lion for dinner – and don't even get me started about the flying monkeys and the green bitch with a chip on her shoulder," he loudly warned the gently swaying palm trees. "I'm about done with all this fantasy crap. "

He almost told his imaginary audience to give him a good Stephen King plot but thought twice about it. What if this place did give him what he requested? Did he really want some psychotic clown over a bunch of singing Munchkins? He absently patted the pocket of his shirt.

"I wish I had a cigarette," he said.

He waited for one to magically appear. When it didn't, he sighed. He hoped that his lack of a wish-granted cigarette meant there wouldn't be any magically appearing serial killers either.

He ran his hand along the curved, intricately carved stone handrail at the top of the staircase. While he appreciated the artwork, he knew he was really procrastinating. He sighed again, rolled his shoulders, and stepped onto the narrow path that led away from the cliff.

"So much for that nice Waikiki bar filled with beautiful wahines and lots of nice ice-cold beer," he muttered, still hoping against hope that there was a water fountain nearby because his throat was sore and his mouth felt like it was filled with the pebbled-sand from the beach. So far things weren't looking too promising. The path leading into the woods looked more like the ones at the State Park back home.

He walked along the narrow path, turning in a tight circle at one point to stare up at the trees. His eyes warily scanned the canopy above for any sign of danger. He swallowed hard when he thought he saw one of the trees move – like really move! He shook his head, deciding that he must be so dehydrated he was beginning to hallucinate. Surely trees – even fantasy ones – couldn't walk?

He shook his head and refocused on the path ahead of him. Beautiful flowering plants in a rainbow of colors lined each side. He stopped to examine one that had dark red leaves and brilliant yellow flowers. In the center, a light mist floated up like the little misting fountain he had given his mom last Christmas.

He waved his fingers through the mist. A startled yelp slipped from his lips when tiny white filaments greedily reached up to wrap around his little finger. He jerked his hand free and shook it when he felt his skin begin to tingle. Rubbing his hand on his shirt, he warily stepped back onto the path.

"You're definitely not in Yachats, Ross. Keep your hands and feet away from the man-eating plants," he muttered, turning in a circle before making sure he was in the center of the path.

He continued along the leaf-strewn track until it suddenly forked. One way narrowed and led deeper into the forest. It looked dark and menacing while the other widened and seemed almost welcoming. He frowned and tilted his head. Through the thinning trees along the wider path, he could see some kind of man-made structure in the distance.

"Dark and scary, or bright and airy – now that's a hard choice," he chuckled with a wry grin.

Turning to the right, he followed the wider, brighter path. He slowed down when he noticed that the trail had become a series of stepping stones. Curious, he knelt, brushing some of the leaves off of the first stone.

He lightly ran his fingers over the surface of it. He rose back to his feet and moved to the next one. He repeated the process for each stone when he noticed that they all had a different pattern on them. The first thing he noted was that each stone was a piece of art with complex designs chiseled into them. If they had been gold, he would swear he had landed in Oz. The second thing he noticed was that each one glowed a different color. The one he was currently standing on was emitting a soft yellow light.

He stood up and stepped back and forth on the stones. An amused grin curved his lips as the colors changed each time he stepped on them. The colorful display moved across the spectrum – from yellow to blue to orange, and more. The changing colors kept him captivated for several minutes before they faded and didn't reappear when he stepped on the stones again.

He glanced back, half-expecting them to have disappeared before he looked up. The pillars of a large stone gazebo stood in front of him, set out on a cliff ledge. But it wasn't the gazebo's ornately carved pillars or even the beautiful view that captured his attention this time.

What captivated him was the stone statue of a young woman – a beautiful young woman – that was situated in the center of the gazebo. She had been partially hidden by one of the thick pillars.

She looked fragile as she held out her hand in a silent plea for help. The expression on her face conveyed horror, fear, and sorrow. In a small way, she reminded him of the ash-encased figures from Pompeii that were frozen forever in their final moments of life.

"What happened to you?" he whispered, slowly walking forward until he stood in front of the statue. "Why would any artist want to leave you here?"

He slowly walked around the statue. The finely carved detail had to be up there with Michelangelo's work, though he couldn't help thinking it would have been better if she was unclothed like the Venus statue his high school teacher had on his desk. He'd never cared much for Michelangelo's David, but damn, if the artist had sculpted this lovely lady, he was pretty sure he would have gotten an "A" in art class.

Unable to resist, he reached up and touched the tip of her outstretched hand. He jerked slightly when he felt a strange and powerful electrical zap. It was similar to the static shock he got at the grocery store when he was in the freezer section and wanted to get something out of the case. He started to pull away when the statue's fingers suddenly moved and clung to his hand.

"Holy…" he bit off what he was going to say when he felt warm skin against his.

He instinctively reached out and grabbed the falling figure when the statue became a warm, supple woman in his arms. He gaped in disbelief as the woman took a deep, shuddering breath. His arms cradled her as he carefully guided her to the ground when her legs gave way.

Breathing deeply, Ross carefully turned the soft body in his arms so that he could see her face. Dark eyelashes lay like crescent moons against pale, almost translucent cheeks. The sudden urge to run like hell swept through him as he stared down at the serene face. For some crazy reason, he had an intense, insistent feeling that when she opened her eyes, he might be well and truly ensnared. As if with one look, he would belong to her.

Just when he thought that she might be asleep, she opened iridescent eyes of pale lavender. It felt like he was drowning all over again, only this time it was in the lavender depths of the woman's eyes. He idly thought that he had never seen eyes the color of hers before, and he wondered if she was wearing colored contacts. He focused on her lips when she licked them.

*I should have run while I could,* he thought when he felt a consuming jolt of attraction and a strong desire to kiss her.

Pushing that crazy thought to the side, he steadied her when she struggled to sit up. He was trying to think of what to say when she suddenly twisted around to face him. His gaze was still glued to her lips. If it hadn't been, he might have seen her fist *before* it connected with the tip of his nose. His head snapped back as pain exploded through his face. Before he knew it, he was lying flat on his back.

A loud groan and a string of curses poured from him as he grabbed his offended nose and glared up at the woman through watery eyes. She now stood looking down at him with wide, furious eyes. He pulled his hand away to see if there was any blood. There was none, but it still hurt like hell. Fortunately, he didn't think she'd broken it.

"*Why* did you do that?" he demanded, tentatively touching his abused nose. "You know what? Just forget it. I don't know who you are or what you are, but you need to work on your greeting style," he snapped, climbing to his feet.

"Are you a minion of Wayman or that black shadow?" she hissed, raising her hands out in front of her.

He looked at her with a confused expression. "Listen, lady, I don't know who this Wayman or black shadow is, or even where I am! All I know is I was thrown off my boat, washed up on the beach down below, and I've climbed a shitload of steps to get my nose busted by some fancy mannequin or whatever you are. You were a piece of rock not more than a minute ago, for crying out loud! What's with that? Can someone please just tell me what the fuck is going on?" he shouted, glancing up at the sky as if expecting an answer.

Muttering a string of curses that would have drawn a rebuke from his mother for their creativity, he warily kept an eye on the woman watching him with a suspicious expression while he rubbed his aching nose. Finally he took a deep breath, closed his eyes, and slowly counted until he felt more in control. The only thing the yelling and cursing did was remind him of how much he needed a drink.

*Screw water or beer, I could use something with a little more kick to it,* he silently groused to himself.

Opening his eyes, he took another deep breath and prepared himself to listen – and believe – whatever fantastical story she would probably tell him. Turning to face her, he blinked, his mouth dropping open in shock, when he noticed she was completely transparent now. He shook his head, and closed his mouth, running his hands down his face. He patted his cheeks a few times to make sure he was awake. He even opened and closed his eyes several times to clear his vision.

"Ah, do you know that I can see through you?" he whispered in a hoarse voice. "Like right through you... and are you floating?" Just when he thought this world couldn't get any weirder, it did.

The woman smiled in disbelieving amusement. Ross swore that if she started laughing at him, he wouldn't be responsible for doing something crazy, like jumping off the cliff. Hell, if he was dead, it wouldn't matter anyway.

"Yes, I am aware that I am not in a solid form," she replied, tilting her head and staring back at him with continued suspicion.

"Are you...," he swallowed over the lump in his throat. "Are you a... a ghost?"

She scowled and shook her head. "Of course not! I would have to be dead for that," she replied, pursing her lips together.

Rubbing a trembling hand along the back of his neck, he swallowed again. He hadn't thought ghosts could fold their arms and look so superior, but.... Another feeling of dread coursed through him, threatening to put him back on the ground.

"Am *I* dead?" he asked.

Ross took a step back when she floated closer to him. He warily watched every movement that she made. Her nose wiggled, and she licked her bottom lip. Of course, that unconscious movement caught his attention.

*Damn, but she has some sweet lips on her,* he distractedly thought.

He wondered what she would do if he leaned forward and traced the movement of her tongue with his. It might almost be worth a broken nose to find out, he mused. He was so focused on imagining kissing her that he was startled when she materialized and pressed one of her slender fingers against his shoulder.

"You don't feel dead," she observed before she leaned forward and sniffed. "You don't smell dead, either, so I guess you aren't," she added with a wry smile.

"Well, that's a relief," Ross snapped, suddenly feeling like a fool. "Can you please tell me where I am?"

The woman raised an eyebrow at his question and took several steps back. He returned her unblinking, suspicious gaze. She wasn't classically beautiful, but there was something about her that irresistibly pulled his eyes back to her face. Of course, he had never met a living statue before, but he had never met a mermaid before either and look where that had gotten him – a one-way ticket to Fantasyland!

"You are on the Isle of the Elementals. How did you get here?" she asked with a frown. "My father enchanted the Isle in an attempt to protect us from the Sea Witch and the black shadow that resides inside her, but she and the creature still found us. "

"Your father *enchanted*…," Ross started to say before he shook his head. "I can't even begin to tell you how weird all of that sounds. Like I told you, I was on my trawler. The sea was calm, and I touched this shell a mermaid gave me – now I sound as weird as you do, *I know* – but all of the sudden I was tossed…." His voice faded as his eyes widened and then narrowed. "This Sea Witch, her name wouldn't by any chance be Magna, would it?"

The woman's eyes turned a darker shade of purple, and her expression was absolutely livid. This time he saw the blow coming. He instinctively ducked her swing to wrap his arms around her.

An explosive curse slipped from his lips when his arms went right through her body. He stumbled forward a couple of steps. Before he could catch his balance, a well-placed foot against his ass sent him sprawling in an inelegant heap inside the gazebo, and though he tried to roll to his feet, her boot caught him in his side with her full strength behind it. He grunted at the familiar pain, and for a sickening moment he flashed back to how he'd felt under his old man's boot. Ross twisted onto his back, his face a dark thundercloud, and glared up at her. This bitch had no idea the hornet's nest she'd just made angry.

"Tell me where Magna is and how to kill the black shadow," she demanded.

"Forget it, Lady. You can find your answers from somebody else," he snarled.

She hissed with fury at his angry retort. Ross reached for her ankle when she started to move again. He muttered a low curse when his hand passed right through her. He gritted his teeth in frustration when she reappeared just out of reach.

Alright, so the direct approach wasn't gonna work. How did a guy protect himself from someone who could disappear? His eyes swept over the floor. The only thing within reach besides leaves were a few sticks.

His fingers wrapped around the largest one. He wouldn't hit a woman, but he wasn't opposed to using the stick to keep a bit of distance between them if necessary – though he wasn't sure that it would work. He rolled to his feet, holding the short, fat piece of wood in his hand. He had barely turned to face her when her fist suddenly connected with his stomach, knocking the wind out of him. He parted his lips and he took a wheezing breath.

*So much for that idea,* he thought as the branch fell from his limp fingers. He pressed his hand to his stomach. *Damn, but for someone so small she sure knows how to fight dirty and she sure as hell knows how to throw a powerful punch.*

He barely lifted his other hand in time to catch the fist that was aimed at his nose again. Her eyes flared with emotion and he saw a glimpse of fear flash through them when he wrapped his hand tightly around hers. Unfortunately, he hadn't considered the fact that he had left himself wide open for the knee that connected with his groin.

He blanched when unimaginable pain flooded him. He released her hand and staggered back several steps before sinking to his knees on the ground. His mouth opened and closed like a fish on land.

"Damn it all to hell. That was dirty," he groaned out between clenched teeth and closed his eyes. He clumsily leaned back against the side of the gazebo holding his affected area in his hands. He gritted his teeth and kept his eyes closed as pain pulsed through his body. Part of him wished that she would just get it over and done with. At least if she killed him the pain would be gone. A shudder ran through him as the throbbing slowly began to ebb.

"Don't touch me or – or I'll hurt you even worse," she warned.

He cracked one of his eyes open before he opened the other. She was standing several feet from him with her arms up and her fists clenched and ready. If he wasn't in so much pain, he might have actually laughed when he saw that she suddenly bit her lip and looked down at him with wary uncertainty.

"I can assure you that this is about as much pain as I ever want to feel." He released a shuddering breath and shook his head. "You know, I've only had this happen to me once before. I thought Carly was bad when she accidentally nailed me, but this – this is way worse. Unless you plan on killing me and putting me out of my misery, I'd just as soon call this as bad enough," he informed her in a strained voice laced with residual pain.

"Wait – are you saying you know Carly Tate?" she hesitantly asked.

# CHAPTER FOUR

Ross closed his eyes again and leaned back against the pillar. His balls still hurt, along with a few other parts of his anatomy, but he was trying to relax. He had closed his eyes again mainly because he didn't want to see if she would follow through on his invitation to kill him. He wondered if dying would reset this whole adventure and cause him to wake up back on his boat.

He finally forced one eye open, then the other one when he heard her hesitant question. Dark spots still danced before his eyes. Did he know Carly Tate? This woman obviously did; he hadn't mentioned Carly's last name.

He took a slow, shallow breath – breathing through his nose and releasing through his mouth as he tried to push the pain away. There was no way in hell he was ever getting close to that one-woman wrecking crew again if he could help it. He stared back at her with a wary expression.

"If we're talking about the same Carly Tate from Yachats, Oregon, then yeah, I know her," he muttered.

She was silent a moment before she spoke again. "You are not much of a fighter. I'd have thought the Sea Witch's warriors would be better – if I'm right and she did send you," the woman observed with an piqued sniff.

"She didn't send me! Okay, well, maybe technically she did, but that doesn't mean that I'm one of her *warriors*. I am definitely *not*. I have only met her a couple of times, but she didn't seem like an evil over-lord to me. Unlike *you*, she also didn't try to beat the shit out of me for no reason," he pointed out in a dry tone.

"The Sea Witch is evil. She is the one who turned me to stone!" she snapped.

"Yeah, well, the Sea Witch I met seemed like she just wanted to be left in peace," Ross said, slowly releasing his injured groin so that he could gingerly rise to his feet.

"Then why did she send you? *She* sent you to me, and a friend of Magna's is an enemy of mine," Gem accused with a pointed glare.

"I don't know! Maybe she didn't even mean to. She gave me a magic shell. I was holding it when I was pulled overboard. That doesn't seem like the best way to send in enemy troops. That just sounds like a fucking joke, and a bad one at that!" he retorted.

"A shell? Why would she give you a magic shell? Are you from the same Isle as Carly? I've only seen a couple of your kind here," she said.

She raised her hands in a braced defensive motion when he moved. Ross lifted one of his hands, palm out, and gingerly stepped away from her, imagining lightning or some shit about to shoot out of her palms. He decided keeping more than a little bit of distance between them would be a good idea.

"My kind? Listen, lady, I'm not from any Isle. I don't even know what you're talking about. I'm just a fisherman from Yachats, Oregon. I was on my boat, minding my own damn business, when I got pulled over-board and ended up out there." He pointed to the water far below. "I'm lucky I didn't drown! I swam ashore, climbed way more steps than I wanted to, and found you all hard and tragic looking. I touched you – which, let me tell you, was a huge mistake that I'm currently regretting – you came to life, and since that moment, my nose has been almost broken, my ass was kicked, and my nuts were kneed so hard I'll be lucky if I ever have any kids – not that I want any – but still, *I'd* like to be the one to make that decision. So in case you can't tell, I'm having a really piss-poor day, and I'd rather be back in Yachats where at least I can be miserable in a place where *I DAMN WELL KNOW WHAT IS GOING ON!*" he finished, his voice getting louder with each word.

He didn't care that he was shouting by the time he finished his long-winded rant. He was so fucking thirsty, tired, hungry, hurting, and he badly wanted a cigarette and a beer to rustle up some small bit of happiness in his miserable fucking life. He turned his back to her, scooped up his jacket and sweater, and started back down the path toward the beach. He'd actually found something worse than those god-damn stairs, and if he never saw her beautiful face again, it'd still be too soon.

Gem watched the man who had freed her from her stone prison walk away. Guilt surged through her. Why *had* she attacked him without giving him the chance to explain himself? She'd felt so much danger buzzing against her skin, but unless appearances were very deceiving, which they absolutely could be, that man was more lost and confused than she was.

Gem warily looked around the gazebo. Now that she wasn't fighting for her life, she noticed that something was dangerously wrong with the Isle. She sensed it in the magic around her, felt an impending doom vibrating in her bones – and she was alone, terrifyingly and ominously alone on her Isle. The clearing was as silent as the grave.

Gem straightened her shoulders and followed the man Magna had sent to her. There was still no reason to trust him – except for the fact that he didn't *appear* to be evil – but he was a necessary part of solving the problem at hand, she could feel it. Perhaps he was a clue or even an unwitting ally if she managed to stay one step ahead. If anything, he reminded her a little of Ashure Waves, the Pirate King, except that Ashure knew how to fight.

"Where are you going?" she called out when he kept walking away from her without looking back.

"Down to the beach," he replied in a curt tone.

She frowned. "But… why?" she asked, hurrying to catch up with him.

He stopped suddenly and turned, then wrapped his hands around her arms to prevent her from running into him. A flicker of surprise crossed his face when his hands didn't go through her, his scowl of irritation turning to a frown of confusion as he blinked down at her.

Wavy strands of different colors linked them together. The silvery-blue, smoky threads followed him when he pulled his hands away from her.

"What is happening now? Every time I touch you I get a shock and now there's a rainbow-colored light show going on. I feel like I'm tripping on some kind of weird, hallucinogenic drug! So for the last fucking time, what – the – fuck – is – going – on?" he asked grimly.

Gem pursed her lips together and looked away from the colors. Instead, she reached out and grabbed his arm when he tried to wave the colorful strands away.

"You can't wave them away," she said with a shake of her head.

"Obviously. I swear everything is just getting weirder and weirder," he muttered.

"You can't escape what is happening," she stated in a tense tone.

He raised his eyebrow. "Listen, *sweetheart,* if you're not going to explain, fine. I don't *care* what's happening. I'm fed up! It isn't my monkey. It isn't my circus. I will tell you what I'm going to do, though. I'm going to go park my ass on the beach and hope that a genie in a bottle washes up so I can order a case of beer, a big-ass steak, and a comfy chair with a nice little umbrella while I wait to wake up from this nightmare," he replied, tugging his arm free.

She sighed. "Perhaps we should begin again. My name is Gem Aurora LaBreeze. You may call me Gem," she said, stepping around him to block his exit.

He shot her a suspicious glare and started to push her aside. He paused, and his frown deepened when the smoky threads still clinging to his arm moved over his dragon tattoo, outlining the shape.

"Okay – Gem. I'd say it was a pleasure to meet you, but I'd be lying, so I won't. What I would like to know is if this smoky stuff is going to make my arm fall off," he warily responded.

"No, your arm will not fall off. You haven't told me your name," she reminded him.

He looked back at her with a distracted frown. "It's Ross – Ross Galloway," he answered.

He looked back down at his arm. Gem smirked when she heard him release a long breath of relief after he noticed that the colorful threads had disappeared and his arm looked normal again. She knew that the threads were just the first of many issues that they would have to eventually deal with – just not right now. She wasn't ready to deal with the meaning of the threads just yet.

At the moment, she wanted to focus on convincing him that he was now going to be a part of her quest whether it was his monkey/circus or not – whatever that meant! The only monkeys that she knew about were Nali's sea monkeys, and they were horrid little beasts. She impatiently waited for him to finish examining his arm.

"I need your help," Gem blurted out when he remained silent.

He looked up to meet her eyes and she watched several expressions cross his face before he settled on wariness. He shook his head, and she pursed her lips, flashing him an irritated look. He was not going to make this easy for her.

Of course, she probably would have been a touch wary if their roles were reversed. Still, considering that Magna was the last person she'd seen before she'd been turned to stone, she felt she had a right to be a little on the defensive side.

She folded her arms across her chest when Ross opened and closed his mouth before he actually responded.

"My help?" He outright laughed. "Lady – Gem – in case you missed it, you just kicked my ass and pushed my nuts up into my throat. I don't think you need any of my help," he said as he turned away from her.

Gem grabbed his arm and turned him to face her again. "The fact that I pushed your nuts up into your throat is not the point. I need your help, and you are going to give it to me," she firmly stated.

Ross's eyes blazed but he pressed his lips into a thin line. Gem was pretty sure he had been about to say some very disparaging words, but he was holding himself back. That was good. He might be resistant to her orders, but he was afraid of her, and that would work in her favor.

"Well," Ross finally said, his eyes boring into hers. "If you're gonna twist my arm, I don't have much choice, do I? You gonna tell me *why* you need me?" he growled.

She took a deep breath as she decided how to phrase this. "I would if I could, but something tells me that you must help me, and since I feel that way, you will," Gem insisted.

He gave her an incredulous look. "Something tells you, huh? Well, you know what? Something is telling *me* that I need to hike my hairy, white ass back down to the beach and wait for my shell to appear or some other random magical shit to happen," Ross stated caustically with a wave of his hand. He stepped around her and started walking toward the staircase again. "Welcome back to the land of the living, lady. I hope your next adventure works out better than your last one," he added with a sharp salute.

Fury and desperation flared inside Gem. She needed his help. The colors – she shook her head. She refused to think about the colors that now bound them together. She would deal with the ramifications later.

Frustrated, she dissolved and swept through him before materializing again. She splayed her hand on the center of his chest, forcing him to stop. Her lavender eyes glowed with determination as she stepped closer to him.

"I need your help, and you are the only one here who can assist me," she repeated through clenched teeth.

He reached up and removed her hand. Folding his arms across his chest, he glared down at her. She curled her fingers into a fist in an effort to keep from doing something drastic – like freezing his feet to the ground.

"And if I don't, what are you going to do – kick my ass again?" he asked softly, his intensity making her breath hitch in her throat.

"If you don't, then we are all going to die." She swallowed, feeling smothered by the weight of this responsibility. "The Isle is sinking and there are only two people who can stop it from happening. We have to find them before the Isle crashes into the ocean and disappears forever," she quietly replied.

A skeptical expression swept over his face, and he dropped his arms to his side. "Okay… this sounds like crazy bullshit, but I'm listening. Tell me more," he demanded.

She raised her hands to her sides, her palms facing downward. "I can feel the disturbance in the Isle. If we don't either renew the spell or undo the one that was created, the Isle will crash into the sea. Not only will our Isle be destroyed, but possibly all the other Isles as well when a mass this large hits the ocean and causes a tsunami in all directions. Only my mother and father have the strength and knowledge to control something this complex," she explained.

"Your parents?" he inquired, surprised.

"Yes, my parents. They are the rulers of the Isle of the Elementals and can control all of the elements. When I left them—" her voice faded as she thought of the last time she had seen her parents. She took a deep breath before she continued, "—when I left them, they were in the palace maze. "

He stared at her in silence for several seconds. She curled her fingers into tight fists when she saw that he still didn't believe her. The longer he was silent, the more desperate she became. She was just about to ask him if he understood what she was saying when he spoke.

"Never had a girl *want* me to meet her parents before," he joked half-heartedly. He took a breath, then another. "I don't suppose it's as simple as finding our way through this palace maze? They've been turned to stone too, haven't they?" he muttered, his eyes narrowed to slits as he tried to deal with this latest news on top of a helluva lot of other shocking developments.

When she hesitantly bit her lip and said "Something like that," he paused, then responded with a heartfelt sigh of resignation.

"Fine. You think you need a useless sidekick? I've got your back. But just so you know, Princess, I'm no hero. I'll get you to your palace only because it appears that is the only way I'm going to be able to get off this floating rock in one piece. When this is done, you, your dad, or *the tooth fairy* are going to send me back home. Deal?"

Gem was silent for a moment before she slowly nodded. "Yes, when this is over, I will ask my father to find a way to send you back to your world, Ross Galloway," she somberly agreed.

# CHAPTER FIVE

Half an hour later, Ross sat on the top step of the gazebo and watched with a disgruntled expression as Gem studied each stone on the path and in the floor of the gazebo. After they'd come to their tentative agreement to help each other, she'd informed him that she needed to know more about what had happened after she was turned to stone, and the runes or whatever were going to tell her. Apparently magic messages were relayed through stones here, and she was expecting mail from her parents.

He had been sorely tempted to make a mad dash down the rock staircase when she'd stepped around him and walked back to the gazebo. He probably would have if he hadn't felt the ground tremble. He knew what an earthquake felt like, and the idea of being on the stairs or the beach in the event of a major collision with the water far below didn't sound like much fun.

Not to mention he had made a promise to help Gem find her parents. After a brief argument with his conscience about whether he wanted to die like a piece of shit burying his head in the sand or die being a man of his word, he had grudgingly turned around and followed her back to the gazebo.

What could he say? He wasn't a team player, but he was here, that was enough for now. It wasn't like he could actually help with whatever it was that she was doing. Tired and more than a little sore, he had parked his butt on the top step and taken the opportunity to observe his frozen princess while she was preoccupied with reading the stones.

Ross put a hand over his mouth to stifle the snort of amusement when she wiggled her fingers near her head, and her hair floated upward. He knew that she did it to get it out of her way, but it looked like her hair was caught in the wind from a leaf blower. Of course, now that her hair no longer concealed her face, he could study her lips again.

He was angry at himself for it, but fuck, he was a man, wasn't he? And damn if she didn't make him fantasize about big beds and messy sheets, with that long dark brown hair spread out beneath him, her head falling backward as he rode her, those full lips tilted in a smile with a dangerous edge, the golden highlights in her hair shining in the sun. Her slender nose was kissable and those stormy, lavender eyes—

"Where did you meet the Sea Witch?" Gem asked, pulling him out of his fantasy.

"What? Right, Magna, well, I was diving off the coast, and you could say we bumped into each other. Do you have many mermaids here?" he asked, picking up a stick off the ground and breaking pieces off of it.

She looked up at him with a frown. "Not here. I told you, we are Elementals. We can control water but not on the same level as Orion. He can control the oceans," she replied.

Ross looked at her with a quizzical expression. "Orion? Like the constellation?" he asked.

"Like the King of the Isle of the Sea Serpent and ruler of all of the merpeople," she corrected.

"Of course, that Orion. How remiss of me to confuse the two," he dryly replied.

She straightened and studied him for a moment. "Are you mocking me?" she inquired.

He grinned at her. "Maybe," he replied.

Gem raised an eyebrow. "You are going to be very irritating during our quest, aren't you?" she asked.

"Every chance I get, Princess," he retorted.

She shrugged her slender shoulders. "Suit yourself, but be warned that I do not irritate easily, and when I am…" She paused and smiled at him. "… I can be very difficult. "

"Oh, I'm sure you can, Princess. I look forward to seeing you all fired up," he replied in a suggestive voice.

"How are your nuts? Have they slid out of your throat yet?" she inquired in a falsely sweet voice.

Ross instinctively reached for his groin and eyed her warily. She chuckled and returned her focus to the stones. He had to hand it to her; she didn't easily fluster.

"When was the last time you saw Magna?" she continued.

"Don't know exactly. It was the middle of the day before I left my world and then all of a sudden it was the middle of some night here, so I'm not sure what the hell the time difference is, but it feels like I saw her a couple days ago. At the restaurant in town – Yachats, that is, in Oregon… on Earth, where I live. She was having lunch with Gabe and Kane, her guys. I saw her and Kane come into the pub, so I went to have a chat with her when he went to the bathroom. I asked her if she was real, she said yes, then she handed me the shell. I left after that. That was it. I decided to take my boat out soon after, and I ended up here," he said, breaking off and throwing tiny pieces of the stick on the ground as he spoke.

"Who are Gabe and Kane?" she asked.

"Well, they were born on Earth, I can tell you that much. Gabe works for the US Fisheries and Kane is the local doctor. They have this relationship thing going on with Magna – you know, a ménage thing with two guys and one woman," he explained with a grin.

Gem looked up at him. "You sound surprised," she said.

The grin on his face faded, and he shrugged. "Yeah, well, it isn't all that common where I come from," he muttered.

"Ah," she murmured.

Ross frowned. "What is that supposed to mean?" he asked.

This time she shrugged. "You sound jealous or perhaps you are just prudish," she suggested.

"Listen, Princess, I'm about the least prudish guy you'll ever meet. If that's their thing, more power to them. I don't like to share. I'm selfish that way," he stated with a glare.

"Ah," she replied.

Ross gritted his teeth. She had a glitter in her eyes that he couldn't place. Skepticism, amusement... pleasure? Fucking woman and her inscrutable expressions. When she raised her eyebrows as if she didn't believe him and looked away, he had to clench his fists to keep from wrapping them around her beautiful neck.

He threw the remaining pieces of the stick on the ground and stood up, shoving his hands into his pockets as he stepped over to where she was studying the stones. The designs on the stones were moving. She frowned in puzzlement, muttering that whatever they were saying didn't make sense.

"This can't be right," Gem murmured.

Ross didn't know what she was talking about. All he could see were a bunch of squiggly lines, but honestly he was past the point of caring. Fighting Gem and fantasizing about her had distracted him for a good long while, but now he was so damn thirsty that all he could think about was finding some water. He ran his hands through his disheveled hair.

"Listen, do you know if there is a stream, water fountain, spring, or even better yet, a bar anywhere around here?" he asked with growing desperation.

She looked up at him and frowned. "There is a river deep in the forest, but until I understand what the stones are saying, it is not safe to continue our journey. Why do you ask?"

He shrugged and slid his hands back into the front pockets of his jeans. It didn't look like he would get anything to drink any time soon. Pulling one hand out, he rubbed his dry lips.

"I'm dying of thirst," he admitted with a crooked twist of his lips. "I feel like I swallowed half the ocean last night, and I haven't had anything to drink since. "

Her expression cleared, and he saw what looked like a flash of guilt cross her face before she hid it. She walked over to a plant that had extremely large, pitcher-shaped leaves. She carefully plucked a leaf off and brought it over to him. He took it from her when she held it out.

"Hold this. I should have thought of that when you so calmly explained what happened to you," she said with a sympathetic smile.

Ross chuckled and shook his head. "Calm, yeah, right," he mumbled and frowned as he looked down at the leaf. "So, what do I do? Eat it?"

Gem laughed and shook her head. Lifting one hand to support his, she moved her other hand slowly over the leaf. As she did, droplets of water formed and began to pool in the bottom of the green bowl. Ross snapped his head up and stared at her in amazement before looking at her hand again as she moved it in a slow circular motion.

"How are you doing this?" he whispered, pushing past the dryness.

"I told you. You are on the Isle of the Elementals," she replied with a small smile, indicating with her hand that he should drink the water.

"My people can control the elements while we are on this island. We can do it on others as well, but our control is not as strong as it is here. Here, we are one with fire, water, earth, air, plants, ice, light, and darkness. "

"This is pretty cool. About the only thing *I* can do is piss off the back of my boat on a calm day without falling overboard," he muttered.

Her delighted laugh told him that he'd not only spoken out loud, but clearly enough for her to hear what he'd said. An uncharacteristic flush rose in his cheeks. He lifted the leaf and drank the cool, refreshing water. The action helped to fight his thirst *and* briefly hide his red cheeks.

*Way to impress her, genius,* he thought with a hefty dose of self-disgust.

"I probably shouldn't have shared that," he finally said.

"It was a very... uh... visual image," she acknowledged with a grin.

"Can I get a refill?" he asked.

"Of course," she replied.

She reached up and cupped his hand again when he held out the leaf, then waved her hand. A small cloud formed where her hand was circling and it rained into the leaf. He grinned when the leaf filled with water again.

Lifting the leaf to his lips, he drank deeply from it. He looked up and connected with her beautiful lavender gaze. He swallowed the cool liquid, feeling the dry, scratchy soreness dissolving when the moisture washed over it.

Finally he felt satisfied, and his mind was no longer on his thirst. Instead he took in her gorgeous features as she stood close to him, probably watching him to see if he was alright now. A faint line of freckles caressed her nose. Her face was heart-shaped, and her lips were perfect for.... Some of the water went down the wrong way, and he began to cough. Damn, he needed to stop making a complete ass out of himself in front of her. He couldn't even take a drink without choking.

"Thanks," he choked out, wiping his mouth with the back of his hand and taking a deep breath as he lowered the leaf. "What do the stones tell you? Did your dad show you how to get past whatever he was warning you about?"

Gem continued to stare at him for several seconds before she flushed and turned her head to look back down at the stones. Her hair danced around her face when she shook her head, and he had to clench his fingers around the leaf to keep from reaching out and touching the swirling, shimmering mass.

"No. I don't understand what they are saying. I mean, I do, but it doesn't make any sense," she said, turning to walk back to the first stone. "The warnings are not from my father or mother. "

"Who are they from then?" Ross asked, grabbing his jacket and sweater off the railing of the gazebo before walking over to stand next to her.

Gem looked up at him with a troubled expression. "They are from the Sea Witch," she replied in a quiet voice.

"I told you that she didn't seem like she was so bad," Ross muttered. "So, what do we do first?"

# CHAPTER SIX

*Magna, the Sea Witch* had warned them that there would be obstacles ahead, but the warnings had been nearly indecipherable. It would have been helpful if they had included more details. She wasn't even sure if they could be trusted!

There had also been no mention of the black shadow that had chased her. There was the warning her father had given her – that he would place traps to slow the creature down. She was a bit more familiar with what he might do. While she knew that none of the traps her father would place would be lethal, she couldn't be so sure of the ones that Magna had warned her about. They would need to proceed with caution until she had a better understanding of what everything meant.

She looked away from the stones to cast a quick glance at Ross under her eyelashes. *He* confused her too, and if she was honest with herself, frightened her more than a little. Her energy liked and was drawn to him.

Each Elemental was perfectly balanced, both with nature and with their people. This resulted in a harmony with the world around them that allowed Gem's people to interact with the Elements. He was her balance – Goddess help her!

*I don't know what is worse – finding my potential mate just before I'm probably going to die or discovering he is the exact opposite of what I was hoping for – right before I die! It also doesn't help that he is completely oblivious to our connection and its importance to me. Maybe it is just as well since he wants to leave if we live through this!* she silently grumbled.

She shook her head, and took a deep breath as she felt the island shudder and groan again. She pursed her lips in determination. There wasn't time to think about what the colors connecting them meant. Right now, they had even bigger things to worry about. She looked at him and realized he was gazing back at her with an expectant expression.

*At least he isn't heading for the beach like he planned to do earlier,* she thought.

"We head through the forest to the palace," she replied in a clipped tone before she turned on her heel and walked away.

She could feel Ross's stare on her stiff shoulders. At the moment, she didn't care. She had more important things to worry about right now than her feelings for this strange man. If her calculations were correct, they had three, maybe four days, at the most, to make it to the palace and find her parents.

Ordinarily, that wouldn't have been an issue since the path to the palace would normally only take a half a day at most if they walked it. The problem was that the path had changed. It was now littered with dangers. They would have to proceed with caution.

"Hey, what about the booby-traps? What did the stones say?" Ross asked from behind her.

"We will deal with them when they occur," she replied over her shoulder.

Gem gasped in surprise when Ross's warm hands spanned her waist, and he lifted her up off the ground. She glanced over her shoulder, speechless as he turned around and placed her on the path behind him. A dark scowl creased his brow.

"Listen, Princess, you're a lot more important to this mission than I am. If there's danger, I go first," Ross retorted in a slightly strained tone.

Gem released her breath when he pulled his hands away from her and quickly picked up his jacket and sweater from the ground where he'd dropped them. She stared up at him in surprise when he straightened up and leveled a look at her that brooked no argument.

"But..." she responded. He took a step closer to her, and the small space between them filled with heat. She swallowed. "Alright." She reluctantly smiled.

He grimly smiled back. "I'll tell you what, though," he casually remarked, "if I get in trouble, you can kick whatever it is in the ass after I distract it." His smile turned genuine and impish for a moment before he turned his back to her.

It took Gem a moment to realize Ross was teasing her. She chuckled and shook her head. He continued to surprise her.

*Score one for the strange man,* she thought with a grimace. *Well, maybe two. First my energy accepts him and now this unexpected gallantry!*

Shaking her head again, she started after him. She admired his body as she followed him. His dark brown hair was shaggy as if he had trimmed it himself, and he had a good day's growth on his jawline. Over the past few hours his brown eyes had sparked with his fighting spirit and glowed with warmth and reserve as if he had been hurt and was trying to hide it. He had broad shoulders that pulled his black cotton shirt taut across them, and his figure tapered down to a narrow waist. He also had a very cute butt.

She flushed at her thoughts. Still, her gaze moved down again. She smiled in amusement. She bet he didn't know that he had a hole beneath the corner of his back pocket, giving her a tantalizing glimpse of...

"You aren't wearing underclothes!" she squeaked before blushing a bright red.

Ross stumbled on the uneven path, turned around and stared at her with a stunned look on his face. She blushed even more when he hiked up one of those devilish eyebrows in a silent question. She looked away from the intense stare.

"How would you know that?" he asked.

Gem returned her eyes to his face and boldly stared back at him. Biting her bottom lip, she fought the smile that tugged at her lips, trying to hide her reaction. She keenly felt his scrutiny of her every move, but she couldn't help inspecting him from the front as well, knowing that he'd know she was checking him out. She paused in her study when she reached the zipper of his pants.

"You have a hole – near your back pocket. I could see that you weren't wearing anything underneath," she mumbled, embarrassed.

Ross took a step closer to her, touched her chin, and tilted her head back a little. She looked up at him with a wary expression, wondering what he would say about her confession. She really wished she could learn to keep her mouth shut.

She gaped at him when he bent his head, pausing when his lips were just a whisper away from her mouth. Her pupils dilated as heat spread inside her again, this time not from embarrassment, but from a sudden overwhelming need to kiss him and see if he tasted as good as he looked.

"Underwear is uncomfortable," he murmured against her lips. "I hate being confined. "

"Oh," she breathed, laying her hand against his chest, her imagination running wild at the thought of him 'not confined'.

Gem blinked when he suddenly pulled away.

"I've always liked my freedom," he muttered as he turned back around.

Gem huffed, aggravated and frustrated at the loss of his nearness. She glared at his back again, refusing to let her gaze stray to the small hole.

*Well, I'll keep it from straying later,* she amended, watching as he bent over and picked up a long, thick stick.

"What are you doing?" she asked, curious.

He waved it around and tapped it against the ground several times. He grinned at her with a mischievous grin. She silently swore. He knew exactly how frustrated she was with him.

"A walking stick and a possible weapon, just in case," he replied. "By the way, all of my jeans have a hole there for some reason. "

Gem immediately looked down at his ass again and groaned – loudly. His low chuckle showed that he had known she would look. He even had the nerve to wiggle his butt.

"You are a very strange and disturbed male," she growled, glaring daggers at the center of his back.

"Yeah, but the women I've dated tell me I have one cute ass," he retorted.

"I'm sure they were sadly mistaken," Gem grumbled in a haughty tone as she followed him down the dark path.

"You'll just have to find out for yourself, won't you, Princess?" he laughed as he continued down the path.

The forest quickly closed in around them as they moved away from the coastline. Gem warily glanced around her. She could feel a dark presence. It felt as if they were being watched. Swallowing, she shook her head. The first stone had warned her to be careful of the river. She knew it would take them at least half an hour to get there.

"Tell me about the place you come from," she asked, stepping over a large root.

Ross glanced over his shoulder with an unconscious grimace of unease before turning back around. He swung the long stick in front of him, knocking away any cobwebs that might be in the way.

"What do you want to know?" he asked in a nonchalant tone.

She gritted her teeth. "I don't know… Perhaps, what it is like would be a good start," she muttered.

"It's a place," Ross replied, glancing at her again. "You know, fog, rain, trees, water, mountains, fog, fog, rain, fog, rain, cold, and did I mention the fog and rain?"

Gem bit back a chuckle. "You might have said something about that," she admitted. "I take it that you don't care for rain and fog?"

"Or the cold," Ross said. "I have plans. I'm moving to Hawaii or one of those nice Caribbean Islands, though they have to deal with hurricanes. Hawaii has them as well, but not as often. So, I think Hawaii is where it will be. A nice little place near the beach. "

"What is so special about this Hawaii? Does it not have rain and fog? Is it warm?" Gem asked, stepping up so that she could walk beside him.

Ross glanced down at her and grinned. "Darling, you can LIVE on the beach there it is so warm. Sparkling water, sexy ladies, palm trees, sand, sun; it is paradise on steroids as far as I'm concerned," he replied with a sigh.

Gem scowled. "We have sun, sand, and sparkling water here," she replied. "I don't see what is so special about that. "

Ross laughed. "Yeah, well, in Hawaii, I don't have to worry about people getting turned into stone or islands in the sky falling down to annihilate everything. "

Gem waved her hand in dismissal. "When we get to the palace, we will find my father and mother and then that will not be an issue. We also have trees," she added.

"Yeah, but do you have the sexy ladies?" Ross asked, raising his eyebrows up and down in a suggestive movement.

Irritation flashed through her, and she curled her fingers into her palm. She had to bite her tongue to keep the retort she wanted to make from escaping. He was *a lot* like Ashure Waves! He should have landed on one of the Pirate ships.

*Sexy ladies? What in the hell does he think I am? Unattractive?* she thought in aggravation, not knowing why it bothered her.

"We have a few," she finally answered in a stiff voice.

Once again, she couldn't help thinking that he wasn't the kind of man she would be attracted to under any circumstance, especially not when there were more important things that she needed to deal with – such as saving her people and the Seven Kingdoms from utter destruction. Still, it rankled that he seemed oblivious to the fact that her essence weaved into his in a way that only a mate's could. The thought that someone so annoying, aggravating, and rude could be her mate was enough to make her want to scream.

There had to be some kind of a mistake. Maybe once the Sea Witch's spell was broken, the link between them would be severed. She really hoped that was the case because if it wasn't, there was no way she could promise that she wouldn't send a few rain clouds, a frigid wind, and a hefty dose of fog to surround him while he was finding *the sexy ladies.*

"Well, since you're the only one here at the moment, I'll have to take your word for it," he teased.

"If the place you lived was so distasteful, why did you stay there? Surely with a boat, you could have traveled to this Hawaii if it meant so much to you," she retorted.

Silence greeted her question. When it continued, she glanced up at Ross's face. His expression was closed, and all signs of the teasing humor that she was beginning to associate with him were gone.

"Sometimes life gets in the way of your dreams," he finally said, step-ping ahead of her as the path narrowed. "Stay behind me, Princess. I need you to watch my back. "

Gem slowed and moved behind him. A concerned frown creased her brow. She wondered what had hurt him in his world. Staring at his back, she watched the glowing bands of her essence dance around him as if wanting to whisk away his pain.

Lost in her thoughts, it took Gem a few moments to realize that this part of the forest was much darker than it should have been. She glanced around. The trees were dead and a foul smell hung in the air.

"Is it always like this?" Ross murmured, glancing uneasily at a tree as they walked past it.

"No, it was not like this before," Gem murmured. "Here, use this. "

Gem focused, pulling together the thin streams of light that fought to filter down through the trees. Pulling it into a ball, she handed the dimly glowing orb to Ross. She did it again so that she could have one.

"Yeah, right, I forgot you could do cool stuff like that. I guess it saves on buying batteries," Ross muttered, staring at the orb in his hand for a moment.

"Batteries? What are...? Oh!" Gem cried in surprise when the ground shook violently under their feet.

"Hold on! What's going on?" Ross muttered, releasing the orb to turn and grab her around the waist.

"The Isle is sinking. We only have a few days at most before it happens," she said.

"Are you sure we have a few days?" he asked as another quake, this time not as strong, shook the ground again.

She looked up at him, her eyes filled with concern. "N... No, not completely," she admitted, gripping his forearms to keep from falling. The orb she had released when she grabbed him briefly floated between them before moving off.

They held on to each other tightly in the dark, their faces scant inches apart, until the world stopped quaking a minute later.

"You, Princess, are just as dangerous as this island," he muttered, staring into her eyes.

"Why… Why do you say that?" she stuttered when she realized that he was pulling her closer instead of letting her go.

"Because the ground is shaking, the air smells like rotten eggs, I swear there are eyes in the trees, and all I can think about is kissing you," he stated in a gruff tone.

"Even if I'm not a sexy beauty from your Ha-wy?" she asked in a slightly haughty voice.

Ross chuckled, leaning closer. "It's Hawaii; and yes, even then. There's something sexy about a woman who can create a floating flashlight just when you need one," he murmured a breath away from her lips.

Gem was trying to decide whether or not he had just insulted her when he pressed his firm, warm lips against hers and the thought vanished. He touched his tongue to her bottom lip and she instinctively opened for him. A soft groan slipped from her when his tongue swept inside her mouth and tangled with hers. She slid her hands up his forearms, wrapped her arms around his neck, and tilted her head so he could deepen the kiss.

# CHAPTER SEVEN

The kiss was amazing. Every cell in his body was alive, the feel and taste of her was beyond hot, and Ross couldn't figure out what in the hell was wrong with him. All his thoughts were centered on one thing, and it had nothing to do with getting home.

No, they were on this deceivingly delicate female who could kick his ass with a wave of her hand if she so desired. He had been doing everything in his power to irritate the hell out of her in an attempt to put up a wall between them, but the wall was made of a child's clay instead of bricks, and now he was kissing her.

He decided right then and there that the few brain cells he had before he fell off his boat must have washed out of his ears. This was dangerous, and it was crazy. He was caught in some bizarre dream world on a heroic quest to save a magical race and their mythical world, and he was kissing a beautiful princess. His tongue was stroking her tongue, her soft breasts were pressed against his chest, she was making these addictive, barely-audible sounds, breathing him in as if she couldn't get enough, and he was doing the same – and he was definitely *not* going to worship her with his touch and have his wicked way with her in the middle of their quest because it was wrong on so many different levels.

He was the last person in any world to be considered heroic. He had never given a damn about anyone except his mom, and even then, he had kept a healthy emotional distance between them. He'd had to, once upon a time, because he'd been too little to protect her when she'd clearly needed somebody to. But, just now, when the ground shook and Gem gasped, all he could think about was protecting his powerful companion, like some silly fairy-tale knight, stalwart and true, and then before he knew it, he was pulling her into his arms and kissing her.

The world could have ended and he wouldn't have noticed. For just a few stolen moments, it felt like there was an obscenely large breach in his protective wall, and everything felt absolutely incredible and he wanted more. What the hell was she doing to him?

Their soft moans reverberated in the quiet, reminding Ross of the fact that they were in the middle of an enchanted forest. He shivered and reluctantly released her lips, running his tongue along her bottom lip one more time for good measure before pulling back to stare into her eyes. He frowned when he realized that something was different.

"Either you are growing or I'm shrinking," he muttered. Gem quickly conjured the floating orbs of light so they could see better.

Ross tried to take a step back and almost fell on his ass. Gem grabbing onto the front of his shirt was the only thing that prevented him from sprawling on the ground. He harshly cursed when he realized that his feet were sinking into the soft mud.

"I can't get my feet out," he growled, grimacing when he tried to pull his leg up. "For crying out loud, this is what happens when you distract me!"

Gem flashed him a look of annoyance. "When *I* distract *you*?" she asked incredulously, grabbing his arm to try to pull him out. Ross twisted back and forth in an effort to break at least one foot free of the mud. "The stone warned of the first major obstacle near the river," she declared, trying to push her feet more firmly into the solid ground on her side while she pulled him. He grunted at the strength of her grip. "Technically, we are not that far from it," she huffed, "and I have been looking for traps this *entire* time, but in case you forgot, a few seconds ago, we were a little busy!" The only thing that happened when she tried to pull him out was she ended up closer to him. She emitted a startled squeak when the ground beneath her feet became soft. The mire was growing.

"Let go and back up," Ross ordered, releasing her.

Gem staggered back several feet and stared at him. Ross glanced around, tightening his lips when he felt the thick ooze slide over the top of his boots. It was almost to his knees now.

"Get me a thick branch or vine," he said, remaining as still as possible.

Gem nodded, turning in a circle, and frantically looked around. The stick he had been carrying was nowhere to be found. She hurried over to a tree and pulled on a long, thick vine. It snapped and fell around her. She picked it up and dragged it toward him.

"Catch," Gem said, throwing one end to him.

Ross grabbed the end of the vine. Unfortunately, it turned to dust in his hands. Gritting his teeth, he pulled more of it toward himself, but the faster he pulled, the more it dissolved.

"The mud must be enchanted," Gem exclaimed.

Ross watched her turn around and hurry back down the path. She soon disappeared around the bend of the trail. The mud crept up to his waist and he was forced to lift his arms higher. If they became stuck, he would be in some serious trouble. He was about to call out to Gem when she reappeared with a long branch.

"Here, try this," she said in a breathless voice.

Ross wrapped his hands around the end of the branch and held on. Gem dug her heels into the soft soil and pulled. For a moment, Ross felt a shift in the mud and could feel himself moving upward instead of down. Hope flared inside him until he heard a loud crack, and Gem fell onto her butt.

"Oh, for crying out loud. Really?" he swore. The branch disintegrated in his hands before he could toss away the broken piece. "Can you find something that won't break? Like a boulder or a crane or something?"

"I'm trying!" she snapped, rising to her feet and wiping the dirt off of her backside. "The curse has made everything near the ground brittle and whoever cast the curse has made it immune to my ability to change the elements, but I... I can talk to things, not things enchanted with the dark curse, but, I can talk to something that is not cursed," she added with a grin.

Ross followed Gem's gaze. High above in the top canopy where the sun was shining brightly, the leaves were still green and lush. He glanced at Gem when she began softly whispering and waving her fingers. Small sparkles of light floated up into the air, swirling and twirling as they rose higher and higher. When the sparkle of magic reached the top thick vines, where they were green and healthy, they began to expand.

"Hurry, Gem. I think the mud knows you are up to something," he informed her in a hoarse voice.

It was true, he could feel the mud sucking and pulling on his body, making him sink at an alarming rate. A shudder ran through him when some of it seeped down the back of his pants. The slimy mixture in such a private place felt – wrong.

"Come to me," Gem breathed, holding her hands up. "Help me. "

Ross lifted his hands as far as he could and took a deep breath when the mud reached his chin. He wanted to open his mouth and tell Gem that she had better sweet talk the damn plant a little faster, but he was afraid he would swallow some of the black ooze.

He held his breath and closed his eyes when his head was pulled under. Now, only his hands were free. To keep from panicking, he tried to slow his pulse rate by thinking of something calming, like the beach in Hawaii. This was different from the time he was thrown overboard, this was darker, thicker, and paralyzing.

Black spots began to dance in front of his eyes, and his chest started to burn. He fought to take control; He wanted to open his mouth to draw in a deep breath of air, but he knew that was impossible. Fear started to blossom inside him when the mud reached his wrists. He was almost out of time and oxygen. Flexing his fingers, he ignored the burning in his lungs and, instead, focused on the image of Gem right before he had kissed her. If he was going to die, he wanted her face to be the last thing he remembered.

The first touch of something on his hand made him think that maybe the mud had reached them. He knew that wasn't it when the thing suddenly wrapped around them. Curling his fingers, he felt the sudden shift in the mud. Instead of sinking, he was being pulled upward. Fighting off the darkness from lack of oxygen, he knew that this was a make-it-or-break-it moment, whether he would live or die.

The moment his wrists were once again exposed, the vine wrapped around them. The further he was pulled up, the more the vines entwined around his arms. The second his head was clear of the mud, he parted his lips and pulled desperately needed oxygen into his starving lungs.

He kept his eyes closed due to the thick sludge running down his face. He shook his head, trying to fling the oozing mess from his nose and mouth. It took almost five minutes before he was completely free of the mud pit and lying on the firm, damp soil of the forest floor.

When the vine released him, he pushed up into a sitting position. Shaking his head again, he wiped the mud off his eyes and opened them, scowling at his filthy clothes and body. He looked like he had been mud wrestling with a passel of pigs. He was just about to make that comment when he was doused with a torrential flood of warm rain from above.

Closing his eyes and tilting his head back, he let the warm water wash the mud from his face and hair. Now, all he needed was a good shower for the rest of his body. He opened his eyes again and flashed a mischievous grin. Impending death had a way of bringing out the humor in life. Rising to his feet, he pulled his shirt over his head.

"What – What are you... you doing?" Gem asked, waving her hands back and forth while her attention remained locked on his broad shoulders.

"Honey, I've got mud in places I don't even want to think about. You keep up the warm shower for just a little longer 'cause I sure as hell don't want to be walking around with caked dirt rubbing between the cheeks of my ass," he replied, dropping his shirt and reaching for the button on his jeans. He was already hard. Not all that surprising given the sexy woman standing before him who couldn't take her eyes off his body. He wondered just how flustered she'd be at the sight.

He toed off his boots and pushed his pants all the way down. The water heated up a few degrees. He watched as Gem's mouth dropped open. She continued to move her hands, but he had a feeling she wasn't aware of it. Raising his arms, he scrubbed his dark hair until it was no longer gritty. Once he was done with that, he continued rubbing his face, arms and torso before moving lower.

"Watch the temperature, Princess. You're getting a little hot there," he teased with a knowing grin.

"What?! Oh, I'm sorry," she whispered, her eyes following the movement of his hands.

When Gem licked her lips, Ross's manhood began to throb in frustration. At this rate, he was going to have to ask her to turn on the cold water. Gritting his teeth, he turned his back to her and finished washing. He bent down and picked up his clothes, biting back the groan that threatened to escape when she gasped again. Taking his time, he turned each piece inside out, allowing the fresh water to rinse away the dirt before wringing it out.

"You can turn off the water now," he replied in a tight, gravelly voice. He held his clothes in front of him. "Now I just need a way to dry them. "

Gem lowered her trembling arms and glanced down at his dripping clothes. What had started out as fun was quickly turning into blue balls. He'd never been this hot and unable to do a thing about it. He should have kept his dirty clothes on and ignored the caked mud. After all, it wasn't like he had never worn dirty clothes before.

"I can help," she whispered, licking her lips and staring at his waist.

Before he could respond, she waved her hands out toward his clothes. The moisture was pulled away in a long stream that ran through the air and disappeared into the forest before a steady, warm breeze encircled him. Within minutes, everything was dry again.

"Damn," he muttered, staring at Gem in appreciation. "Could you tell me how you do that again?"

Her startled gaze moved up his bare chest, and a rosy blush flushed her cheeks when she locked eyes with him. Ross curled his fingers around his dry clothes. She looked so damned adorable that all he wanted to do was kiss her again. If it wasn't for the fact that he was standing bare-assed naked in dangerous territory, he might have taken advantage of the situation. Instead, the feeling of eyes burning holes into his rear end was enough to dampen his desire – at least a little.

"I think it might be better if you turn around while I get dressed," he suggested.

Gem's eyes widened. "Why?" she choked out, staring at him.

He grinned. "Because, Princess, I am very turned on, and this isn't a good place for me to do anything about it," he replied with a sardonic chuckle. "Unless you are sure there aren't any more mud holes for me to sink into; then I might just say to hell with it and give it a try. "

"Oh… No, there may be more… mud pits – traps – spots," she stuttered before turning on her heel. "Are you alright?" she called over her shoulder.

Ross slid his leg into his jeans, pausing at her question before looking down at his body. He was still hard. Grimacing, he quickly stepped into the other leg and pulled up his pants, making sure to adjust himself so he didn't get anything crucial caught in the zipper. It didn't take him long to finish dressing.

"I'm fine," he replied as he bent over and picked up his sweater, jacket, and a new walking stick several feet away from the mud pit. "I think we better get moving. It feels like it's getting to be early afternoon, and personally, I don't relish the thought of being stuck in this forest once the sun sets. "

# CHAPTER EIGHT

Ross stuck the walking stick into a patch of thick leaves. Sure enough, it sank into oozing mud, and the end of it dissolved. After trying it a few more times in various places, he and Gem soon came to the conclusion that the round leaf-covered areas were a trap and they made sure they avoided them. Unfortunately, this made their journey seem more like a game of hopscotch than a hike.

Almost an hour after his near-death experience, they finally reached the river. He leaned against his fourth walking stick and glanced back and forth along the river. It wasn't extremely wide, approximately thirty feet, but the water was deep and turbulent.

"We can cross there," he said, nodding at a large tree that had fallen across the river.

"I don't like this," she murmured, staring at the river with a frown. "There used to be a bridge here. I can't imagine why the Sea Witch destroyed it and not the tree. "

Ross turned around and studied the path that ended at the riverbank ten feet in front of them. There was definitely no bridge, and they couldn't wade across the river – the current and the depth made crossing too dangerous. The only way was to cross over on the fallen tree or follow the riverbank until they found a different place to cross.

"Maybe the tree fell after she left. We might not have enough time to keep searching for another crossing. It's big enough to walk across. I'll help you if you're afraid," he said.

Gem shook her head. "I'm not afraid, it's just... The stone said to stay true to the path," she murmured, rubbing her forehead.

"What, like walk on the water that's in front of the path? That makes no sense! If we cross using the tree, that's still part of the path. Besides, she didn't say anything about the mud traps, did she? Maybe the Sea Witch wasn't being as helpful as we hoped she was," Ross reasoned.

Gem glanced at the tree. Her gut was telling her to stay away from it, yet her eyes were telling her that there was no way they could stay on the path. Biting her lip, she shook her head.

"I just don't think we should go that way," she murmured. "Something doesn't feel right. "

He sighed and faced her. Sliding his hand along her cheek, he tilted her head back until she looked him in the eyes. He smiled when he saw the worry and uncertainty in them.

"I tell you what," he said, rubbing his thumb over her lip. "I'll go across and make sure it is safe first. If it is, I'll come back for you. "

"What if it's not?" she asked, glancing at the tree again before looking at him. "What if it is another trap?"

Ross chuckled. "Then you get to save my ass again, Princess, and you can even say 'I told you so'," he replied, brushing a quick kiss across her lips.

❧

Gem raised an eyebrow at his recklessness with his life and his assumption that he could casually kiss her whenever he wanted to. Yes, it was nice, but they weren't – well, they were, but... he was an extremely frustrating male who was casually kissing her before he went off possibly to die in a very stupid manner! He shot her a flirty wink as if to punctuate her conclusion before he turned around and stepped away from her.

The stone had not given much information, just a pictograph of the river with the words 'Stay the path' underneath. She looked once more at the path where it ended at the water's edge. Before the Sea Witch's visit, there had been a wide wooden bridge with a decorative iron railing across the broad expanse.

She started to walk toward the spot where the bridge would have begun. She was almost to it when she looked over at Ross. He was climbing over the massive roots and up onto the long, thick tree trunk. Once past the roots, he had taken only a dozen steps when Gem saw movement at the base of the tree. Fear swept through her when she realized that her gut feeling had been correct – it was a trap.

"Ross!" she yelled, as she starting running toward him across the loose gravel bank. "Ross, get off! You can't cross there. It's a trap!"

Horror gripped Gem when the tree suddenly rolled, and the long, thick branches began to move as the tree started to rise. Ross slid against the rough bark, grabbing hold of a knot and clinging to it as the tree groaned and pushed upward. It was alive!

Ross carefully examined the tree before he reached up, gripped the tangled roots and pulled himself up onto it. He tested a few places before putting his full weight down in case there were any rotted sections. Overall, there appeared to be enough nooks and crevices for him to get a good foothold.

He quickly reached out to steady himself when the tree suddenly shook and shifted under his feet. He wobbled unsteadily, bent forward, and scanned the tree trunk until his gaze reached the top of the tree.

He wondered if the island was doing another moan and groan. He turned his head when he heard Gem's frantic shout above the roaring sound of the rushing water below him and the tree. Straightening up, he frowned and started to release his grip on the branch when he saw her running toward him.

It took a moment for her words to sink in. When they did, a grim horror swept through him.

Glancing back at the top of the tree, he groaned when it suddenly twisted and two dark, empty eyes looked back at him.

"This is one messed up world," he muttered just as the tree rolled, and he found himself hanging onto a large, gnarled knot in the trunk for dear life.

The branches of the tree were like arms while the trunk was its body and the roots were its feet. Ross reached for a branch to get a better grip and dizzily swung around in a circle as the tree pushed against the boulders with its thicker branches near the bottom. Its trunk bowed slightly as the tree began to stand.

Ross looked down and tried to determine just how far it was to the water below. This really wasn't the way he wanted to test the river's depth. If it was too shallow, he could break a leg – or worse. If it was deep – well, he had been in over his head before.

The decision to release his grip on the branch or not was quickly taken out of his hands when he caught a movement out of the corner of his eye. A long, pointed branch was heading straight for him. Releasing his hold on the branch, he folded his arms across his chest and bent his knees as he fell.

Cold water closed over his head, forcing the breath out of him and pulling him down. He wildly rolled along the riverbed, then pushed up from bottom and swam upward, fighting against the turbulent water until he broke the surface. Gasping for air, he barely saw the large boulder before he was being propelled toward it. He flailed desperately for any hold.

Elation burst through him when he was able to wrap his fingers around a tree limb that was jammed into a crevice. Dragging himself hand over hand, he pulled himself closer to the boulder and away from the swiftly flowing water, just in time to hear Gem's battle cry.

Fear unlike anything he had ever experienced swept through him. His biceps bulged as he pulled himself up the limb and out of the water to crouch on the rock. He now had a clear view of one of the larger limbs of the massive tree slamming into the ground near Gem. The force of the blow was so powerful that the water in the river actually rose up and the power of the wave caused the boulder under him to shift. With a hoarse shout, Ross stood and jumped onto a smaller rock. Then he jumped into the shallow area near the bank.

"Gem!" Ross roared, pushing out of the water and sprinting across the loose gravel beach.

The tree turned around when it heard his yell. Waving his hands, Ross darted to the side when it bent over and violently swiped at him. When it missed him, Ross swung around, running parallel to the spot where he had last seen Gem. He was almost to the path they'd been warned to stay on when a branch slammed down in front of him, blocking his way. Sliding to a stop, Ross fell backwards, bracing his hand on the ground to steady himself as he twisted around.

He glanced up, then lunged and dodged another murderous branch. As the tree wound up for its next swing, Ross heard Gem calling his name from the other side of the tree. Deciding the best plan to get past it was to run as close to the base of the tree as he could, he turned toward the tree and ran straight for the tangle of roots that were slithering along the ground like the tentacles of an octopus.

Jumping over several of them and ducking down, he rolled under the tree and emerged on the other side. He still had an obstacle course of swaying roots to weave through that would have put any military course to shame. Diving over one root, he rolled under another before he was clear of the thrashing mass.

"Over here!" Gem called as she lobbed a current of strong wind at the tree again and again in an effort to slow down its movements.

She was standing in the air several feet over the water. The sight was so unexpected that he stumbled to a stop, but the loud groan from the massive tree as it turned in his direction quickly reminded him that he had no time to stare.

"RUN!" Gem cried, waving her hand at him to hurry. "The bridge is here, you just can't see it."

"Why does that not surprise me?" Ross groused.

She was waving her hands in a pattern and muttering now, her attention focused on the tree behind him. As he sprinted forward, he watched two long columns of water rise up out of the river. He hit the end of the path, and kept running as the water shot past him toward the tree.

He didn't let himself slow down as the edge of the river rushed toward him. He just had to trust Gem. Drawing in a deep breath, he leaped toward the swift current, and his feet hit a solid surface a couple of feet above it. Rolling to cushion his landing, he found himself facing the tree as it was blasted by the twin jets of water, forcing it to retreat until it disappeared back into the forest with an angry groan.

Beneath him was a bridge. Apparently it was only visible if you were standing on it – or sitting on it, in his case. He stood and turned to look at Gem, taking several deep breaths. With a shake of his head, he grinned at her in relief. This was definitely on his list of the weirdest things that had ever happened to him.

"Are you alright?" she asked in an unsteady voice.

She reached up and cupped his cheeks between her hands. He returned her concerned gaze with a wary one of his own, and he gave her a wry grin.

"Yeah, I'm alright. I need my clothes dried again, though. Remind me to listen to your gut feelings from now on," he ruefully chuckled.

Her soft, lilting laughter filled the air. She waved her hands, and he was surrounded by warm air as the moisture was pulled out of his clothing. She followed the line of his body with her hands, but her eyes never looked away from his. Ross rested his hands on her hips and gently pulled her close as the dampness in his clothes faded.

"I think that deserves another kiss," he murmured.

Her eyes glittered with an emotion he didn't quite understand, but he liked it. "I think so, too," she whispered, rising up onto her toes. "You know, this is beginning to become a habit. "

Ross paused a breath away from her lips. "What? Me kissing you?" he asked in a low voice.

"No," she chuckled with a twinkle of amusement in her eyes. "Me saving your ass. "

# CHAPTER NINE

"Thank you, again – for saving my life," Ross said.

A wave of warmth swept through her at Ross's murmured admission. Shadows cast by the trees danced across his face. They stood near the edge of the forest. The rock-strewn bank had turned to dirt. They would be entering the forest again. She had stopped, needing time to gather her wits about her and take a moment to appreciate that they were still alive.

Her hands unconsciously twisted in the fabric she was holding and she looked down at his jacket and sweater that she was carrying. She'd never returned them after the incident on the other side of the river. Instinctively, she looked back at the bridge. From this side, she could see it clearly.

She bit her lip and turned to look ahead again. "I promised I would," she said, meeting his gaze. "You were brave, too," she said softly, "and nimble. " She sent a mischievous glance his way and held out his jacket to him.

He huffed a laugh. "Yeah, that was Olympic medal stuff right there. "

His smile faded. "I should have listened to you. You know this place better than I do. "

Gem's throat tightened when he looked away from her and slid his jacket on. In the brief moment before he did, she caught a glimpse of several emotions – regret, vulnerability, and something else that she couldn't quite put her finger on.

"We had no way of knowing what would happen." She sighed. "And I… did not trust my instincts enough. My father and mother taught me that a good leader knows when to compromise and when to stand firm. I have always had such trouble with that. You may have noticed that I do not always ask nicely when I should," she wryly stated, ruefully meeting his eyes. "But the other part is difficult too, when I have doubts, when I don't always know what to do. At the time I just wanted to act *quickly*, and the tree was the obvious route.

"I was impatient," she whispered, "and you could have died because of it, we both could have, and then my people…. "

Ross reached out and tucked a strand of her hair behind her ear. Faint swirls of the elements rose up to wrap around his wrist, and again he was oblivious. She gripped his hand when the Isle shuddered under their feet, but this tremor didn't last long.

Ross stroked her cheek for a moment. "No one expects you to know everything all the time, Princess. We just gotta keep moving, keep trying," he quietly countered.

She nodded and softly sighed when he pulled back, turned away, and began walking down the path. Her mind went to the stones. There hadn't been a warning for the mud pits, but the warning from the stones about the river had been right. They should have stayed true to the path when they came to the river.

At this point, Gem was deciding to trust that Magna was trying to help. Ross seemed to think she had changed, and when the Sea Witch had turned Gem to stone, the shadow had seemed angry with Magna. Perhaps that had been the only way to keep Gem alive and unpossessed. So, now all Gem had to do was correctly interpret Magna's other messages.

She scanned the forest. The next warning on the stones flashed through her mind and a shiver of unease ran through her. Each obstacle was growing progressively more dangerous and deadly. Those by her father had been designed to delay and confuse – like the mud pit. An unwary traveler would not be killed, but the stones hadn't warned her of his decoys – only those created by either Magna or the alien that controlled her.

The sudden thought occurred to her that the traps Magna had warned her about had been placed not to stop someone necessarily, but to capture them. The creature was looking for more hosts – those that it could not capture, it would kill to protect itself.

"The next warning on the stones said to be wary of the living bloodsuckers," she cautioned.

Ross was sweeping his walking stick back and forth and paused in mid-swing. He looked over his shoulder with a frown. Gem gave him a rueful smile of apology.

"Living bloodsuckers," he dryly repeated.

She nodded. "Yes," she replied.

He warily scanned the forest. "Nice, real nice. Is there any chance you could perhaps expand upon that a little? Are we talking mosquitoes or vampires? It would be nice to know what we are up against so that…. Never mind, I think I've figured it out," he murmured, looking up.

She followed his gaze, and instinctively stepped closer to him, curling her fingers into the back of his jacket as she stared upward with fascinated horror.

"I think you are going to need a bigger stick," she whispered.

"To hell with a stick, I need a frigging flamethrower," he responded in a hoarse voice.

The canopy above them was filled with thick threads of silk, in some places so thick it was impossible to see through. While they couldn't see the spiders, there was no doubt what type of creature had created the webs.

"Move very quietly," Gem murmured, pushing against his back.

He reached behind him, gripped her hand, and began pulling her along the path. He held the stick out in front of him. They both continually glanced up from the path to the webs above them as they walked.

Gem tightened her grip on Ross's hand when she thought she saw a shadowy movement among the dense threads. He must have seen it as well because he began to walk faster. She moved her hand to the hilt of her short sword.

The sound of a cracking branch drew her attention away from the webs above to the thick cluster of trees to their right amongst surrounding ferns. A giant, hairy leg rose into the air and pushed against a tree. The movement caused a rippling along the silky ropes of the web above.

"I've landed in a fucking Stephen King novel," Ross growled.

"I do not think I would like to read this Stephen King's stories," she replied, watching in horror as the web split and thousands of small, dark shapes began to appear through the tear.

"I think it's time to say to hell with stealth and run – run fast," Ross muttered.

Gem nodded. She fully agreed. The monstrous spider was made from dark magic and something else she couldn't place at first. Then her eyes narrowed in horror when she realized the creature was a grotesque creation formed by a part of the malevolent alien.

Rage built inside her even as Ross pulled her behind him. The spider shoved the tree aside, sending thousands of smaller spiders cascading down to the forest floor. A gasp slipped from her lips when Ross reached around, grabbed her by the waist, and pushed her in front of him.

"Go!" he ordered.

She ran as fast as she could down the path. She had covered several hundred yards when she realized that she didn't hear Ross's footsteps behind her. She skidded to a stop and turned around. He wasn't there.

"Ross!" she hissed with dismay.

Ross backed up with a sinking feeling as the huge spider took a step forward. He jumped when the heel of his boot sank in the soft soil. The sound of a loud hiss and the smell of rotten eggs filled the air.

"Come to me," the spider hissed.

Shock swept through him. "What the fuck? Spiders can talk here?" he exclaimed in a startled voice.

"I can give you power," the spider replied.

Ross raised an eyebrow and warily stepped back when the spider slowly advanced. He gripped the long stick with both hands and held it out in front of him. He didn't even bother trying to make sense of the fact that he was preparing to battle a talking spider the size of a Sherman tank – and that he was more than likely going to die. His only thought was to give Gem enough time to get far away.

"Yeah, well, you know something? I've seen what power can do to someone and it isn't pretty. If it is all the same to you, I think I'll pass on the superpowers," he retorted.

The spider paused, as if processing his response. Ross could see his reflection in the two largest eyes of the creature. He wasn't overly impressed by what he saw. Stepping to the side, he jerked when his heel sank into a soft spot and the foul odor of sulfur filled the air again.

*Great! If I don't get turned into a spider-kabob, I can sink into a pit of methane,* he wryly thought.

"You are weak compared to the other and of no use to me. The other is very powerful," the spider concluded.

"Yeah, well, whatever you say. I should warn you that I made a promise to help the Princess find her parents, and I've got this really weird thing about breaking my word once I've given it," he said in a voice filled with more bravado than he felt.

"They are no more," the spider hissed, taking a step forward.

"I hope you're wrong or we're all in a shitload of trouble – not that you would probably care," Ross replied.

He wobbled unsteadily when the ground beneath his feet shuddered. Multiple popping noises and the stomach-churning smell of rotten eggs filled the air. He stumbled forward a step and grimaced when he caught sight of the ferns moving with a black wave of hairy legs.

"Kill him," the monstrous spider ordered.

Ross watched with growing horror as the tide of spiders advanced on him. He tried to keep his focus on them and the freaking monstrous one behind them at the same time. He stumbled backward until he bumped into a tree. The damn things were emerging from the ferns onto the path now.

Muttering a curse, he turned, grabbed a low branch, and started climbing. His fingers slipped when he tried to grab a branch while still holding the long stick. The stick slipped from his fingers, and he tried to grab it but missed.

His eyes widened when he saw the mass of moving bodies below the tree. He turned and climbed higher as quickly as he could until there were no more limbs beneath the webs. Twisting around, he looked down at the spiders that were beginning to surround the trunk of the tree.

"Death by spiders is right up there with – okay, nothing," he muttered before turning his attention to the monstrous spider.

"I will find the powerful one. She will not escape us this time," the spider gleefully informed him.

Ross narrowed his eyes and took deep calming breaths. He looked up at the thick layer of web above him before looking down at the ground again. The spiders were beginning to climb.

He tightened his grip on the limb and bent his knees when the ground shuddered again. Dozens of popping noises echoed in response to the Isle's moan. He glanced at the ground and back to the creature that had been speaking to him.

Ross released his grip on the tree and patted the pockets of his jeans. Not finding what he was looking for, he reached into his jacket pocket. His fingers wrapped around the familiar metal housing of his lighter. He might have given up smoking, but he'd never stopped carrying a lighter.

Pulling out the lighter, he popped it open and flicked the metal wheel. The lighter was one of the old-fashioned kind that didn't have a safety on it. It was the only thing he had kept from his dad.

The wick ignited and the flame danced. He reached out onto the limb and broke off a dead branch from it. Lifting the branch up, he snagged some of the spider web above him, wrapping it around the tip until there was a thick coating of web.

He held the end of the web-coated stick to the flame. The silky threads caught fire, sending a scorching wave of heat toward his hand. He pulled back just as the smell of rotten eggs began to reach him. He smiled and looked out at the alien spider with a raised eyebrow.

"I don't think so," Ross replied as he held up one hand and lifted his middle finger while he released the flaming branch from the other hand.

The branch rotated as it fell. The gas that had been released from the thin layer of moss when the ground shook flared into an intense flash fire that rolled across the ground. The accumulated layer of gas was almost ten feet deep.

Ross hissed, closed his eyes, and hugged the tree trunk as the intense heat rose. The explosion caused more vents to open, releasing even more gas and fueling the already horrific fire. Bowing his head, he pulled his leather jacket up and tried to protect his face while peering through his fingers at the massive spider.

It had turned to run, but became entangled in a blanket of webbing that had fallen from the canopy. The webbing caught fire and melted around the large body.

Flames flared out toward him and his clothing was beginning to smolder. He closed his eyes – waiting, wondering, and hoping that being burned alive wasn't as painful as it looked on television.

He was surprised when a draft of çool air suddenly surrounded him, and the thick miasma of rotten eggs and smoke vanished. He cautiously opened one eye before he opened the other and lifted his head. Rubbing his eyes, he blinked several times before wryly smiling.

"Saving my ass again, Princess? If you aren't careful, I might get used to this," he teased.

He didn't know if she could hear what he was saying. Hell, he wasn't even sure if Gem was here or if she was just creating the shimmering bubble that protected him from the burning inferno beneath. Either way, he appreciated being saved from a fiery death.

The thought of death drew his gaze back to the white-hot skeletal remains of the black spider. The creature had collapsed and looked like it had tried to roll. The spider's long legs stood straight up and still glowed from the heat, the tips burning like Tiki torches.

Ross rubbed his hand, wincing when he touched his blistered skin. Opening the hand, he looked down at the silver lighter. He slid his thumb over the image of the fishing boat etched into the casing. For the first time in a long, long while he thought about his dad without resentment. It felt good.

"I never thought I'd say this, but thanks, old man," he murmured before he slid the lighter back into the pocket of his jacket.

It took almost twenty minutes before the flames died down enough that it was safe to descend. There were still spot fires burning where thin funnels of gas continued to rise, but at least there were no more spiders. Late afternoon sunlight shone down through the canopy of trees now that the spiderweb above was gone.

Ross was about to start climbing down when the bubble surrounding him moved and lifted him off the branch. He reached out and steadied himself when it began to move, warily holding his breath as the skin of the bubble gave slightly under his hand. At first, he was worried that the bubble would burst and send him tumbling nearly ten feet to the ground. He sighed in relief when it remained intact.

The sphere floated downward, occasionally bobbing upward to avoid a patch of still-burning gas before drifting closer to the path. Through the glossy, transparent film, Ross could see Gem standing twenty feet away. Her arms were stretched out in front of her, and her hands moved as if she were conducting a beautiful symphony.

The bubble dissolved when he was a foot off the ground. He dropped and stumbled forward several steps. Partially twisting to look behind him, he couldn't help but think that the forest looked like a firebomb had been detonated – which of course is exactly what had happened thanks to his lighter and some swamp gas. He dispassionately watched as the legs of the spider crumbled.

Returning his gaze to Gem, he saw her standing with her hands by her side now, her eyes focused on him. A wry smile curved his lips, and he strode down the path. She met him half way. Opening his arms, he wrapped them around her waist and pulled her close.

"You didn't run very far," he teasingly chided. She glared at him. "What? What did I do this time?"

She answered him with an inelegant sniff. He rubbed his cheek against her hair and closed his eyes for a moment. A myriad of strange feelings were engulfing him. He didn't know if it was from having so many near-death experiences in a short period of time or the fact that ever since he first saw Gem, he had been feeling off balance.

"You have got to be either the craziest man I have ever met or the dumbest," she finally muttered in a voice thickened with emotion as she tugged his hair in reproach.

# CHAPTER TEN

By late afternoon, they had made it past another obstacle. This one hadn't been as frightening – or as dangerous – as the ones before. Gem chuckled and shook her head when she heard Ross muttering about it under his breath while he pulled lumps of viscous plant sap out of his hair.

"I'm going to need another shower," he informed her in a gruff tone.

The thought of seeing him without his clothes was still firmly burned into her mind, and it sent a flash of heat through her. She barely stifled her groan at the memory. She clenched her fists as she resisted the urge to offer help in taking his clothes off.

*Get a grip, Gem,* she silently admonished herself.

"You have some goop on the tip of your ear," she replied instead.

He reached up and ran his fingers along his ear. She laughed when he muttered a few colorful words and swiped the plant sap away. She decided now was not the time to tell him that he had a large glob on the back of his head.

"I'm so done with being almost buried alive, stomped on, sucked dry, burnt to a crisp, and eaten – all in one day, too!" he dramatically exclaimed.

Gem giggled. "I know it isn't funny, but – it is funny. I did try to warn you," she reminded him.

"Ha ha ha," he dryly replied before he lifted a hand and found the glob coating his hair. He snorted in laughter. "You know, every Halloween, that's a holiday back home, the owners of the local bar would play Little Shop of Horrors. I swear I'll never be able to watch that movie again with the same enjoyment," he vowed.

"Why not?" she asked.

Gem stopped walking when he turned to face her. She plucked a piece of plant fiber from his hair and scowled in distaste when she felt how sticky it was.

"Your expression pretty much says it. The story is about a huge plant that likes to eat people. Being eaten by an oversized Venus Flytrap gives me a whole new understanding of what an insect must go through," he explained.

She nodded. "You are lucky that you were able to escape as quickly as you did. The sap of the plant would have begun dissolving the flesh right off of your bones in another few minutes," she said

"Are you serious?" he demanded with dismay.

The snort slipped from her before she could stop it. The expression of disbelief and horror on his face was priceless. She created a small rain cloud over her hands so she could wipe the sticky residue from them before she wiped the tears of laughter from the corners of her eyes as she shook her head.

"No, not really. The plant would have sucked you down through its stem and into its stomach. It would have taken weeks before your body was finally dissolved, but I would have cut you out way before then," she replied with a straight face.

Ross shot her a haughty glare before shaking his head. "I have goop in places that goop should not be. This is the second time today that I've been in this predicament. Someone should have warned me that this hero business is much harder, messier, and slightly more embarrassing than I thought it would be," he informed her.

Gem laughed at his dramatically pained expression. "Well, I think you've been a *great* hero. If it makes you feel better, I can make warm water and air dry you again," she teased, wiggling her fingers at him.

His expression softened and his lips curved into a rueful, crooked smile. "Yes, you can," he conceded.

They stared at each other for several seconds. She didn't know what was going through his mind, but she hoped it was similar to her own thoughts – she wanted to kiss him, then she wanted to help him out of his clothes and….

"I think we should stop for the night. It will be dark soon and too dangerous to proceed," she suggested in a slightly breathless voice.

"Good idea. So, is there a place that you think would be safe? I mean, like, there aren't going to be any night-swarming flesh-eaters, ghosts, or weird monsters trying to eat us while we sleep, are there?" he half-heartedly inquired as he looked around them.

"Of course not – at least I don't think so. By the way, monsters are not weird. In fact, most of them are very polite and sweet," she informed him with a pointed look.

She tried not to laugh at his expression of disbelief. He shook his head and lifted his eyebrow at her amusement, then he stepped closer to her. She parted her lips in anticipation. He lifted his hand and placed a finger under her chin.

"You, Princess, have a very sassy sense of humor," he murmured.

"Is that a bad thing?" she asked.

Gem watched as several different emotions – confusion, hesitation, desire – appeared on his face. It was the last emotion that held her spellbound. How was it possible to desire someone so much after just meeting them? She didn't believe in love at first sight.

*Perhaps this isn't love – just desire,* she thought.

"No, it isn't a bad thing," he replied in a gravelly voice.

"I know of a place where we should be safe. There is – there is a cave near here that I have used before when I needed to seek shelter," she said.

"Sounds good," he quietly responded.

Gem was disappointed when Ross dropped his hand to his side and stepped away from her. She had hoped that he would kiss her again. Chiding herself for her wayward thoughts, she walked around him.

"I'll lead the way. It isn't far but can be easy to miss," she said.

"Lead the way, Princess," he said before muttering under his breath. *"Besides, it will be a hell of a lot nicer looking at your ass for a change."*

She almost missed his barely audible remark – almost. She smiled, not bothering to hide her pleased expression because he couldn't see it with her back to him. Striding forward, she continued down the path feeling like she was floating on air.

Ross stared in awe at the spot Gem had chosen for the night. There was a short but wide waterfall that emptied into a small pool. The pool flowed down into a series of smaller waterfalls before it ran into a narrow creek.

Behind the main waterfall, he could see a dark recess that opened into a cave. Ross suspected that the cave had been formed by a lava tube at some point based on the weathered volcanic rocks that lined the opening. Thick tangles of plants grew from the rocks. Flowers of all different shapes, sizes, and colors were interspersed among the ferns and moss.

"We should be safe here," Gem murmured.

"This looks like the photos of Hawaii that I've seen," he responded without thinking.

Stepping around her, he walked over to the edge of the clear pool. He stared down into it for several seconds before he turned and looked at her. He nodded toward the water.

"Is the water safe?" he suddenly asked.

He gave her a questioning look. She had started, as if she had been a million miles away, when he had asked about the water and now she was blushing. It might be interesting to know if she was thinking about his earlier shower – or maybe contemplating joining him this time.

"Yes. I've often enjoyed a swim here. The water is nice because there are several hot springs further up that feed into it so it is not cold," she said.

"Oh yeah," Ross groaned, tossing his jacket and sweater onto the ground and reaching for the hem of his shirt.

"Oh!" she exclaimed softly. "I—" She bit her lip as he pulled his shirt over his head, revealing his very appealing torso. "You shouldn't be —" she said in a rush as all her breath left her.

He shot her a grin as he tossed his shirt down along the bank. He bent over and untied his boots. Hopping around, he pulled one boot off and then the other. He tossed them down next to his shirt.

"If you don't want to get another eyeful, you might want to turn around – unless you'd like to join me?" he added with a wicked smile.

He pulled off his socks and straightened up. Her eyes followed the movement of his hands when he reached for the button on his jeans, and they widened as he slowly pulled down the zipper. He softly chuckled, fully aware of what he was doing to her.

He sighed in regret when she suddenly turned her back to him. He pushed his pants down, but he continued to study her stiff shoulders. Deep down, he had really hoped that she would decide to join him.

"I'll gather some food and set up camp while you get cleaned up. If you toss your clothing onto the bank, I'll dry them for you," she added before she hurried away.

Ross pulled off his jeans and held them in one hand as he watched Gem weave her way toward the entrance to the cave. Shaking his head at the thoughts coursing through his mind, he dropped his jeans on the pile of clothing before diving into the pool. The water was a mixture of warm and cold currents, and it reminded him of the thermoclines he often encountered while diving.

Breaking the surface of the water, he shook his head and turned in a circle. It was the magic hour when the stars begin to appear. He blinked when he saw a small green bar floating above him.

He reached up and grabbed it before turning to face the mouth of the cave. Holding up the soap, he nodded his thanks to Gem who quickly turned around and went back into the cave. He chuckled again.

"It would appear my magical Princess is a little shy," he murmured.

He swam over to the edge of the pool. Lifting the soap to his nose, he sniffed it. A surprisingly pleasant scent of pine wafted through his nostrils. He grunted in response and began to lather his skin. The soap produced a mild, refreshing tingle. He scrubbed his skin and his hair before ducking his head under the water.

He reached up and pulled each article of clothing into the water after he finished bathing and scrubbed off the sticky sap. He stood and spread each piece out on the slope of the bank. When he finished, he placed the bar of soap on a rock, turned, and dove under the water again.

Ross swam as far as he could until his burning lungs forced him to surface again. The night had come while he washed his clothes, but the stars, the brightness of the double moons, and the glow of bioluminescent flowers lit up the pool. He sighed deeply and floated on his back so he could stare up at the twinkling stars.

Now that he was no longer worried about dying or wondering if his butt cheeks would be permanently glued together, his thoughts turned to his tantalizing companion. It was hard to believe that they had only met each other a few hours ago when it felt like they had been together for much longer.

*I guess time flies when you are trying not to die,* he thought.

He wondered how much time exactly had passed back on Earth, and thought about the fact that Gem knew Carly Tate – one of the women he'd been accused of killing. Had they all travelled here? The two women and the detective? That picture that Mike had brought back, the one that helped exonerate him, had Carly in it… with *her kids.* She didn't have kids before she'd disappeared. The children pictured had been young and Carly had been missing a long while, but… it was kind-of a mind-fuck. She'd looked happy and healthy, which had been nice.

He was glad she'd found someone, even if she'd had to go to *another world* to find a someone she wouldn't accidentally dismember. He groaned as he remembered that blow to his balls. In that split second, he'd really thought they might never recover – and that wasn't nearly as painful as when Gem had done it.

*I sure know how to pick 'em.* Ross thought with a low, self-derisive snort.

Carly was sweet, though, one of those wholesome women who a guy could fall in love with and marry. Ross was the kind of guy who liked one-night stands – no attachments, no expectations, and no regrets, but he'd gone out with Carly four times because he'd started to worry that he'd never be able to make real, human connections.

His mom and he sort-of had a built-in bond, but Ross had no true friends, no 'lovers' who really… loved him. So he'd tried, but after Carly had almost emasculated him and nearly burned down his boat, he'd decided that 'nice and wholesome' women like Carly were too damn dangerous to be around.

"Are you alright?"

Ross jerked when he felt an unexpected touch on his arm and accidentally slipped under the water in surprise. Surfacing, he coughed and sputtered as he treaded water. Lifting a hand, he wiped the water from his eyes and pushed his hair back. He frowned in confusion when he saw Gem in the water beside him.

"What – Is everything alright?" he asked, looking around before returning his worried gaze to her.

She looked back at him with a slightly wary expression. "I called you to let you know that I dried your clothes and that I found some food for us, but you didn't answer. I heard you moan and thought you might be in pain," she explained.

"Oh – Everything is okay. I was just thinking of a girl I dated," he answered without thinking.

Her expression changed. "Oh. I'm sorry I disturbed you then," she replied in a frigid tone.

Ross reached out and grabbed her arm when she started to turn away from him. She shot him a haughty glare. He smiled in amusement.

"She wasn't my type," he said, pulling her closer.

Her eyes narrowed. "I wasn't asking if she was," she retorted.

"No, you didn't, but I wanted you to know," he quietly replied.

"Why – why should you care what I think?" she softly demanded.

"I don't know why. I just do – care. I care," he murmured.

He pulled her close, and she looked into his eyes. Their legs moved in unison, keeping them afloat.

"Ross…. "

She took a deep breath and brushed a light kiss against his lips. A shiver ran through him when she glided her hand up his arm to his shoulder. He was vaguely aware that she was wearing some type of swimsuit. The thin material did little to protect him from the feel of her soft curves.

He pressed his lips harder against hers, and she parted them under the pressure. He swiftly deepened the kiss until they were in danger of sinking beneath the water. She tangled her fingers in his hair and wrapped her legs around his waist. He kicked his legs harder to keep them afloat, and each kick pressed his growing arousal against her.

He finally broke their kiss. He stared into her eyes. Breathing heavily, he wrapped his hand in her hair and held her tightly for a moment as waves of need crashed like a tsunami through him.

*Hell, forget a tsunami! It feels like a fucking atom bomb going off inside me,* he thought.

"We'd – we'd better go," she breathlessly suggested.

Ross released her when she pressed her hands against his shoulders and pushed away. He watched her swim to the bank and climb out, and hissed when he saw the form-fitting green suit she was wearing.

"Down, boy," he muttered to his cock when it jerked with approval.

He slowly swam to the bank. By the time he climbed out, Gem had already done her magic and was dried, dressed, and heading to the cave. He shook his head in wonder.

"Keep your head on straight, Ross, or she'll pull your heart right out of your chest and roast it over one of her magical fires," he cautioned himself in a low, strained voice. "Damn if I won't end up with a set of blue balls by the time I get back home. "

The thought of leaving had a sobering effect on his libido. A startled oath slipped from his lips when a strong current of warm air surrounded him, moving from his feet up to the top of his hair. He shook his head.

"Thank you," he called out.

"You're welcome," she replied without looking back.

He chuckled and picked up his clothes. He slowly dressed, giving both of them time to collect themselves. Pulling his socks on, he was surprised to find his boots completely dry as well.

"I'm really going to miss this," he sighed.

After he finished dressing, he looked back up at the glimmering stars. For a moment, he was lost in their beauty. The last twenty-four hours had been surreal. He didn't know what tomorrow would bring, but for once, he was excited to find out.

"I'm going to eat your food if you don't come and get it," Gem shouted.

His stomach growled in protest. Laughing at her obvious lie, he turned toward the waterfall and followed the path to their retreat. He already knew that it would be a very long and challenging night – and he was going to enjoy every second of it.

# CHAPTER ELEVEN

Ross stepped behind the curtain of water and paused. The glow of a small fire lit the back of the cave. Shadows from the flames danced against the walls. He had been right – the cave was actually the remains of a lava tube.

"Something smells good," he said.

Gem grunted in response. He walked over and sat down on a log that apparently had been dragged into the tube at some point. Markings on the walls captured his attention. He started in surprise when Gem suddenly blocked his view.

"Here," she quietly said.

He took the bountiful offering, and focused on her face. She was avoiding his gaze.

"Thank you. Hey – are you okay?" he asked in a low voice, wrapping one hand around her wrist.

She briefly lifted her eyes and looked at him, her expression troubled, before she nodded, pulled away, and returned to her seat on a log across from him. He lowered his hand and looked down at the wooden plate. He was shocked to see a variety of fruits and nuts along with a round husk filled with a thick, yellow steaming liquid.

"We need to remember that once I find my parents, you will be leaving," she said, picking up her plate of food.

He silently studied her. She kept her head bowed, but he could see that she was picking at the food on her plate. He was surprised to see a slight trembling of her hand when she picked up a piece of fruit and bit into it.

"Yeah, well, who knows – I could get used to all of this magical hocus pocus. It's kinda growing on me now that I'm over the initial shock. I mean, I have a great meal, great company, my own waterfall with a swimming pool, glow-in-the-dark flowery things, and...," Ross commented before his voice faded.

She looked up at him with a raised eyebrow. "And...," she prodded.

He gave her a crooked grin. "And where else would I have my own sexy, kickass warrior woman to make sure I don't get myself killed?" he finished.

"You don't have a kickass warrior woman back home?" she asked.

Ross swore he could feel himself falling forward into her luminous eyes. Her mixed expression of skepticism and pleasure poured over him like warm honey on a sweet roll. Hell, he could feel his mouth watering for a taste of the juice on her lips.

*And a few other places,* he silently groaned.

"No – no kickass warrior woman – or any woman for that matter," he finally replied.

"Not even the one you mentioned earlier?" she dryly reminded him.

Ross didn't try to hide his grimace. "Hell, no! Especially not Carly. Actually, I've been meaning to ask you about her, since you seem to know more about what happened to her than I do," he said.

"Carly...? You dated Carly? The Dragon King's mate?" she asked, her expression shocked.

Ross muttered a curse when he sloshed some of his soup onto his hand. He lifted his hand to his lips and licked it off. The burst of flavors swept over his taste buds, and he looked down at the soup in surprise.

"Yeah, heh, Dragon King. That sounds like someone who could survive her. How *do* you know Carly?" he asked.

"I met her when she and Drago attended a meeting to determine how to kill the Sea Witch," she replied.

"Huh, well, since the Sea Witch isn't dead, guess *that* didn't go according to plan – but Carly, she's ok? Happy? Nothin' bad happened to her? I saw a picture of her that Mike Hallbrook brought back from here and it looked like she was happy in the photo. It's kinda hard to wrap my head around the fact that Carly is with a dragon. I'm not quite sure how that works, but if I remember correctly, Carly was obsessed with the creatures, so who cares? I have to admit that I can see Carly taking one look at a dragon and deciding to take him home," he mused.

Gem smiled. "Yes, she seems happy. I don't know all the details, but Drago is besotted. I think he would have died if she had not come to give him hope. It's enough to give anyone hope, really, the fact that *Drago* found happiness. He's the last dragon left in the Seven King-doms. The Sea Witch turned his people into stone like she did me," she said.

They were quiet for a few moments, and Ross was grateful for the soothing sound of the waterfall. It blocked out the eerie silence of the rest of this Isle. Except for the spiders, they hadn't seen any other animals so far. He wasn't sure if it was because of the spell that had been cast over the Isle, if the alien had eaten everything, the animals had been frightened away, or hell, maybe he was just used to living where he could always hear cars and people.

"This soup is really good. What is it made from?" he asked, lifting the bowl to his lips and taking a mouthful.

"Slugs," she casually replied.

Ross glared at Gem. A shudder ran through him as he swallowed the tangy broth. It wasn't until he warily looked at the creamy mixture that he heard Gem's snort of smothered laughter and knew that she was teasing him.

"Slugs, huh?" he wryly repeated.

She shook her head. "You are so easy to tease. It is a soft potato root from the vines that grow along the rocks. It is perfectly safe to eat," she reassured him with a grin.

"I'm going to have to keep my eye on you," he said, waving his finger at her.

She sniffed at his warning. "You'll have to keep up with me first," she retorted.

Ross chuckled when she added a mischievous grin and swirled her fingers at the fire. He watched as dancing figures appeared in the flames, twirling as if they were at a lavish ball. He was reminded once again that he was in a magical world where monsters, witches, elementals, and even dragons thrived.

*I am so in over my head,* he thought, looking across the fire at Gem. *But who the hell cares? Since I can only live once, I might as well enjoy the ride.*

Several hours later, he sat on a rock gazing up at the stars. He didn't remember them ever being this bright and clear. He turned his head when he heard Gem climbing the path back to the cave.

When she stopped beside him, he scooted over. She sat down and looked up at the sky. They didn't say anything at first.

He picked up a flower that he'd found a few minutes earlier. The white bloom still glowed. Turning toward her, he placed the flower behind her ear.

"Why...?" she started to ask before falling silent.

"It reminded me of you," he murmured, sliding his fingers through her hair.

"You confuse me," she softly admitted.

He chuckled. "Sometimes I confuse myself," he said with a shrug.

"Would you like to see something?" she asked.

"Sure – as long as it isn't monsters, dragons, humongous alien spiders, bone-breaking trees, mud pits, or people-eating plants," he dryly replied.

"It won't be *all* of those," she cheekily promised.

"Lucky me," he muttered.

He wasn't kidding when he said that he sometimes confused himself. Right now, his mind was like a tangled ball of yarn after the cat had played with it, and he had a funny ache in the center of his chest.

"Watch this," she murmured, raising her hands.

Ross gaped in awe when some water from the pool rose up in the shape of strange creatures. They looked like half-dragons/half-sea horses. They danced across the water, frolicking like the porpoises back home.

Wisps of mist floated across the pool and began to gather and change. He chuckled when he saw the dragon-shaped sea horses change to birds and the mist turned into trees. Glowing blooms from the surrounding forest swirled amongst the mist-created trees and floated upward.

He looked at Gem's face, enjoying the pleasure reflected in her eyes and the slight flush to her cheeks. He loved the way she bit her lip as she added more detail to the scene she was creating.

Reaching up, he absently rubbed his chest, feeling the strange ache again. He looked back at her creation when her hands stopped moving. His breath caught when he saw the two figures frozen in the center. A man stood with his arm around a woman who leaned heavily on him.

Ross stood up when he saw the look of pain and determination in their eyes – and saw the spiral of sparkles sliding from the woman's side. Her parents. Had to be. Who else would be on her mind? He turned and looked down at her as the image began to fade when she lowered her arms. A single tear coursed down her cheek.

"Gem...," he murmured in concern.

"That is what my parents looked like the last time I saw them. My mother was wounded. They realized that the alien creature was stronger and far more dangerous than they could defeat without help, but they knew they had to keep it from escaping," she murmured, staring at the pool of water.

Ross ran his thumb tenderly across her cheek, capturing the tear. She looked up at him with a troubled expression. Struck by the haunted look in her eyes, he pulled her into his arms and held her tightly.

"Everything will work out. I promise," he vowed.

They silently embraced. After several minutes, he reluctantly released Gem when she lowered her arms and pulled back. She looked at him without speaking before she turned away. She paused after taking a couple of steps.

"We better get some sleep. According to the stones, the traps will become more treacherous the closer we get to the palace," she murmured.

"I'll be up in a moment," he replied.

He watched as she slowly climbed back up to the cave. Only when she had disappeared behind the curtain of water did he release the breath he'd been holding. He hadn't realized he wasn't breathing until his burning lungs began to protest. That is what she did to him

– made him so freaking confused he didn't know his ass from his head!

He leaned back to look up at the stars. Shoving his hands in his front pockets, he contemplated once again how his life could get so fucked up in such a short period of time. 'If' – all of the questions began with 'if. '

*If I had moved away instead of sticking around Yachats. If I had not seen Magna. If I had minded my own business. If I wasn't such....*

Ross stopped the negative thought, and patted the pocket of his T-shirt, wishing for the thousandth time that he had not chosen to quit smoking. He dropped his hand and sighed deeply.

"Whether you want to be a hero or not, Ross, doesn't matter. Gonna help that wickedly enchanting Princess save her home or die trying. My old man would be laughing his ass off if he could see me now," he muttered to the diamond-encrusted sky.

Shaking his head in self-deprecation, he turned around and climbed the narrow path up to the cave. Mist from the waterfall coated his face, and he wiped it off. He smiled tenderly when he saw that Gem had made a pallet out of moss and leaves for him on the other side of the fire from herself.

He studied her with a strange mixture of concern and admiration. She was using his sweater as a pillow. Her arms were wrapped around it, and her face was partially buried in the Merino wool fibers. He was glad he had worn it instead of one of his cheaper ones. The fibers were finer and didn't itch.

He didn't know why that thought had popped into his head or why it would even matter, but it did. He looked at the wall of water. Making a quick decision, he picked up the pallet she had made for him and placed it beside hers. The move did three things: it allowed him to face her and the opening instead of having his back to it, it put the fire between them and the opening, and it allowed him to use his body heat to help keep her warm. He had not missed her slight shiver nor the way she unconsciously rubbed her cheek against his sweater.

He lowered himself onto the pallet. Lying down, he turned on his side and pulled his jacket from where she had neatly folded it so he could use it as his pillow and he spread it over both of them. She immediately scooted back against him and relaxed.

He frowned when he noticed a strange pattern of colors dancing from her skin to his when he wrapped his arm around her waist. As he folded his other arm under his head, he noticed the same colors in her hair. They caressed his face, spreading a tingling sensation of warmth before gradually disappearing.

He was too tired to care what they might mean. They could mean everything or nothing, but they weren't killing him at the moment. In fact, the colors felt really nice, so Ross closed his eyes, and slowly relaxed.

He would only keep his eyes closed for a little while. He was used to getting very little or interrupted sleep from spending a lot of time on his fishing boat. He needed to stay awake – just in case.

*I've got to protect my Princess,* he exhaustedly vowed, even as he fell into a deep, deep sleep.

# CHAPTER TWELVE

**The high seas of the Seven Kingdoms**

With a disgruntled groan, Gant lowered the sails of the medium-sized schooner, and stepped toward the railing, warily peering through his spyglass at his quickly approaching visitors.

Either he was having a really bad day or his mission had been announced to half of the Seven Kingdoms! From the east, he could see a ship flying Ashure Wave's all-too-familiar flag. From the north, he could see the distinctive outline of two dragons in the sky. When he turned to the west, the vivid lightning in the clouds told him that Nali, the Empress of the Monsters, had also spied him. It didn't take them long to converge on his location.

The two dragons were the first to land. Drago, the King of the Dragons, shifted first, followed by his Captain of the Guard, Theron. Gant clenched his jaw when the two dragon-shifters walked across the deck of his ship as if it belonged to them. He bowed his head to Drago in greeting.

"King Drago, welcome aboard my ship," he wryly greeted.

Drago flashed him a sharp-toothed grin. "Thank you for the invitation," he retorted.

Gant smiled at Theron's knowing chuckle. The dragon grinned back at him. Gant studied the telltale scar of a dragon's burn along the captain's right cheek and down his throat. Only the king's dragon fire could produce such a scar on another dragon.

"It looks like you have more company," Theron commented.

"Yes, I noticed that as well," Gant replied.

The three men turned to watch Ashure Wave's magnificent ship glide toward Gant's port bow. With the Pirate King's usual flare, he waved a nonchalant hand and half a dozen grappling hooks flew through the air. Gant waved his hand in defense, and four out of the six fell to the water as if they had hit a transparent wall. He would allow the pirate two hooks – bow and stern – but not six! He didn't care if the man was a king. Gant was still pissed off about his unexpected swim off the dock thanks to the damn sea monkeys that Ashure had unleashed.

"Gant! Still upset with me, I see," Ashure laughed. "What brings you to my part of the world?"

"Ashure," Gant replied with a brief bow of his head. "Koorgan would like the return of the mirror. "

"Mirror – ah, yes, well, I seem to have misplaced it. Once I find it, I'll be happy to have it delivered to your king," Ashure assured. "Good day to you, Drago. It is good to see dragons once again flying through the skies. "

"One of your ships fired on me and Theron, Ashure. The next time I'll burn it down to the waterline," Drago snapped.

Ashure raised his hand in a placating motion. "I will speak with my captains, Drago. No need to get upset. I'm sure the captain meant no disrespect to you or your man," he half-heartedly defended.

The snap and crackle of electricity in the air drew their attention.

"Hold on!" the crew on Ashure's ship shouted as Nali's ship descended from the clouds. Gant gripped the handrail and watched as the massive vessel carried by four Thunderbirds descended for a landing. He could feel his hair standing on end from the static electricity produced by the Thunderbirds.

Nali's ship gracefully glided across the water and pulled up on his ship's starboard bow. Gant gritted his teeth when it rocked his schooner back and forth.

"Hold her steady," Ashure ordered in a booming voice.

Drago bent his knees and took the movement in stride while Theron muttered a few words about monsters and pirates that would have had him on both Nali's and Ashure's black list. Gant straightened up, then scowled when Nali jumped and landed on the bow of his ship.

"Well, it would appear that the only one who hasn't invaded my privacy is… never mind," Gant grumbled when Ashure swung from a rope down to the deck of the schooner.

"This *is* a bit of a surprise," Ashure commented, rubbing his hands together. "I believe this calls for a drink, don't you, my lovely empress?"

Nali shook her head. "Only if you are supplying it, my dear pirate," she retorted.

Ashure shot Gant, Drago, and Theron a pained expression. "She wounds me. Gant, do you perchance have any of the brandy that I left behind?" he inquired.

"You took all of it when you took the mirror," he replied.

"Ah, well, I guess since Drago and his man did not bring a ship, I will have to sacrifice a bottle that was destined for the lovely Isle of the Monsters and its beautiful Empress," Ashure tsked with faux regret.

"If I may be so rude as to inquire, why are you all here – on my ship? Did Koorgan send you?" Gant quietly demanded.

Ashure cheerfully answered. "Nay, I knew you were searching for the Isle of the Elementals and thought you could use some assistance. I'm always up for a new challenge. "

"I came because Ashure is here," Nali bluntly stated.

"I came because Orion sent a cryptic message that sounded ominous. Now, seeing Ashure here, I can only imagine he must be behind it," Drago growled.

"Why am I always the one who is blamed?" Ashure demanded in mock outrage.

Theron chuckled. "Because you usually *are* behind it. We heard about the sea monkey catastrophe on the docks," he informed Ashure.

"That is something else I need to discuss with you at a later time, Ashure," Nali snapped, pointing a waving finger of warning at Ashure. "My sea monkeys are not to be used in your antics." With that, she curtly turned away from him. "Now that our reasons for being here have been explained, let us get down to business. Drago, the alien creature still lives. We need your and Orion's help to kill it," Nali stated.

"I am here," Orion replied.

Gant hissed with surprise when he saw Orion gliding in on a wave of water. The King of the Sea People stepped onto the railing and then down onto the deck. The trident in his hand glowed for a moment more as the funnel of water retreated into the ocean. Orion gave Gant a brief nod before turning his attention to Nali.

"I received your message," Orion said.

"I'm glad you came so quickly and you were able to convince Drago to join us," Nali murmured graciously.

"Given the contents of your message, I could hardly afford to wait," Orion dryly replied.

"Gant, your journey and ours are intertwined. Is there a place on your ship where we can talk?" Nali asked.

Gant saw that Nali's eyes no longer held amusement but a deep concern. "There is an office below deck – with refreshments," he added, looking at Ashure.

"Brilliant," Ashure murmured.

"You cannot go, Ashure," Nali snapped.

"Perhaps if you would explain why I cannot participate in saving the Seven Kingdoms instead of using vague hints and dire threats, I would agree with you," Ashure replied in an uncharacteristically sharp tone.

"It is too dangerous. If the alien were to inhabit your body—" Nali began before she bit off her sentence and shot an expressive glare at Ashure that Gant didn't quite understand. "I think you know why that would be a problem."

Ashure stood and walked over to Nali. He gently grasped her hand and lifted it to his lips. Pressing a kiss to her fingers, he stared down at her with unblinking eyes. Gant swallowed when he noticed a strange swirling of colors in the pirate's eyes that he had never noticed before. Koorgan had told him of how Ashure's eyes had changed before LaBluff had dissolved – was this what Koorgan had talked about?

"If anyone should be afraid, it is the alien creature, Nali, not I," Ashure reassured her.

"My mirror said otherwise," Nali stated.

For a moment, Gant thought the Empress was talking about the magic mirror that Ashure had taken. That mirror had been enchanted to show the possessor the thing they wished for the most. It wasn't until Drago growled in disapproval that he realized there must be another mirror.

"You had better tread carefully, Empress," Drago warned.

Nali turned to face Drago with a raised eyebrow. "The Goddess's Mirror showed me the truth before, did it not?" she retorted.

"What did the Goddess's Mirror show you this time?" Ashure asked, shooting a sharp glance at Drago.

Nali turned and looked at the group. Gant lifted the crystal bottle that held the Silver Rum. It might not be brandy, but it was close enough. He carefully topped off the glasses. Theron grinned, held his up, and bowed his head in thanks. Nali lifted her glass and stared into the crystal clear liquor.

"The mirror is not always easy to interpret. There are times when the images are clear and other times when they are not," Nali admitted.

"Well, that helps us a lot," Ashure dryly commented, returning to his seat and picking up his drink.

Nali glared at Ashure. "The first time the mirror was very clear that Carly's appearance was a catalyst. With Drago awake, we now have our best chance to defeat the dark shadow. The image that appeared this time didn't make sense at first, but I now understand the reason for Marina's warning that you should not be near the palace the day we faced Magna and the alien creature. If you were to avoid being near the creature the first time, it only makes sense that you would still be in danger this time," she explained.

"Not necessarily, though I would have appreciated knowing Marina's fears instead of everyone trying to keep me in the dark and sending me on wild goose chases, but I digress. What exactly did the mirror *not* show you this time?" Ashure asked with a sigh.

Nali frowned. "Without Magna's power, the alien creature is not as strong, but it is fragmented. I do not yet know exactly where all the pieces are or how best to destroy them. I have seen glimpses of many things," she explained.

"Well, there are enough of us," Drago pointed out. "You, Ashure, Theron, and Gant can find them and Orion and I will destroy them," Drago said, looking at Orion for confirmation.

Orion nodded. "It would be best to stay close, but if it comes at us from multiple points, we will be ready," he agreed.

"There is more," Nali said, grimly looking at the group.

"Isn't there always?" Ashure muttered with a roll of his eyes and a grimace.

Drago and Theron snorted at Ashure's pained expression. "What is it?" Gant asked.

Nali looked at him with a dark, unfathomable gaze. "This time, one of us will die," she softly said.

# CHAPTER THIRTEEN

Gem woke the next morning feeling refreshed and warm. The fire, made of magic, still burned brightly in the fire pit. She could feel the warmth against her back.

She could also feel the warm body she was curled up against. She slowly opened her eyes and was greeted by Ross's morning shadow of dark stubble. Her hand lay over his heart, and her head was tucked against his shoulder.

She could feel one of his hands on her hip while the other hand lay across her waist. Amusement filled her when he smacked his lips in his sleep and sighed. She didn't know what he was dreaming about, but from the low rumbling growl coming from his stomach, she imagined it was food.

With regret, she faded into a mist and reformed several feet away. Ross grumbled incoherently in his sleep and gathered the sweater she had been using as a pillow in his arms. She wrapped her arms around her waist and studied his relaxed features.

She'd thought that if he were to stay, that would simplify matters, but now that he had admitted he cared for her and he might not go back to his world, Gem was even more conflicted. The colors marked them as a perfectly balanced pair, but she just didn't know....

Obviously she found him attractive, that wasn't in doubt. She had never before thought someone so scruffy could be so appealing! His dark brown hair was almost to his shoulders and there were shorter pieces sticking out all over. She couldn't see him ever bothering to style it smooth, because he didn't strike her as someone who worried about how it looked, unlike most of the men she knew. His face was tanned, and there were faint wrinkle lines near the corners of his eyes and mouth as if he spent a great deal of time outside.

She curled her fingers against her waist as she remembered the sensation of his calloused hands against her skin. It was obvious he was used to hard work. His hands also had scars that would never be found on someone who spent their days immersed in court politics. Gem decided that she liked that about him.

His nose had a slight bump in the center, and there was a tiny, thin scar running along the ridge that told her it had been broken before. She grimaced when she saw the fading bruise where she had struck him. Guilt washed through her. She reminded herself that she had struck him before she realized he was not a threat.

The more she studied his face, the more she saw. This was a man who had lived life and had a strong moral compass. He was also sexy and funny.

*Which makes this journey even more alarming,* she suddenly thought.

Shaking her head at her thoughts, she silently exited the cave. She would gather some food for their morning break and decide on the best route to the palace. Yesterday's traps had made it difficult to cover a lot of ground, and she could feel the fragile magic straining to hold the Isle aloft. There was no doubt in her mind that time was running out for her people and her heart.

～

Ross sat up and wildly glanced around him. His heart was pounding, and he rubbed the center of his chest. The dream had been incredibly vivid – it would have been nice if he could remember what it was about.

"God, I hate dreams sometimes," he groaned, rubbing his face.

He groaned again when he registered the sound of water. Cursing under his breath, he looked at the spot next to him. It was empty except for his sweater. Scrambling to his feet, he scanned the cave.

"Gem," he called.

His voice echoed in the cavernous space. Bending over, he scooped up his jacket and sweater and headed for the entrance to the cave. The chilly mist from the waterfall helped to chase the lingering cobwebs from his mind. He carefully stepped along the path and scanned the area near the pool.

He sighed when he saw Gem gathering fruit from a tree and placing it into a basket. He gaped, his mouth wide open, when the tree bent over so that she could pluck a piece of fruit that was beyond her reach. At first, he thought he had imagined it, but the tree next to her did the same thing before pointing in his direction.

Ross wiped his damp face with his hands, and he started forward when Gem turned around and smiled at him. She said something to the tree which shook in response. Several pieces of fruit rained down around her. The pieces stopped in mid air before floating over to land in her basket.

"Welcome to the Twilight Zone. I really hope today goes better than the last two!" he muttered.

It was cooler this morning, so he pulled on his jacket. Tucking his sweater under his arm, he worked his way down the path and walked along the edge of the pool. He warily looked up at the trees when they turned as if to look down at him.

"Uh, good morning," he greeted in an uneasy voice.

She smiled at him. "Good morning," she said.

"Here, take my sweater. It is a little chilly out. I'll hold the basket for you," he offered.

"Thank you," she said.

He held out his sweater with one hand and reached for the woven basket with the other. He didn't miss the slight flush on her cheeks when they exchanged items. Clearing his throat, he looked up at the trees.

"So, I take it these are good trees? They aren't going to – like – try to step on me or smash me into little pieces, are they?" he inquired.

Gem finished pulling his sweater over her head and looked at him with wide, startled eyes before she smiled again. She pulled her hair free of the sweater before she reached out and caressed the trunk of one tree. Ross bit the inside of his cheek to keep from making an asinine remark that was sure to embarrass them both.

"No, these trees have not been bewitched," she said.

"Cool," he replied.

He felt strangely tongue-tied. He looked at the trees again before looking at her and then the basket. His stomach rumbled, and he grinned at Gem when she laughed.

"Your stomach was rumbling earlier, and you were smacking your lips. I thought you might be hungry, and the trees were kind enough to share their fruit with me," she teased.

"I feel like I could eat a horse," he confessed.

"A horse? Do you eat them where you come from?" she asked with a frown.

Ross shook his head. "No, I don't eat them. I don't mind a good steak every once in a while, but that is usually a little more than my budget allows. I pretty much eat seafood – you know, fish, shrimp, crab, scallops – that kind of stuff," he said.

"Oh. My people mostly eat the harvest given to us from the trees. The forest is filled with an abundance of food that does not require eating meat," she replied.

"Uh, okay, so you guys are like vegetarians or vegans," he deduced.

She frowned. "We eat many vegetables. I do not know what a vegan is," she confessed.

Ross chuckled and shook his head. "Hell if I know either – I just see the stuff in the grocery store and keep on walking. If it is too healthy, there has to be something wrong with it," he replied.

She stared at him in confusion for a moment before she shook her head. "I do not think I understand that logic," she said.

Ross reached out and grasped her hand. "Don't bother trying. So, what do you do with this bounty of whatever it is?" he asked, looking down at the woodsy-looking fruit in the basket.

"I'll show you," she replied.

She pulled free and started walking back in the direction of the cave. He feasted his eyes on her retreating figure. She looked cute in his sweater.

"She'd look really good if that was all she was wearing," he murmured, admiring the sway of her hips.

He started in surprise when he felt a slight sting on his ass. Looking over his shoulder, he caught the tree behind him straightening up and pulling back a thin branch. He scowled at Gem's woodsy guardian.

"A guy can look, can't he?" he defended himself.

He ducked his head and hurried after Gem when the tree shook, sending down a shower of small nuts.

*Great! I'm in a land where prudish trees live!* he thought with a wry smile and a rueful shake of his head. Of course, that didn't stop him from looking again – or appreciating Gem any less.

Half an hour later, Ross cleaned up the remains of their breakfast and dumped it into the fire. The woody husks quickly burned to a fine ash. Throughout their meal, they had kept their conversation light, trying to avoid thinking about what lay ahead, but that easy, peaceful time had come to an end when the Isle violently shuddered, sending a cascade of small rocks down near the mouth of the cave.

"So, what kind of things are we looking at today? Godzilla? Thanos? The Minions?" Ross asked in a half-joking tone.

Gem looked at him and frowned. "I am not familiar with those things. Are they bad?" she asked.

Ross rubbed the back of his neck and dryly laughed. "Only one of them really. It was a bad joke," he said with a crooked smile of apology.

She stared at him for a second and nodded. "Oh. I'm sorry, I didn't know…, " she replied.

"Nothing to apologize for. Different worlds – jokes don't always translate the same. I was just wondering if you had any idea what we might encounter today," he awkwardly finished.

She bit her lip and thought for a moment. "The stones did not show me everything we have encountered so far. I assumed Magna could see what the alien creature had planned, and broke free of its control long enough to convey what she learned to the stones," she explained.

Ross frowned. "Which traps from yesterday did the stones show?" he asked.

"The tree at the river was the first one and the spider was the second. There were a total of six warnings," she said.

"So, what about the mud pit and the human-eating plant? Who did those?" he asked.

She looked at him with a bemused expression. "I suspect my father created those," she said.

"So, we have four more from the stones and no idea about what else might happen. I have to tell you that I'm not getting a good feeling about this," he confessed.

She nodded in agreement. "The mud pit surprised me; the plant did not. My father has a gentle soul. He would rather restrain than kill if at all possible. I suspect that you would have fallen through the mud pit to an underground cavern and been lost for days before finding a way out. "

Gem waved her hands in the air. Ross stepped back when a mist appeared showing what could only be a three-dimensional map of the Isle. He walked around it, studying the Isle's layout. Along the far cliffs – as far as a person could go on the map, of course – was their final destination, the palace.

"We are here," Gem said, pointing on the map. Between them and the palace there was a whole lot of ground to cover.

"The palace really isn't that far, it only appears to be," she said, contradicting his thoughts on the distance.

"I was just thinking that," he lied.

"The four other warnings do not specify the location of the traps, but if we go by the order written in the stones and the fact that the river trap and the spider were here and here, then I believe the next one will be here," she said, pointing to a narrow canyon on the map.

"What did the stone say?" he asked in an uneasy voice as he imagined them walking through a creepy Canyon of Doom.

"'Take the passage through the rock but beware, for life exists where none should be'," she recited.

A shiver ran down Ross's spine. "I don't like the sound of that. I vote for finding a different way. This has ambush written all over it –

narrow passage, lots of rocks, no place to escape.... What if we went this way instead?" he asked.

He pointed toward a section that looked like a miniature desert. They could cross it in a few hours. It would also cut half a day off the trip.

"The stone was very clear, take the passage through the rock. Remember what happened before when you ventured off the trail?" she pointed out.

"Yeah... the stomping tree. How could I forget that? Okay, we take the passage through the rocks. What happens when we get through it?" he asked with a grimace of distaste as he stared at the map.

"We go through the Field of Fire and then across the lake," she said.

"How long did it take you to get to the gazebo when that creature attacked?" he asked with a hint of disbelief.

"I created a wind tunnel. It allowed me to travel at a much greater speed. If I created another one, the alien creature would detect the shift in power and be aware that we are near," she explained.

Ross frowned. "Right, but if you could zap yourself to the palace and bam – wake your folks, then everything would be okay," he said.

She shook her head. "My parents and I could not defeat it the first time. We need to save the island without the creature realizing I am awake. My father warned that I could not let the alien creature take control of my body," she softly said.

"Then wouldn't it have made sense for you to get off the island once I unfroze you? You could have brought in reinforcements to fight the creature," he exclaimed in exasperation.

"There wasn't enough time! It would take days, if not weeks, to hunt down Drago, Orion, Nali, and the others! Then more time to get them to agree and return – if they *ever* agreed. The island is sinking, and we will be lucky if we can get to my parents in time to prevent it from happening," she groaned with frustration.

"Okay, no time, I get that. But, from the sound of it, the creature is still there, and if you go back, you'll be in the same danger you were in before. What if – what if I went ahead? I could find your folks and wake them up while you go for help," he offered.

She was vigorously shaking her head in disagreement. "You would never make it alone. Look at what happened yesterday. If I hadn't been there – Ross, you could have been killed," she contended as she waved her hands in agitation.

He reached out and gently grabbed her wrists. Pulling her close, he hugged her tightly. He waited until she relaxed before he spoke.

"I've got this, Gem. Now that I know what I'm up against, I've got this. Yeah, there might be a little magic, a few monsters, an alien, some people-eating plants, a few trees that want to stomp me…," his voice faded when she reached up and placed her hand over his mouth.

"I'm going with you. Someone has to watch your back," she said in a firm voice.

He chuckled, pressed a light kiss to her fingers, and mumbled, "I was hoping you'd talk me out of being an idiot," he teased.

He tightened his hold on her when the ground shook. They stared at each other for a moment before pulling apart. Ross patted his pockets and looked around to make sure he wouldn't forget anything while Gem put out the fire.

"Okay, we'd better get this show on the road," he said, stepping closer to her.

Gem nodded and started to turn away before she twirled on her heel and pressed a brief, hard kiss to his lips. She turned back just as quickly and hurried out of the cave. Ross stood bemused for a moment before he snapped out of his reverie and followed her.

"Focus, Ross. You can't save the Princess if you go weak in the knees every time she kisses you," he muttered to himself.

# CHAPTER FOURTEEN

Two hours later, Gem followed closely behind Ross. They were making good time and hadn't encountered any unnatural obstacles, though the tremors were happening more frequently now, so they were finding toppled trees on the path.

The trees became more sparse and widespread as they neared the rocky passage in the canyon. Gem had always loved the canyon. It made her feel a sense of awe and wonder that such a barren place could be so beautiful, colorful, and unique.

Her mother used to tell her when she was a child that the Goddess had made the Isle of the Elementals by mixing the sands of time with the ocean, leaving this chasm of exposed sandstone as a reminder of their origins. The brilliantly colored sediment running through rocks sparkled when the sun hit them a certain way. The walls were smooth and beautiful, and natural bridges crisscrossed the canyon in many places. Small pools of water from rainfall often gathered in the shadowed craters.

She hissed in surprise when she felt a sudden frigid blast of air, and she rubbed her hands on the sweater she was wearing to warm them.

The path opened up as they cleared the last stand of trees, and she could see the entrance to the canyon ahead.

"Damn, but it's cold," Ross commented, zipping up his jacket.

"Yes," she replied in concern.

She stepped up next to him and warily studied the canyon's entrance. The canyon should be warm this time of year. Based on the position of the sun, winter was still several months away.

"It should not be cold. This is not normal," she said.

"Great, okay. Listen, wait here. I'll be back in a second," he said.

"I – alright," she replied.

Gem watched in confusion as Ross retraced their steps back into the forest. She impatiently waited, growing more concerned as the minutes ticked by. She shivered when another frigid burst of air from the canyon swirled around her. It took a split second to register that it wasn't the wind surrounding her, but an icy hand. With her arms trapped against her sides, she couldn't break free. Before she could dissolve, the chill seeped through her clothing and to her skin, and she knew she was being frozen again, this time into ice.

"Ross!" she cried out before her throat froze, and the fine crystals imprisoned her in their icy grasp.

Ross searched for the fallen tree they had passed a few minutes earlier. He grunted in satisfaction when he found it. Wading through the tall ferns, he reached down and pulled a large piece of bark from the trunk.

He weighed it in his hands. It was thick and heavy but manageable. Now he needed a way to hold and control it with one hand like a shield.

He made a handle with a limber green branch along with some vines, courtesy of the trees that had heard his unconscious muttering for the items during his search. He held the shield up, swung it around, and took a few steps as if he were battling an invisible foe.

"Okay, that should work. A bit clumsy but better than nothing," he said and looked up at the large tree with a wide grin. "You wouldn't happen to have a lance hidden among your branches, would you?"

The tree shook in response. Ross hadn't really expected a reply, so when it came, he uttered a startled list of his favorite go-to words that would have made his mother wash his mouth out with soap if she were still alive. He barely jumped back when a six-foot branch impaled itself in the ground less than a foot away from him. The branch was at least three inches thick, straight, and devoid of leaves. It also had a very, very sharp point, which he discovered when he pulled it out of the ground. He studied his new weapon for a second and looked up at the tree with a wary expression.

"Uh, thanks. This is perfect," he said.

The tree shook again. This time, leaves fell around him like a gentle summer rain. His laugh was cut short when he heard Gem's loud cry of distress. All humor disappeared, and he turned around.

"Gem!" he shouted.

Taking off at a run, Ross held his new shield and lance tightly against his body. He burst through the opening in time to see an enormous creature which was the icy white-blue color of a glacier. It stood at least twenty feet tall and it was carrying an unconscious Gem into the canyon. A second creature of equal size stood near the curve in the canyon.

Ross sprinted forward, clenched his jaw in determination, and focused on Gem. He was almost to the mouth of the canyon when the creature standing near the entrance raised a large icy club and struck the ground. Ross cried out in outrage when a wall of ice shot up from the ground.

He hit the wall and bounced backward, almost falling on his ass. Dropping his shield, he lifted the lance and held it with both hands. He struck the ice wall over and over, but every crack he made in the ice sealed up before he could make another.

Tossing the lance aside, he beat on the wall of ice in frustration. His heart pounded frantically in despair as he watched the creatures walk away. He raised his fist and struck the ice again.

"No, damn you! I swear if you hurt her... Gem... Damn it, no!" he shouted in frustration.

His breath fogged the ice, and he impatiently rubbed the sleeve of his jacket against it. He watched with growing hopelessness as the creatures disappeared around a curve in the canyon. He let his hands slide down the ice wall and dropped them to his side when he could no longer see Gem.

"Gem – what have I done? I promised...," his voice faded, and he bowed his head in grief.

Once again, he had failed to protect the person he loved. Tears burned his eyes as he thought of his mother – his life – Gem. He took a shuddering breath and looked down at his handmade shield. It looked small and insignificant now – a child's toy in the face of magic. He had been stupid to think he could be a match for such creatures. He was an idiot to believe that he could ever be anyone's hero. He was a loser – just like his father – just like everyone back home thought.

He stepped back and studied the ice wall. It was at least twelve inches thick. The walls of rock on each side were flat and also covered in ice, making it impossible to climb. He clenched his hands into fists.

He'd done some mountain climbing when he was in high school. He'd also spent a good deal of time climbing around on a rocking boat. If there was a way up and over that damn block of ice, he would find it. He would not give up.

With grim determination, he pulled a couple of vines free and tied the shield and lance to his back. He would need a weapon when he made it over to the other side.

"Hang in there, Princess, I'm coming for you," he muttered.

~

**Nali's airship: Just before daybreak**

Gant watched with a deepening frown as Theron approached Nali's airship, the Thunderbirds screeching a challenge as he came closer.

"I see one of our illustrious explorers has returned. I wonder what happened to Drago. Perhaps *he* was turned into stone this time," Ashure dryly commented.

"You don't care for the dragons?" Gant inquired.

Ashure flashed him a broad smile. "Of course I like dragons – or should I say I like their gold when I can get them to part with it," he replied.

"I can see how that could be an issue, then," Gant chuckled.

"Yes, and the fact that they are rude, arrogant, and tend to burn my ships to the waterline when they are in a bad mood – which unfortunately tends to be frequently – doesn't help their likability," Ashure added with a sigh.

"You know, you might get a little more gold and a lot less burning if you didn't try to steal from them all the time," Gant reflected.

Ashure looked at him, affronted. "Now where is the fun in that? How can a pirate of any stature and honor truly call himself a pirate if he doesn't pillage? An honorable pirate would never be able to look in a mirror if they behaved like – Goddess forbid – a normal merchant!" he argued with a shudder of distaste.

Gant raised his eyebrow at the indignant tone in Ashure's voice. He didn't want to point out the oxymoron of an honorable pirate. What he did want to ask about was the mirror that Ashure had absconded with when he left the Isle of the Giants.

"Speaking of mirrors—" he began only to be interrupted by Theron's arrival.

"Theron, what news?" Nali asked, stepping onto the deck with Orion.

"We found the Isle of the Elementals – due west and less than an hour's flight from here," Theron quietly responded.

"Where is Drago?" Orion asked with concern.

"He remained on the Isle. I am linked to him, so he can guide us to it," Theron explained.

"I am impressed, dragon. I have searched for Ruger and Adrina's kingdom for the past several years and have never been able to locate it. I never thought of looking up for it!" Ashure said.

Theron looked at Ashure and nodded. "It is well hidden. We would have missed it if we hadn't literally flown into it. We were flying through a thick layer of cumulus clouds when we came upon it. The clouds were actually a concealment spell. We landed on the beach, noticed fresh tracks and followed them up to a gazebo. Drago spotted additional footprints, smaller than the first, so we know that there are at least two people on the Isle. The tracks were no more than a day old and led into the forest. Drago is following them. I will guide us to the Isle with your permission, Empress Nali," he said, turning toward Nali.

"Granted – of course," Nali replied with a regal bow of her head.

"Surely Drago knows the dangers of going alone. What if the alien creature captures him? You saw what it did to Magna. The alien would be nearly indestructible if he had the power of the Dragon King," Orion said with concern.

Theron looked at the Sea King. "And that is one reason why we should hurry. Drago is aware of the danger and will be cautious. We had little choice, your Majesty. The Isle is unstable. I will be able to warn you if he is compromised," he assured them.

Nali nodded. "Time is of the essence, Theron. Please take the helm. Prepare for possible battle," she shouted to her crew.

Gant moved to the bow of Nali's ship while Theron and Nali moved to the helm. Ashure and Orion followed him. Around them, the Cyclops, Gargoyles, and other monsters worked in unison arming themselves and readying the airship.

The Thunderbirds balked at first when Theron took over the helm. A sharp command from Nali quickly settled the birds. Lightning snapped between them, sending a burst of electricity through the airship that caused the hair on Gant's arms to stand on end.

He gripped the railing as the massive ship surged forward at an incredible speed. Cool air swept across his face, and he couldn't help but enviously wonder if Nali would be willing to part with a few of her precious birds. This form of travel was much faster than the schooner he was using.

He looked up at the bird closest to him. Large talons, each the size of a warhorse on the Isle of the Giants, gripped a specially designed metal perch. The support for the perch was encased in a magically enhanced clear glass. He could see bolts of electricity traveling through the tube that would rival any that were cast down from the clouds on a stormy day.

He leaned over the railing to look toward the stern. The glow from the twin propulsion systems could be seen. He looked over his shoulder when Ashure spoke.

"Nali's use of technology combined with magic and the Thunderbirds is amazing. You know, I once tried to steal a couple of their chicks from her," he commented with a sigh.

"How well did that go for you?" Orion chuckled.

Ashure grinned. "As well as you might expect. It took months for my hair to grow out again and even longer for Nali to quit sending her blasted sea monkeys to attack my ships, not to mention a year's worth of brandy," he replied with a deep sigh.

"You never learn, my friend. Nali has a memory almost as long as a dragon's," Orion said.

"Don't remind me," Ashure humorously retorted.

"There," Gant said, pointing toward the clouds before them.

The two men next to him grew quiet. The clouds looked ordinary – except the rain that should have been falling from the clouds was going upward. Rolling bands of dark mist and flashes of lightning lit the cumulus clouds from within. Gant's breath caught when he saw the outline of the Isle through the illuminated veil of clouds.

"The spell that created this is very old. The lines are pure. I've never seen anything quite like it before," he murmured.

Orion looked at Gant with surprise. "You can see the magic?" he asked.

"Yes," he replied.

"Prepare for a rough landing," Nali shouted above the growing howl of the wind.

Gant knew Nali must have seen the magic mixed in with the storm as well. Nali always appeared to know more than she let on and he knew that her own skills with magic were very powerful. The Thunderbirds leaned forward and surged through the cloud. Lightning swirled around the airship. An explosive bolt struck the deck. Three gargoyles were thrown in different directions. One of the gargoyles shifted to stone when pieces of wood flew outward.

Gant instinctively lifted his hands and created a protective shield around Orion, Ashure, and himself when a massive bolt hit too close for comfort. Another bolt struck the mainmast. The impact splintered the top section and ran down the rigging, which disintegrated under the intense heat.

A loud cracking warned Gant that the tip of the mainmast was frac-tured. Without the support of the rigging, it would fall to the deck. He immediately glanced at a Cyclops who was kneeling over an unconscious Gargoyle.

"Ashure!" he shouted, unable to help without exposing them to more of the deadly lightning bolts.

"I see them," Ashure replied.

They were in the thick cover of cloud now. Lightning struck the airship from every direction. The Thunderbirds' screeches filled the air until his ears rang. They sounded joyful, and he realized that of course they would be immune to the lightning and were perhaps even drawing it to the airship.

"Orion, you have to tell the Empress to shield her birds. They are attracting the lightning," he gritted out.

Orion nodded and sprinted across the deck. Gant clenched his teeth together and projected his shield as far as he could, muttering a strengthening spell under his breath as he concentrated. The ancient spell protecting the Isle of the Elementals was pressing against his magic, and it felt distinctly unwelcoming.

He was distantly aware of the pandemonium raging around him. Through the cloud's mist and the smoke from the fire on the ship, Gant saw Ashure helping the Cyclops pull the Gargoyle to safety and Theron struggling to control the airship. He could hear Nali's crew shouting out to each other as they fought to help those who were hurt and Orion yelling to Nali.

His legs trembled, and he sank down onto one knee. Nali lifted her hands and the Thunderbirds immediately tucked their wings to their sides. The airship began to sink quickly without the power of the mighty birds to keep it aloft.

Gant lowered his hands when the airship suddenly dropped as it passed through the last cloud barrier. He pressed his hands to the deck to keep from falling face first onto the wooden planks. They were descending too quickly. He struggled to his feet, hanging onto the railing as the distance between the water and the airship narrowed.

"Brace yourselves!" Nali ordered.

Out of the corner of his eye, Gant saw Orion lift his trident. A huge wave of water rose up from the ocean below and cradled the ship's hull. It took Gant a moment to realize exactly what the Sea King was doing. The airship settled on the wave that gradually descended with its burden, gently pushing the great ship toward the beach.

Cheers erupted from the crew when the airship glided across the water until the hull dug into the soft sand and bottomed out, stopping the ship fifty feet from shore. Gant breathed a deep sigh of relief and looked up at the Thunderbirds. He chuckled when the one closest to him shook, sending a small shower of electrically charged feathers crackling to the deck around him. The movement caused the bird's feathers to fluff out.

A firm hand on his shoulder startled him, and he quickly turned around and stared into Ashure's eyes. The pirate's eyes glittered with a speculative expression. Gant warily waited for Ashure to ask the question that he knew he could not answer.

"Interesting, very interesting," Ashure murmured before dropping his hand to his side. "Many thanks, Giant, for your protection. "

"My pleasure, your Majesty," Gant replied with relief.

Ashure turned and smiled at Nali. "Well, Empress, another thrilling adventure awaits us. It is time to see which of us lives – or should I say, doesn't live – in this prophecy of yours. "

# CHAPTER FIFTEEN

Ross lay on his back with his eyes closed. There wasn't a place on his body that didn't ache. He gingerly did an external assessment to make sure he hadn't broken any bones. He groaned when his body protested the movement.

"I see you are not dead," a deep voice said.

Ross snapped his eyes open and scrambled to his feet with his fists up, ready for a fight. Two things flashed through his mind. First, nothing was broken, and second, he was going to need more than his fists to defeat the tall guy standing only a few feet away.

"Who the fuck are you, and where did you come from?" he hoarsely demanded.

"I am Drago, King of the Dragons. You are not an Elemental. What Isle are you from?" Drago replied.

Ross slowly put his arms down and warily moved to the side when Drago stepped past him and touched the wall of ice that he'd been trying to climb for the last two and a half hours. He absently rubbed his bruised buttock.

"I'm not from around here. I'm Ross Galloway, King of Yachats – well, of a fishing boat anyway," he said, muttering the last part.

Drago turned around and ran an assessing look over him. Ross straightened, stiffened his shoulders, and returned Drago's gaze with a steely one of his own. He would be damned if he felt like he was standing in the principal's office. He hadn't been cowed when his father was in a rage or in high school when he got caught doing some stupid shit, and he wasn't about to do it now – King of the Dragons or not.

"Wait a minute – are you...?" Ross started to say at the same time as Drago's expression darkened.

"Ross – are you the human my Carly...?" Drago said.

Ross ran his hands through his hair. "Your Carly.... Yeah, right, Carly Tate. " He looked Drago up and down before he gave him a crooked grin and shook his head. "And you're still alive! Still have all your parts too, as far as I can tell. I don't mean that in a bad way – I mean, well done! You know, it's just that she – Carly – tended to be – but what with you being a dragon... and all," he disjointedly tried to explain without pissing off the guy. He finally gave up and shoved his hands into his front pockets. "I'm glad she's alright. "

Drago gave him a sharp-toothed grin. "She almost emasculated me with a broom handle – more than once. She is afraid of mice," he admitted, folding his arms across his chest. "What happened to the Elementals?"

Ross clenched his jaw. "I don't know for sure what happened to all of them. I do know that Gem needs my – our – help," he stated.

Drago's eyes narrowed. "Where is Princess Gem?" he asked.

Ross waved his hand at the wall of ice. "She was taken. The island is filled with traps – some of them were set by Gem's parents, others by Magna – or at least the alien creature that caused all of this mess. I know it sounds weird, but what I'm telling you is the truth. We've been battling them since I found Gem yesterday morning. Magna had turned Gem into stone. Somehow the stone dissolved when I touched her. Which leads me to ask how in the hell did you find us – me?" he suddenly asked.

The suspicion that this could be another trap had just dawned on him. Gem had said it could take days or weeks to find one of the others who could help her. It was a little suspicious that this guy suddenly popped up out of nowhere.

"You left enough tracks that a child could follow you. Dragons have exceptionally keen eyesight. It was faster to fly," he replied.

Ross couldn't argue with Drago's logic. He looked back at the ice wall before turning back to face Drago. The clock was ticking, and he was still no closer to finding Gem.

"Listen, Gem wanted to ask you and some other magical people to help her, but there wasn't time to find and convince you guys. The spell that keeps the Isle afloat is weakening. She says she has to find her parents. They are the only ones who can stop it from crashing into the ocean. Oh, and like I said a minute ago, there is this alien creature. We toasted a small bit of it, but Gem says there is more." Ross paused and looked at the ice wall again as a wave of desperation hit him. "I don't know what took her. It looked like a Yeti – an abominable snowman – back home. They aren't real, but whatever took her sure as hell was. There are at least two of them. "

"Then it is good that I arrived," Drago replied.

Drago lifted his fist and struck the ice wall with a bone-shattering blow. Ross curled his fist against his side, thankful that their meeting hadn't ended in an exchange of fists. He had no doubt that he would have been as fractured as the cracks forming in the ice wall. He opened his mouth to warn Drago about the enchanted ice, but swallowed the warning when the man struck the wall again with supernatural speed.

Thin fissures ran in uneven lines, fanning outward before resealing almost as quickly as they had formed. Drago frowned and took a step back. He rubbed his knuckles.

"Magic ice. I've tried everything. As fast as you break it, it reseals. I've tried climbing over it. That doesn't work either. I wouldn't bother trying to climb over it if I were you. It would be as useless as hitting it. The walls and the top are covered in ice as well," Ross said.

"I do believe that dragons are full of fire. Surely you have enough hot air in you that you could melt a doorway for us," another deep voice dryly commented from behind them.

"Son-of-a-bitch!" Ross exclaimed, turning to look at the group slowly descending from the air. "What'd you guys do? Come from a costume ball?"

"I won't begin to tell you how humiliating this is, Nali," the man stated with an indignant sniff.

"Oh, trust me when I say I've seen you in far more humiliating situations," the woman carrying him retorted before she dropped the man the last couple of feet to the ground.

Ross warily watched as the man straightened up and adjusted the brocade cuffs of his ornate black coat. The guy looked like he had just stepped off the set of a pirate movie. The woman landed beside the pirate and gave Ross an assessing look. Ross staggered back when she lifted her long, lustrous black wings behind her and folded them into her back.

A man with a glowing trident landed on the other side of the pirate while a real, live, fire breathing dragon carrying another man landed behind the group. Ross gaped in surprise when he realized the man with the trident appeared to have markings that looked an awful lot like—

"Are those scales?" he murmured under his breath to Drago.

"Yes. He's a merman," Drago replied in a tone laced with amusement.

"Merman – dragon, pirate, I don't have a clue, and—" Ross said, pointing to each of them.

"Nali is the Empress of Monsters and Gant is a Giant," Drago replied when Ross's finger stopped on Nali and Gant.

"Ah, of course, can't forget about the monsters and the giants," Ross mumbled.

"What took you so long?" Drago demanded.

Ashure waved a hand at Theron. "It would appear that while the Isle's magic might not have been as hazardous when you and Theron approached, it did not care for Nali's airship," he stated.

"The lightning was attracted to my Thunderbirds. What have you discovered? Who is this?" Nali asked with a wave of her hand.

"This is Ross Galloway. He is from Carly's world. He confirmed that the Isle is in danger of collapsing back into the ocean below, the alien creature is here, and Gem has been taken," Drago explained.

Nali stepped forward and touched the ice. "The ice is enchanted by a very powerful spell," she murmured.

"I was about to try melting it," Drago replied, shooting a glare at Ashure.

"Do you know who or what took Gem?" Ashure asked, pulling a sword from his belt.

"It looked like a Yeti – an abominable snowman. They are a myth back on my world, but apparently not here. We were warned that there would be a trap here," Ross explained.

"Why did you not take a different path, then?" Orion asked.

"Because the same thing that told us to be careful also told us to come this way. The last time we tried to take a detour, I almost ended up flattened by a demented tree," Ross answered with a touch of exasperation. "Listen, I don't mean to be rude, but if you guys came to help us, can you do that? Those – things – took Gem hours ago. Who knows what has happened to her since then. "

"Drago," Nali said with a nod.

"Stand back. Theron, we will do this together. The ice will reform almost immediately. There will only be a small window of opportunity," Drago warned.

"I will assist as well," Gant stated, stepping forward.

Ross bent down and picked up his shield and lance. He rolled his shoulders in anticipation, then hissed and shook his head when Drago suddenly transformed into a large, solid black dragon.

Swallowing the lump in his throat, he stepped out of the way when the dragon named Theron moved forward along with Gant. Ross exchanged glances with the 'giant' as he stepped around him. The guy looked normal to him.

"Interesting weapons," Ashure murmured with a hint of amusement in his voice.

Ross pulled his shield closer to his body. "The store was out of rocket-launchers," he retorted.

"Ready – go," Gant said.

Drago and Theron each released a strong, steady burst of super-heated blue fire. Ross lifted his shield to protect his face from the intense heat. Gant held his arms out, hands extended. Ross didn't understand what the man was doing, but whatever it was appeared to keep the narrow hole that had formed from closing.

"Hurry!" Nali ordered.

Ross was already in motion. The moment he saw an opening large enough for him to safely pass through, he sprinted forward. He held the shield and lance out in front of himself and dove through the center as Drago and Theron paused to draw in a deep breath. From this side he could see that the entire top of the canyon was sealed with ice too. The only way to get into the canyon was through the opening they had made, and almost immediately, it began to close.

*"Ring of fire open wide the ice that is meant to create a divide,"* Gant gritted out as he kept his hands spread.

The opening that the dragon fire had created remained thanks to whatever Gant was doing, but a thin layer of ice crystals was beginning to form along the edges. Ross stepped back as Nali, Drago, and Orion dove through the opening after him. Ashure was a touch more reserved. He broke away the edges of ice and stepped through.

"Gant, release your spell and stand back. Theron will open it again from that side while I open it from this one," Drago shouted.

Gant dropped his arms and stepped back. Ross glanced back and forth between the group and the passage. Drago and Theron had shifted back into their dragon forms and were once again releasing a long blast of fire. Nali and Ashure stood to the side watching them.

Gant jumped through the opening the moment it was wide enough for his large frame, barely making it through before the ice sealed the hole. Ross reached out and steadied Gant when he stumbled.

"Thank you," Gant muttered.

"No problem," he replied with a brief nod.

Then the dragons blasted the ice one last time, but this time, it held firm.

"The ice is no longer melting. Theron cannot get through," Nali said with concern.

"Drago, you release your dragon fire and I will use the power of the trident to try to create an opening for Theron," Orion instructed.

Drago bowed his large black head. Ross wasn't sure how Drago did it, but he was able to communicate with Theron through the thickening ice. Theron shifted forms and rolled his shoulders. Lifting a hand, Theron nodded to them on the other side of the ice. Ross stumbled back a few steps when Nali gripped his arm and motioned for him to retreat.

"It might get dangerous," she said.

"Why – damn!" Ross began.

The rest of his sentence was cut off when dragon fire combined with powerful bursts of dark blue balls of energy hammering the ice wall. Ross lifted the wooden shield as large chunks of ice flew toward them. Peering out from behind the shield, he was shocked to see that the ice remained intact. It was as if the magic that had caused the ice to form was adapting – as if it were alive – and now it was attacking them.

"Stop!" Orion shouted.

The small group stood gazing at the thick wall of ice. The silence was broken by the sounds of crackling ice. Nali and Ashure stepped out from behind him.

"Well, this isn't good," Ashure said with an uneasy expression.

Drago shifted back to human form and walked over to the wall. He reached out to run his hand over it, but quickly drew back when Gant grabbed his wrist. Gant nodded to the ice crystals greedily reaching for Drago's hand.

"This is old magic," Gant murmured.

"How is it that a Giant knows so much about magic?" Ashure casually inquired.

Ross didn't miss the way Gant's expression hardened. From the reaction of the others, neither did they. Gant relaxed and shrugged.

"I'm not at liberty to share that information," he replied.

"Drago, warn Theron about the ice. Perhaps he should return to my ship. We may need it, and your link to him will be helpful," Nali said.

Drago gave a brief nod. "Done, he will return to the airship and await further instructions," he said.

"Ah, guys – and Empress – I think we should get moving," Ross suggested.

"I second that," Ashure said with a wave of his hand toward the wall of ice. The crystals were voraciously reaching toward them.

Drago and Gant's curses blended together. Orion pulled both men out of the crystals' reach. Ross looked at the small group. If he had to be in this mess, this seemed like a good cavalry to have on his side.

"Just so that you know, Gem said the stones warned her that things that shouldn't be alive are, or something like that," Ross said.

"Something like that? It might be helpful if you could remember exactly what she said. There is a large amount of gray space when it comes to magic," Ashure dryly commented.

Ross shot the pirate an irritated glare. "I was too busy trying not to get killed. You guys are the ones who live in Fantasyland, you figure it out," he retorted before he turned and began walking away.

"How did you come to our world?" Nali curiously asked.

Ross carefully scanned the walls of the narrow canyon as they walked. "Damned if I know," he responded.

He'd learned his lesson well and was not going to mention his encounters with Magna any more than he had to. From Gem's reaction, it wasn't hard to deduce that Magna wasn't very popular in this world. Turning people into stone and creating deadly traps would do that. Still, it was hard to reconcile the things he was learning about her past with the woman he had met back home.

"One minute I'm on my boat, the next I'm swimming for my life. I ended up on the beach here, found Gem, and we've been fighting to stay alive ever since," he said with a shrug.

"Interesting," Nali commented with a speculative expression.

"So, Orion is a merman, right?" he casually asked.

Nali glanced over her shoulder at Orion. "Yes, why?" she inquired.

"I was just wondering how he can be out of the water," Ross said with a shrug.

Nali chuckled. "The merpeople live both above and below the water," she said.

"What about the giant? He doesn't look all that big," Ross said.

Nali raised an eyebrow. "Oh, he can get much bigger. It is his ability with magic that I find intriguing. He has an unusual skill that deserves closer examination. Before you ask, Ashure is no ordinary pirate. I would not cross him. His skill with a sword is legendary, but there is more to Ashure than meets the eye," she explained.

"Okay, the giant can get bigger and don't piss off the pirate. What's your story? They call you the Empress of Monsters. Are you like their mother or what?" he asked.

Nali tilted her head back and laughed. Ross flushed and grinned. The other guys stopped the quiet conversation they were engaged in to look at them with curious expressions.

"I am the most fearsome of all monsters, Ross. I protect and care for them. In return, they follow me," she said with an amused smile.

"She is also wickedly beautiful and very stubborn," Ashure added.

Nali looked over her shoulder at Ashure. "I'm still mad at you for using my sea monkeys and don't think I've forgotten about your theft of my sea stags to use them in one of your illicit schemes," she said.

Drago and Orion chuckled. "I would quit while you are ahead, Ashure," Orion suggested.

"How is Lady Jenny doing? Is she tired of you yet?" Ashure asked.

"Jenny – Jenny Ackerly? Is she— Look out!" Ross warned when he saw the cascade of rocks out of the corner of his eye.

The group dove for cover when a large section of rock suddenly broke loose. Ross rolled and protectively covered Nali and himself with his shield. He uttered a pain-filled grunt when several fist-sized rocks hit his lower back and legs.

*More bruises to go along with the ones on my ass and face,* he silently grimaced.

He lifted his head when the rumbling stopped and peered out from under the shelter of his shield. The feel of hands pushing against his chest caused him to look down. He shot Nali an apologetic look before he rolled to the side. He stood up and held out his hand to help Nali to her feet. She gripped his hand and rose to her feet when he pulled her up.

"Thank you," Nali said.

"What happened?" Orion asked, rising to his feet.

"Ah – I don't think you want to know," Ashure replied in a voiced laced with wary reservation, his eyes widening with alarm. The pirate tightened his grip on his sword even as he took a step back. Following Ashure's gaze, Ross took a deep, hissing breath. The rocks that had fallen were rolling across the ground and beginning to link together.

"I do not like the looks of this," Nali commented in a slow, measured tone.

"I agree with the Empress," Gant muttered.

The clump of rocks straightened – towering above them. Ross cautiously bent over to pick up the lance he'd dropped when he dove for cover. He paused, his fingers an inch from it, his eyes frozen on the rock creature when the creature suddenly looked down at them. He almost fell on his ass when it hunched over and roared at them.

"I think now would be a good time to run," Ashure said, turning on his heel and taking off.

"For once I agree with the pirate," Drago muttered.

Ross grabbed his lance and twisted around as Nali sprinted past him. He snapped his head up when the rock creature lifted its arm. The creature smashed its fist down on the ground like a hammer right in front of him, and the ground shook from the powerful blow. Ross ducked when the rock creature swung its arm out again, barely missing his head.

"Son-of-a-bitch! If it isn't mud, trees, and spiders trying to kill me, it's rocks!" he groaned.

He scrambled sideways before taking off in the fastest run of his life. Two things quickly occurred to him. First, he was glad once again that he'd quit smoking but wished he had done it years ago; and second, the others were either in a hell of a lot better shape than he was, or they had super-human speed because they had already disappeared around a curve in the canyon path.

Ross didn't bother to look over his shoulder to see where the creature was – he didn't need to because of the shaking ground, loud crunching noises, and billows of dust rolling past him. He instinctively bent forward and ducked his head when he heard a swoosh of air and was pelted by rocks. Fortunately for him, the rock creature had hit the side of the canyon wall as it swung at him.

Unfortunately, bending forward shifted his center of gravity, and at the speed he was running, he lost his balance. He stumbled and tried to catch himself but tripped when his foot caught the lance's shaft. Realizing he was going down, Ross tucked and rolled.

"Shit!" he choked out when he saw the rock creature raising its foot to stomp him.

# CHAPTER SIXTEEN

Ross raised his shield in a futile attempt at some protection. He was in the process of turning his head away and silently preparing to meet his maker when a burst of cold air swept over him and covered him in a thin crust of frost.

"What the fu—?" he hoarsely muttered.

"Don't question the help, just move!" Ashure and Orion instructed at the same time.

Ross felt their hands under his arms lifting him up and dragging him away from the two creatures that were locked together in combat. He watched in disbelief as one of the huge Yetis fought the rock creature. The canyon shook when their bodies slammed into the walls. Ross's feet slipped on a layer of ice the Yeti had left behind and he fought to get his footing while he was dragged away by Ashure and Orion.

"What the hell is going on?" he demanded.

"A fight," Ashure replied, his tone implying that Ross should already know the answer.

"I can see that, but—" Ross started to say.

"This way," Nali urged.

"Holy Mother of Mary," Ross whispered.

Standing in front of him was Gant – except the man wasn't the same as he'd been earlier. Gant had grown – a lot! Ross swallowed.

"Right – giant. Now I get it," Ross muttered.

He scrambled to his feet and pressed his back against a stone wall as Gant passed him. The ground shook as the rock creature tossed the Yeti over its shoulder. The Yeti slid across the ground before rising back to its feet. By then, Gant had wrapped his arms around the rock creature's waist and was lifting it up off its feet.

The rock creature came apart in his arms. Large and small rocks fell to the ground, only to roll back together and reform. The Yeti grabbed the rock creature by the arm and swung it into a canyon wall. Over and over, Gant and the Yeti tried to defeat the creature, but it was difficult to defeat something that was made by magic.

"Gant, it would help if you could keep it in pieces," Ashure called.

"If you – think – this is – so damn easy, Ashure, you are welcome – to take – my place," Gant gritted out.

"You need to break it apart," Ross muttered.

Ashure looked at him with a raised eyebrow. "They have been, but it rolls back together," he pointed out in a slightly amused tone.

"No, like blast it apart – like with dynamite and into pebbles," Ross said.

"Orion, your trident," Nali suggested.

Orion smiled, his eyes glinting with eagerness. "Well, if Gant doesn't mind sharing the fight. Gant – you and that ice creature pull the rocks apart again and stand back," he shouted.

Ross was surprised when the Yeti appeared to understand what Orion said. Gant grabbed the rock creature by one arm while the Yeti grabbed it by the other. Together, they ripped the creature apart. As the rocks fell to the ground, Gant and the Yeti fell back while Orion lifted the glowing trident in his hands and aimed it toward the larger boulders, blasting them into tiny fragments when streams of blue electrical charges shot out from the trident. Ross had a whole new appreciation for the power behind these mythical people. He would never think of the Little Mermaid story in the same way again.

Within minutes, the rock creature was no more than a pile of rubble, and everyone was focusing on the Yeti. Ross wasn't sure whose side it was on. On the one hand, the beast had saved him from being smashed to smithereens, while on the other, the creature had kidnapped Gem.

The Yeti took a step toward them, and Gant moved into the creature's path. Orion, Drago, and Ashure each took a stance in front of Nali who rolled her eyes at the men.

"I – we'll watch their backs," Ross muttered, lifting his flimsy shield.

Nali chuckled. "Saving their asses is usually what happens," she dryly retorted.

Ross didn't know what to expect next, but it definitely wasn't what happened. The Yeti shook – slinging large globs of ice and snow outward like a wet dog shaking after a swim – and began to shrink. Ross blinked several times to make sure he wasn't having a hallucination. When a tall, stately-looking man emerged from the blizzard, he was pretty sure he was imagining things. The stranger was about six foot six if Ross were to guess, and broad. His brown hair was long, and he had a bushy beard. Hell, if Ross hadn't seen the man covered in snow and ice and nearly twenty feet tall, he would have thought he was just one of the locals back home.

"King Samui!" Nali hissed in shock.

"King – you know this guy?" Ross asked, looking from Nali to the Yeti-turned-man.

"He is the King of the Giants – long thought lost to this world," she answered.

"Oh – Ah, what world did he get lost on?" Ross asked, feeling suddenly stupid.

"Your Majesty," Gant said.

It wasn't until Gant spoke that Ross realized Gant had returned to his normal size. The man turned to Gant and gripped his shoulder, clearly overcome with emotion.

"Koorgan?" Samui asked in a thick voice.

Gant smiled at the man. "He is well – and still getting into trouble," he quietly replied.

"Samui, is Malay—?" Nali asked, stepping between the men in front of her.

Samui looked behind them for a moment. "She is well. Come, I will lead you to her," he answered.

Ross stood aside, wondering what he should do. He looked at the pile of rocks before turning in the direction the others were going. He scowled in determination. If this man was a good guy, it meant that Gem should be safe. Until he knew for certain, though, he would still be ready for the next challenge.

"What happened to you?" Orion asked.

"There is a dangerous creature – an alien – that fell from the sky. It struck our ship when we were not far from the coast of the Isle of the Sea Serpent. I didn't realize the extent of the damage until we were almost to the Isle of the Elementals. I was working below deck when the alien attacked me. Malay was able to suppress it, but it was a temporary solution. We immediately sought help from Ruger and Adrina, but the alien was becoming stronger, and I weaker. I lost control – briefly. Malay wrapped her arms around me and Ruger and Adrina transformed us into trees to keep everyone safe as we bound the alien to us.

"I don't know how long we remained frozen. Without Ruger and Adrina's magic to hold the spell, we transformed back into ourselves. We were weak, but because we had been in the form of a tree, we were able to avoid the effects of the magical mist that had rolled over the Isle. By then, Ruger and Adrina were gone – and the alien creature had taken over the body of Wayman – Ruger's Chief Advisor. Malay and I journeyed as far as we could before we became trapped in this canyon. The rock creature would not let us pass together, but neither could the alien creature enter the canyon due to the enchantment that Ruger and Adrina had cast. Every time it tried, the ice walls would form and keep it out. We were both too weak to dare fight the alien. We have been using what little strength we have to re-enforce Ruger's ice spell and not provoke the rock creature," he said.

"What about Gem?" Ross asked, stepping forward. "You said she was okay. Where is she, and why did you take her?"

"What about the others? Ruger and Adrina? Do you have any idea what happened to them?" Drago demanded with a deep frown.

"They are still here," Ashure murmured.

Everyone turned to look at Ashure with a surprised expression. The Pirate King's eyes were glowing, and dark shapes moved in the depths of his pupils. A shiver ran down Ross's spine. There was something really strange about the guy – besides the funny way he dressed.

"What do you see, Ashure?" Nali asked, laying her hand on the pirate's arm.

"Shadows – I see nothing but shadows," Ashure said with a shake of his head.

Ross's stomach dropped when the Isle violently shook. They all braced themselves and looked around as pieces of ice above them cracked and fell before the ice sealed again. He instinctively raised his shield, protecting his head from the falling ice.

"Come, it is best to seek shelter," Samui said.

∽

It took Ross's eyes a moment to adjust to the dim interior of the cavern that Samui led them to. He could see a magical fire, similar to the one Gem had created, burning in a ring of rocks. Another Yeti stood on the other side of the fire.

Ross pushed through the group when he saw Gem lying pale and still on a pallet. The Yeti growled in warning. Ross realized that its focus was on the lance he still clutched in his hand. He dropped it and the shield.

"Malay, it is safe. The rock creature was destroyed," Samui said.

Ross knelt on one knee and cupped Gem's hand. Her fingers were like ice. A light coating of frost covered her blue-tinged skin. His heart hammered, and he felt a welling of grief and desperation grip him. He lifted Gem's hand to his lips and blew his warm breath over them.

"She is merely sleeping. It was necessary," a soft voice murmured.

Ross looked up and blinked. Standing on the other side of the pallet was an elegant woman. Her features were as delicate as Gem's, but her hair was longer. She raised her hands, palms down, over Gem. Wisps of frost rose from Gem's body.

Ross quickly looked at Gem again when she took a long shuddering breath through slightly parted lips. Relief swept through him, and he pressed her fingers to his lips when her eyelashes fluttered for a moment before she opened her eyes.

"Hi," she whispered.

"I'm mad at you," he said without thinking.

Her low chuckle warmed the chill that was still flowing through his body. He reached out and gently brushed her hair back from her face. Her cheeks flushed under his touch, and he grinned at her.

"What happened?" she asked with a frown of confusion.

"You were kidnapped by a Yeti, which turned out not to be a Yeti, and left me on my own to deal with the dragons, the pirate, the fish guy, a lady that doesn't look too bad for being the biggest, baddest monster around, and a giant that gives a new meaning to the term growth spurt," he summarized with an emotion-filled chuckled.

Gem glanced behind him and moved to sit up. Ross slid an arm under her shoulders to help her, and she studied the small group staring at her with concern, pausing when she reached the older man and woman. He felt her body tremble.

"You look like my mother," she said in a barely audible voice.

"I'm Malay, your mother's older sister. You were just a little girl the last time I saw you," she replied, her voice shaking with emotion.

"I am Samui. You probably don't remember me," Samui greeted.

Gem slowly nodded. "You used to carry me on your shoulders and grow taller so that I could pick the fruit from the top of the trees," she murmured in a hesitant voice.

"Yes," Samui chuckled.

"Oh, Gem," Malay cried, sliding onto the pallet and wrapping her arms around Gem.

Ross slid his hands from Gem and stood up. He silently watched as Malay tearfully whispered her apologies for bringing danger to her people. Gem clung to her aunt.

Feeling out of place, Ross quietly skirted the group when they began asking Gem what had happened. He stepped outside of the cavern. The brightness of the sun briefly blinded him, but soon he had walked a few feet from the cavern. A large rock lay next to the canyon wall. He gently tapped the rock with the toe of his boot and waited to see if any weird shit would happen. When the rock didn't move, he sat down on it.

He was outside for a couple of minutes before he heard footsteps. He looked up and smiled briefly when he saw Nali walking toward him. He slid over when she waved her hand for him to make room. She sat down beside him.

Neither one of them spoke at first. He leaned back and looked up at the top of the canyon. Sunlight flickered across the ice, and every once in a while, he could see a droplet of water form from the heat only to freeze again before it fell.

"Your quest is not finished," Nali finally said.

Ross blinked in surprise. "Quest? You make me sound like some kind of knight in shining armor out to defeat a foe and save a kingdom," he retorted with a slightly derisive tone.

"Aren't you?" she asked.

Ross looked at her in disbelief before he snorted and shook his head. "No, I'm about as far from a knight in any kind of armor that you can find. I'm a fisherman, and I'm not very good at that either. She and I have a deal, that's all. I go with her to wake her parents, and she'll get me back to Yachats. Now that Gem has you and the other mythical creatures here, I guess I'll just be tagging along, trying not to get in the way until she sends me home," he stated, rising to his feet.

"You are more than that, Ross Galloway," Nali said, sliding off the boulder to stand beside him.

Ross shoved his hands into his pockets, curling his fingers to keep from patting his shirt pocket for a pack of cigarettes that he knew wasn't there. He would damn near kill for one at the moment.

"Is this what you really want?" Nali asked.

Ross glanced down at her outstretched hand, and stilled, his eyes glued on the pack of cigarettes in her hand, his favorite brand.

He clenched his jaw and looked up into Nali's dark eyes. Her mocha-colored skin was smooth, her lips full with the hint of a sarcastic smile lifting one corner. He could see the challenge in her eyes as if she were daring him to give in to his craving – and give up on his promise.

"I gave them up," he said.

"Why?" she quietly prodded.

He flashed a savage smile. "That, Empress, is none of your fucking business," he stated.

She continued to stare at him with unblinking eyes. Out of the corner of his eye, he saw the pack of cigarettes disappear into thin air. He narrowed his eyes.

"Gem must complete this journey," she continued.

Ross shrugged and looked away. "She will. Now that you and the others are here, it should be easier," he said.

"What would you do if I told you that she will die if she continues?" Nali asked.

Ross hissed. He studied Nali's calm face. He couldn't tell if she was asking a hypothetical question or making a prediction. Either way, he didn't like it.

"Are you telling me that she will or that she might?" he demanded.

Nali tilted her head and looked at him. "I am the keeper of the Goddess's Mirror. The visions that it gives are not always clear, but they are never wrong. I saw the death of one of us," she explained.

"One of you? Which one? It can't be that hard to tell if it was a man or a woman – and since you all are pretty damn different, it should be obvious which one," he growled in frustration.

"The Goddess did not share who will die, only that one of us will," Nali admitted.

"Sounds pretty typical if you ask me – build the fear without answering the question," Ross sarcastically commented.

Nali looked at him with a raised eyebrow. "I detect a hint of skepticism in your voice," she remarked.

"Just a hint – I must be getting lazy," Ross retorted.

Nali took a step closer to him and stared into his eyes with a cool, calm intensity that sent a shiver down his spine. She had that same look that he had seen in his mom's eyes when he did one stupid thing too close to the last one and crossed that imaginary line in the sand. He shook his head.

"How did you get here, Ross Galloway?" she asked in a low voice.

He narrowed his eyes. "A magic shell," he replied.

"You are here for a reason. The magic would only work if the Goddess knew that you were needed here. Princess Gem and her people need you. Your belief in yourself may be the difference between success and failure. Would you truly let her down because you simply refuse to try?" she pressed.

He shook his head and looked back at the cavern. Gem stood in the entrance watching him. His heart hammered in his chest as he remembered his fear and frustration when she was taken earlier. He hadn't given up then, had he? It hadn't done much good, true, but maybe next time it would, maybe he *could* be what she needed.

"No, I won't let her down," he answered.

Nali turned and followed his gaze. She smiled in satisfaction. Ross barely registered her murmur of approval. His focus was on Gem who was now walking toward them.

"I will join the others. There is much to be discussed before we continue on our journey," Nali said.

# CHAPTER SEVENTEEN

Gem paused when Nali drew close to her. She forced herself to look away from Ross's face and turned her attention to the Empress. She still didn't know how they had known she needed help, or why they had come, but she was grateful.

"Thank you – for coming here," she said.

"No thanks are needed, Princess Gem," Nali reassured her.

Gem shook her head and looked back at Nali with a troubled expression.

"I should have insisted that we help in the fight against the creature on the Isle of Magic as you requested. I didn't know about the alien creature being here as well. If I had...," her voice faded.

She didn't know what she would have done. She looked over Nali's shoulder to Ross. He was standing in the shade with his hands in his front pockets. Would she have met him if things had been different? Perhaps the timeline of events was necessary in the larger scale of the universe. Without the shell that Magna had given him, they would never have met.

"Everything has a purpose. Sometimes it is difficult to understand the course the Goddess has set for us," Nali answered, confirming what Gem was thinking.

Gem nodded. "True. I know uncertainty is part of the journey, but that doesn't mean that I have to like it," she grumbled.

Nali laughed. "Yes, but where is the fun in always knowing how things will work out?" Nali replied, looking over her shoulder at Ross. "He has a good heart – even if he tries to hide it. "

Gem nodded. "Yes, he does," she said with a small smile.

She stepped around Nali and slowly walked over to Ross. Her heart sped up when he pulled his hands out of his pockets and held his arms open. When he immediately thought better of it and lowered his arms, she quickened her steps and reached for him.

A sense of peace surrounded her when he pulled her close. She buried her face against his neck and took a deep breath. There was something about his scent that made her feel safe and calm.

"What happened – after I…," she asked.

He slowly released her and motioned for her to sit on the rock. A flush of pleasure swept through her when he retained her hand and sat next to her. The colors of her essence flowed along his arm.

"The color thing is happening again. It seems to do it whenever we touch," he observed.

She chuckled. "Yes, it does. So, what happened after I was taken? How did you find the others?" she asked, redirecting his attention.

He looked at the entrance to the cavern. "It was more of a 'they found me' moment. I turned around and there was this long-haired dude who looked like an axe murderer. Turns out that he was just a dragon in disguise," he paused and took a deep breath, "After you were taken, I tried everything I could think of to get to you. A wall of ice had formed over the entrance to the canyon – and over the top. It felt like a freaking tomb once we finally made it inside. "

"Malay and Samui were trapped in the canyon and changed their appearance to protect themselves from the rock creature," she said.

"Makes sense, I guess, but why put you to sleep? Wouldn't it have made more sense to just say 'Hey, guess what? We're here. ' It would have been a hell of a lot easier," he concluded in a gruff voice.

She laughed at the slight pout in his voice. "They placed me in a suspended form of sleep until they could determine if the alien had taken over my body. They know how dangerous it is and weren't sure if it might have been evolving. I suspect they were also hesitant when they saw your rather determined attempts to break through the barrier of ice," she explained.

"I guess I can understand their reasoning, but that doesn't mean I have to like it," he muttered.

"Ross...," she said before biting her lip.

"Yeah?" he responded in a low voice.

"Thank you for not giving up on me," she murmured.

He met her eyes, and his lips twitched before he gave her a crooked grin. He shook his head.

"Somebody has to watch your back, Princess," he gently responded.

"Gant will take Malay and Samui back to my ship. Now that the rock creature is destroyed, Samui and Malay can now pass together through the opening of the canyon. Gant should be able to remove the ice from the entrance with the club that Samui and Malay have enchanted. The rest of us will continue on to the palace. We should reach it by tomorrow night," Nali said, pointing to the map that Gem had drawn in the sand.

"The creature is very dangerous. Perhaps I should—" Samui started to say.

"Samui, no…," Malay softly protested, gripping her husband's arm.

Gem looked up at her aunt and uncle. They were so exhausted that they needed to lean on each other. The prolonged use of their magic to maintain both the protection spell on the canyon and their ice form in order to deal with the rock creature had taken a heavy toll on them both.

"No, Uncle. The creature may sense your essence now that it has inhabited your body," she said.

Orion placed his hand on Samui's shoulder. "Gem is right. We have previously fought the alien. It quickly senses those it has encountered before and in your weakened condition, you would be more of a hindrance than a help," he explained.

Drago nodded. "We know what to expect – and how to deal with it," he added.

"If you are sure," Samui reluctantly responded.

"We will leave immediately," Gant said.

"What about the traps?" Ross asked, looking at Gant before looking questioningly at Malay and Samui. "No offense, but like Orion pointed out, you two look like you've been run over and backed up on."

"I will carry them. In my larger size – and with my magic – I can protect them," Gant reassured him.

"With any luck, if we leave soon we should be able to reach the Great Lake by sundown. We can find refuge along the shore and cross over tomorrow. The palace is on the other side," Gem explained, pointing to the map again.

"May your journey be triumphant," Malay wearily said.

"Whatever you do, do not allow the alien to touch you," Samui cautioned.

"We will be careful," Orion said.

"Ashure—" Nali began.

Gem turned and looked at the Pirate King who had been silently leaning against the cavern wall. He twirled a jewel-handled blade between his fingers, his attention fixed on the map.

"I look forward to our quest, Nali," Ashure lightly assured her.

Nali sighed. "Very well. Gem, we will let you lead the way since you not only know the best way to proceed, but the obstacles that we will face," she instructed.

"I'll lead," Ross stated. He continued when both Ashure and Drago raised a questioning eyebrow. "The Princess and I have this agreement. I find the traps – and she saves my ass. "

Thirty minutes later, Ross waited as Gem reluctantly released her aunt from their tight hug of goodbye. She nodded at something her uncle said before rising up on her toes to give the older man a brief kiss on the cheek. Ross looked down and adjusted the strap of his shield.

"Ross, I thought you may be able use this," Ashure suggested.

He looked up in surprise as the pirate stepped up beside him holding out a sword. He reached for the handle and took the sword from Ashure's hand. He was surprised at the lightness of the long blade. He'd always thought swords were heavy and cumbersome.

"Ah, thanks," he murmured before looking back at Ashure. "But – shouldn't you keep it?"

"A good pirate never gives away his best blade," Ashure reassured him.

Ross watched with a mixture of amusement and awe as Ashure cupped his hands together before spreading them out like a magician in a magic show. A beautiful steel sword with a jewel embellished hilt appeared.

"Wow! Nice trick," Ross commented, impressed.

Ashure shot him an exaggerated look of outrage. "Trick! You don't think that the giant is the only one who knows magic, do you?" he retorted with an indignant sniff.

Ross shook his head. "I wouldn't put anything past anybody or anything since I've been here," he grudgingly admitted.

"Do you know how to use a sword?" Ashure inquired.

Ross stared at Ashure for a moment, unsure how to answer the question. His first impulse was a sarcastic retort that, sure, he carried one around all the time, all fishermen did when they were out at sea. Unfortunately, that kind of statement would probably go right over the pirate's head because, for all he knew, the fishermen here carried swords all the time. He decided it might be in his best interest to admit the truth.

"Humans stopped carrying swords around a couple of centuries ago. I've used a machete, but not for fighting," he conceded.

"Ah, well, perhaps it would be best if I gave you some instruction during our journey, just in case it is needed," Ashure suggested.

"Yeah, I guess some lessons might come in handy," Ross muttered just as Gem indicated it was time for them to leave.

He nodded to Ashure before walking over and standing next to Gem. He followed her gaze, and gasped when he saw Gant shimmer once he was outside of the cavern. Ross watched avidly as the man began to grow exponentially.

He shook his head in amazement. Once Gant was a good thirty feet tall, he bent over and gently picked up Malay and Samui. It was a good thing that the royal pair had dismantled their icy fortress or Gant would have been brushing the top of the ice ceiling that had covered it. He snorted in amusement when Gant turned his head and gave them a brief nod before he took off at a fast walk, retracing the path back to Nali's ship.

"What do you find amusing?" Gem curiously asked.

Ross looked down at her and shrugged. "This gives a whole new meaning to calling for a Lyft," he said with a grin.

She looked in Gant's direction and shook her head. Ross deeply sighed. Obviously, they called ride-sharing companies something different here. The fact that his joke went right over Gem's head was additional proof that he was in way over his own head in this magical world.

"Are you ready to go?" Nali asked.

"Yes," Ross and Gem responded at the same time.

# CHAPTER EIGHTEEN

The Field of Fire was a complete contrast to the icy walls of the canyon. Ross stared out across the scorched ground. Pools of lava bubbled and glowed while plumes of smoke filled the air with the distinct odor of sulfur. Through the bubbling pools of molten rock, he could see a narrow path that weaved its way through the field. In the distance, he thought he could see the shimmering ripples of water – the Great Lake – or a mirage. Whatever the case, their objective was clear – get across the field without getting toasted.

"I think this is the first time in my existence that I almost wish I was a dragon," Ashure murmured with a hint of disdain in his voice.

Drago chuckled. "You would make a lousy dragon, Ashure. I've been on the receiving end of your negotiations," he replied.

"If Nali can carry Ashure across, you can carry the human, Drago. Gem, you are capable of using your powers to traverse across the field, aren't you? This should not be difficult," Orion suggested.

Gem shook her head. "The stones warned against the use of any magic, which would include the alternate forms the Goddess bestowed upon us. None of us can transform," she said.

"So – what exactly will happen if we do?" Ashure inquired.

"Bad things – at least it has every other time we didn't follow the guidelines set in the stones," Ross murmured in response.

"Why don't I test it? Dragons are immune to fire," Drago said.

"I wouldn't—" Ross started to say.

His objection fell on deaf ears – Drago had already shifted. Ross watched with growing reservations as Drago rose into the air, and almost reflexively he reached out and slipped his hand into Gem's. Maybe it wasn't the time for this, but touching her was becoming addictive, especially since they could die at any moment. He swore to himself that he'd let go of her hand as quickly as possible if things went south and she needed both hands to fight. Gem squeezed his hand.

"I don't like this," she murmured.

"Drago is a big boy. He can handle whatever comes his way," Ashure replied with a wave of his hand.

"That is exactly what I thought, and boy was I wrong," Ross retorted, never taking his eyes off of Drago.

Ross had to hand it to the dragon. He looked big and mean enough to handle anything that might come at him. The huge black dragon soared a good twenty-five feet off of the ground. Drago was nearly fifty feet inside the area known as the Field of Fire when Ross began to relax a little. So far, nothing bad had happened. That thought had no sooner flashed through his mind than all hell broke loose.

"Drago, below you!" Gem shouted.

He doubted that Drago could hear Gem's shout of warning, but the Dragon King must have sensed that he was in danger because he swerved at the same instant that one of the cauldrons of lava exploded and shot upward. The eruption of lava was bad enough, but it was the molten hand attached to the wave of magma that horrified the group.

"How fire proof are dragons?" he asked when the hand closed around Drago's body.

"We're about to find out," Ashure reflected.

Ross looked at Ashure with an incredulous expression before returning his focus to the lava monster. He vaguely wondered if this creature would be covered under Nali's jurisdiction. From her growing concern, he suspected it was right up there with the rock monster that had attacked them earlier.

"Orion, can you only make electricity with that trident thing or can you make water, too?" Ross asked.

"We can't use our magic," Gem warned.

Frustration held the group immobile. They had to do something. There was no way that even a dragon could survive a prolonged dousing in molten lava.

"Well, it doesn't look like we have much of a choice. Orion, can you hose that thing down?" Ross asked.

Orion nodded, lifted the trident, and pointed it across the field. Ross released Gem's hand when she pulled away to step up next to Orion. He cursed himself for being a man of his word, even if he'd only promised himself, when Gem pulled away from him.

"She can help Orion," Ashure murmured.

"I know she can," he gritted out between clenched teeth.

Gem could do anything, Ross had never doubted that for a moment. Gem lifted her hands, and the steam rose from the ground, lifting higher and higher until thick dark clouds hung over the lava creature.

"Orion, you must hurry," Nali urgently beseeched.

"Together, Gem. We may only have this one chance," Orion instructed.

Gem nodded. Ross watched in awe as Orion called forth water from the lake on the other side of the field. A funnel of water rose high in the air, then headed toward the creature. Along the field, additional pools of lava began to bubble and spew upward.

Gem lowered her hands, palms facing down, and a deluge of water fell from the clouds she had created just as Orion's blast of water hit the lava creature and covered its body. The red lava hardened, turning black as the water cooled it – and then dozens of lava creatures burst of out of the other cauldrons.

"Drago, hurry," Nali muttered.

Ross was thinking the same thing. Several lava creatures reached out, deflecting the funnel of water that Orion was directing while others threw large balls of molten projectiles at Gem's rain cloud. The heat from the molten rock quickly evaporated the thick cloud.

The seconds ticked by while Orion's water pummeled the creatures and Drago struggled to break free of the stone hand restraining him. There were so many lava monsters that Orion's water wasn't able to concentrate on a single monster long enough to harden them into stone. Soon it'd been almost a minute, and Ross speculated that he wasn't the only one holding his breath. Orion lowered his trident, and as the funnel of water fell with a heavy splash to the ground, the lava creatures returned to their cauldrons, all except the stone hand imprisoning Drago. Thick billows of steam clouded the area as the water seeped into the heated ground and disappeared into the lava pools.

"Look!" Gem breathed.

Ross heard a sharp snap right before the creature's hardened lava hand broke apart. He hissed out a relieved breath when he saw Drago emerge from the severed hand. The lava creature's hardened remains crumbled back into the pit, and the dragon hovered in the air for a moment before he began to fall.

Ross started forward, almost certain that this would be the one time in this world that having absolutely zero magical power would be an asset.

*I can help Drago,* he thought as he stepped onto the Field of Fire, then took another step. Ross winced when the dragon hit the ground with a bone-shattering thud. No lava body parts appeared from the pits though. The rest of the walk seemed to take a very long time with Ross's heart pounding so hard he was afraid he wouldn't hear it if a creature burst into the open from behind him, but finally he reached Drago, and the man shifted back into his two-legged form. Ross froze, frantically looking around to see if the volcanic magic-police would show up again. They didn't.

"Drago. Hey, man, are you alive?" Ross asked, kneeling beside him.

Drago's deep groan was barely audible. Ross gently rolled the man over onto his back. Drago looked a little singed around the edges, but he was remarkably untouched overall.

"Ross, don't move. "

Gem's soft warning caused him to look up. He swallowed when he realized the lava creature had melted, reformed, and was peering out from the pit beside them. He instinctively brought his shield up, not that a piece of wood was any deterrent against fire.

"Drago, can you move?" Nali asked with concern.

Drago opened his eyes. "Of course I can move," he growled.

Drago pushed himself up into a sitting position. Orion and Ashure steadied him when he wobbled. Ross kept his attention on the lava creature. After several seconds, the creature retreated back into the pit.

"So…?" Ross said.

"We are not using any magic," Gem murmured.

Ross rose to his feet and gingerly inched closer to the pit, peering down into it. All he saw was a pool of bubbling magma.

"Okay, no magic," he said, stepping back and turning to face the others. He looked down at Drago. "Can you walk?"

Drago glared at him. "Of course I can walk," he snapped.

"I think the dragon got his feelings hurt," Ashure murmured with a grin.

Drago turned his heated glare on the pirate. "How about we see how well a pirate can withstand being surrounded by lava?" he suggested.

Orion chuckled. "How about we don't – at least until after we finish our journey," he replied.

"Do you see this? Pirates get no respect – none whatsoever," Ashure playfully complained.

"We'll throw you a pity-party when this is over," Drago growled.

Ashure and Orion each bent over and helped Drago to his feet. Ashure brushed some ash from Drago's shoulder before slapping him a little harder than necessary in Ross's opinion. Drago winced and sent another rumbling growl of warning at the pirate.

"As long as the party includes beautiful women, alcohol, and a bounty of dragon's gold and jewels, I would rejoice in the festivities," Ashure replied with a flourishing bow.

"I'm going to kill you," Drago calmly stated before he turned away.

"You're doing better, Ashure. He's only threatened you once so far on this trip," Nali replied with a chuckle.

"I was beginning to think I was losing my touch," Ashure retorted.

"Whatever happens, not a word of this to Carly, do you understand? She'll have my balls on a spit if she hears about what happened," Drago grudgingly requested.

"Of course not, Drago! Not a word to your lovely mate about your bullheadedness," Ashure cheekily promised.

Ross listened to the banter between the strange mixture of royals. It was almost hard to believe they were standing in the middle of a lava field and that Drago had almost died. If he hadn't been a witness to everything, he would swear that he had awoken in some strange parallel universe.

*Wait, I did,* he thought with a rueful shake of his head.

"Are you ready?" Gem asked, touching his arm and pulling him back to the present.

"Yeah. Okay, to make sure we are on the same page, no magic. While Drago may be semi-fireproof, I know for sure that I'm not," Ross warned.

"It would appear that your non-magical self is at an advantage, Ross," Ashure said with a grin. "Lead on, human. "

Ross nodded, then bent over and picked up his sword. When he straightened, Gem touched his arm again, her expression worried, and Ross gave her a crooked smile.

"We are going to do this. By tomorrow, we'll be at the palace," he reassured her.

"I know," she answered.

He frowned when he heard the slight catch in her voice before she looked away. He turned and took a deep, calming breath before he started walking. They had a lot of ground to cover before sundown.

# CHAPTER NINETEEN

Gem held her breath and watched Ross cross a bridge made of hardened lava. She was exhausted. Throughout the day, their journey had been a tedious one requiring one nerve racking decision after another.

The path had continued to change in front of them. There were times when the ground opened up to reveal a river of lava while another section crusted over. The enchantment was meant to catch the unwary. More than once, Gem had grabbed the back of Ross's jacket to steady him when the ground began to crumble under his feet.

By the time the lake was in view, everyone's nerves were stretched to the breaking point. It didn't help that another part of the enchantment was a spell that slowly drained them of their magic. Everyone but Ross was stumbling with fatigue toward the outer boundary of the field.

"I see the edge of the Field of Fire," Gem breathed in relief.

"Thank goodness," Ashure murmured, his voice slightly slurred.

Gem turned when she heard a low grunt. Drago had fallen to one knee. His face was ashen, and lines of pain and fatigue were etched around his mouth. He had one arm across his body as if he were holding his ribs.

"What is it?" Nali gently asked.

"It's nothing," Drago replied.

Gem gasped when a bone-melting wave of power hit her, and she swayed. She instinctively reached out for Ross. He caught her with one arm and steadied her.

"What's wrong?" Ross demanded.

Gem could see the wall of magic, and it suddenly dawned on her that one of the reasons she and the others were feeling this way was because the Field of Fire was a combination of two different magic spells – the first from her parents and the second created by the Sea Witch. The two spells were interacting with each other, to their detriment.

Her legs trembled and gave out on her. Ross dropped his sword and held her. She leaned her head against his shoulder, too exhausted to hold it up. Behind her, the others slowly collapsed next to Drago.

"There – is – a spell. It – is – draining us," she forced out in a barely audible voice. "Can't – move. "

Gem could barely hold her eyes open. She felt as if every ounce of energy was being sucked out of her. The harder she tried to fight it, the worse she felt.

Ross changed his grip on her. The faint thud of the wooden shield and the clank of another metal sword as they hit the ground barely registered in her mind. Even the simple act of breathing was becoming difficult to do.

"Hold on, love. I've got you," Ross urgently told her.

Gem was tenderly cradled in his arms. She knew she was dead weight. Even the ability to lift her arms was too much for her. Her breathing was becoming raspier.

Her mind faintly registered that Ross was carrying her. She forced her eyes open. He was striding closer to the shimmering wall. Fire began to lick at her flesh the closer he got. She bit her bottom lip to keep from crying out as the burning intensified. Her head fell back against his shoulder, and she parted her lips on a silent scream of agony when he passed through it.

Just as quickly as the pain had erupted, it vanished. She raised a trembling hand to touch her forehead. The pressure and fatigue began to fade, and she was able to breathe without difficulty.

"Ross, the others," she whispered with growing concern.

She looked at where the others were lying on the bridge, but for the moment, Ross didn't follow her gaze, he only had eyes for her. "You'll be ok here? You're feeling better?"

"Yes, I'm ok, I promise. You have to help the others," she said in a stronger voice.

He looked back at the barely conscious royals and nodded. "I'll be right back, just – don't get kidnapped this time," he cautioned.

"I won't," she responded.

She could tell he was torn when he gently lowered her to the ground. It wasn't that he was afraid of going back for the others, it was that he didn't want to leave her. Funny how they'd only had a couple of days together, but Gem felt like she knew him well enough to read his mind. He straightened up and looked down at her for a brief, indecisive moment before he turned and sprinted back to the bridge.

He returned with Nali first. Gem was feeling stronger and motioned that she would attend to the Empress while he returned for the men.

One by one he either carried – or in Drago's case, dragged – the others the last few yards. He was in the process of pulling Ashure over his shoulder when a horrendous cracking noise split the air.

Gem was creating water for Drago and Orion to drink when she heard the sound and looked up. She stared in horror when she realized what was happening – the bridge was disintegrating.

"Ross, run!" she yelled.

Ross sprinted across the bridge, his arm wrapped around the back of Ashure's legs as he carried the pirate over his shoulder – fireman style. After a few harrowing seconds, he stumbled to a stop several feet from her. Orion and Drago quickly stood up and pulled Ashure off of his shoulder.

Ross bent forward with his hands on his knees, breathing heavily. Sweat beaded on his brow as he took several deep breaths. Then he suddenly straightened up and looked over his shoulder. The bridge was still there, though it was vibrating and becoming more unstable by the second as vital pieces slowly disintegrated.

"Shit! Hold on," he said, twisting around.

Gem didn't understand where he was going at first. Her lips parted in protest when she saw him run back to the bridge one more time. He slid and almost fell as he changed direction. She saw him grab Ashure's large hat, his own shield, and his and Ashure's swords. She was shaking her head in denial when part of the bridge closest to them crumbled.

Ross tossed the shield and the swords across the gap when the bridge bowed upward. A scream ripped from her when she saw his arms flailing before he disappeared from sight. Strong arms wrapped around her waist, holding her back when she tried to run to him.

"Gem, it is too late. You cannot save him," Nali said.

"No! Ross! No!" She refused to believe he was gone. He had saved all of them – only to perish over a hat, a piece of wood, and a couple of swords. It didn't make any sense. "No! Let me go!" she demanded, struggling to break free.

"You cannot cross the barrier," Drago said, rising to his feet from where he had been kneeling next to Ashure.

"I can—" she argued, placing her hand on Nali's arm.

"Ouch!" Nali hissed in pain.

Ice covered Nali's arm, and she shook it. Drago grabbed her when she tried to pass him. Gem turned and hissed a warning at the Dragon King.

"Release me," she demanded.

"Princess Gem – there is nothing you can do," Orion quietly said.

Gem looked back and forth between Drago and Orion. Her mind was splintering. Fear, grief, and denial hit her with such an intense wave that she began to shake. She curled her fingers into Drago's arm and looked back to the edge of the crevice, her tears blinding her. As she swiped them out of the way, she registered Ashure's hoarse laughter. Fury swept through Gem and she turned to face Ashure, ready to unleash her grief on him when she heard Nali's excited exclamation.

She turned her head to follow where Nali was pointing. A choked laugh slipped from her when she saw a hand holding Ashure's large, purple hat – the feather on it still glowing with a small flame – rising over the edge of the crevice. Drago released her when she pushed against him. In faltering steps, she started forward in a slow, hesitant walk. She stopped at the shimmering wall and brushed a hand across her cheek.

Ross slowly pulled himself over the edge and rolled onto his back. She could see that he was breathing heavily. She laughed again when he lifted the purple hat and patted out the flame on the bedraggled plume. He placed the hat on his chest, coughed a few times, and turned his dirty face toward her. Her heart melted when he gave her that crooked grin.

"Perhaps I should want to be a human instead of a dragon," Ashure mused.

Gem giggled and gave a tearful nod. She watched Ross roll over and stand up. He stretched and looked behind him with a grimace before he walked over and picked up the swords and the shield. She impatiently waited for him to cross through the shimmering barrier. The moment he did, she wrapped her arms around his neck and buried her face against his throat.

"You have got to be either the craziest man I have ever met or the dumbest one," she choked out against his throat.

He wrapped his arm around her waist and held her close. "I think a little bit of both. Next time, Ashure's hat gets sacrificed to the great Fire God," he teasingly threatened.

She leaned back and looked up into his eyes. "I thought I had lost you," she whispered in a throat tightened by tears.

He shook his head. "You can't get rid of me that easily, Princess," he murmured.

"My hat! You saved my hat! Ah, my poor feather. Nali, it looks as if I'll need to come and visit you again for a new one," Ashure moaned as he pulled the hat out of Ross's hand.

"You're welcome," Ross dryly commented.

Ashure beamed at him as he placed the hat atop his head. "You are not so bad for a human," he informed him.

"You're not so bad for a pirate," Ross retorted with a grin.

"I think we've had enough ass-kissing. It will be dark soon," Drago said.

Orion nodded. "Yes, it is getting a bit nauseating," he added.

"They are just jealous of you, Ross," Nali replied with a shrug. "Gem, do you know a place where it may be safe for the night?"

"Yes, there is a place not far from here," she answered with a small, reassuring smile.

"Looks like we're going to have a lot more company than we did last night. I've gotten kinda spoiled with having you all to myself," Ross grumbled near her ear as they walked by the others.

Gem felt a wave of heat go through her. "Well – suffer!" she whispered. "You almost made my heart give out I was so scared – for you!"

He stopped and looked at her. He reached up and gently traced a line on her cheek with his thumb. She knew from the way his eyes followed the movement that he could see the trail left by her tears.

"You've got me tied up in knots, Princess," he said.

"If that means you'll be more careful in the future, then that is a good thing. Otherwise, I might actually tie you up to keep you safe," she replied.

"There are sexier reasons to tie me up – if we ever get any privacy again I'll show you," he teased.

Gem tilted her head in curiosity and Ross smiled, leaning closer, his lips a moment away from brushing her own. She placed her fingers against his lips when she saw four heads turning in their direction behind him. She lifted an eyebrow and glared at the grinning foursome.

"Do you mind? This is a private moment," she snapped.

"Sorry," Orion muttered.

"But of course," Nali demurely agreed.

"Ah, sweet love," Ashure murmured.

"Why should I mind if he wants to kiss you?" Drago demanded.

Gem opened her mouth to give Drago a scathing reply when Nali shook her head and winked at her. Gem tried to keep from grinning when Nali threaded her arm through Drago's and pulled him away. She could hear Nali quietly explaining why she and Ross needed a few minutes alone.

"Are they gone yet?" Ross asked.

Gem looked back up at him and nodded. "Yes," she replied.

"Good. Because I'm going to kiss you like there is no tomorrow, Princess," he warned.

Gem started to say there might not be, but the words were smothered when Ross captured her lips in a deep kiss that left her breathless. She tightened her hold on his neck and kissed him back with even more fervor, fueled by her earlier fear that he had died. He slowed down her frantic kisses, though, and took his time, uncaring that their audience might have returned or that it was getting late.

After several minutes, he reluctantly ended their kiss with a deep sigh. He rested his forehead against hers while they both caught their breath. She pressed a light kiss to his lips.

"There will be a tomorrow," she finally murmured.

He smiled. "You bet your sweet ass there will be, Princess," he vowed with an amused voice.

"It's getting late," Drago called out.

"Ah, Drago, it is good to know I am not the only obtuse one at times," Ashure said with a resounding slap on Drago's shoulder.

"I swear if you slap my bruised shoulder one more time, Ashure, the pirates are going to need a new king," Drago threatened.

"Gem, Ross, the children are getting antsy. I think it is in the best interests of all the kingdoms to get to a place to rest for the night," Nali suggested with amusement.

"I will definitely not pretend that I'm the father to those two children in any universe," Orion stated.

Gem laughed and wrapped her arm around Ross's waist. They passed Drago and Ashure as they continued to trade increasingly rude remarks and ignored Orion threatening both of them if they came to blows. She had never seen this side of Drago – or Orion before.

"Are they always like this?" Ross asked.

Gem shrugged. "I've seen this type of banter between Nali and Ashure, but I've never spent much time with the others. They are actually very entertaining," she said with a glance at the small group.

Ross looked at Ashure and Drago with a raised eyebrow. "I'd place ten dollars on the dragon. Anything that can survive a lava creature has to be pretty resilient," he remarked.

"You might be surprised about the pirate. I've heard tell that almost everyone – including the dragons – have tried to kill Ashure at one time or another," Gem chuckled.

"I can certainly understand why," he murmured when he heard another slap and Drago's answering growl.

# CHAPTER TWENTY

"This is a good spot. We should be safe. There was no mention in the stones about any traps by the lake," Gem said.

"What did the stones tell you?" Nali asked.

Gem bit her lip. *"Beware the waters that you sail, danger lurks with deadly tails,"* she recited as she stared out across the lake. She unconsciously leaned back against Ross when he came to stand behind her and slid his arms around her waist. Since the incident crossing the Field of Fire, they couldn't get enough of each other's touch. She rested her hand on his arm.

"Well, between myself and Orion, I think we can handle just about anything above or below the water," Ashure stated with a dismissive hand.

"Yeah, just like a dragon and a lava monster," Ross retorted.

Ashure grimaced. "Perhaps now might be a good time to give you your first lesson in sword fighting," he suggested.

Gem nodded. "Nali and I can gather some food while Drago and Orion set up camp," she said.

"That sounds good to me," Nali agreed.

Gem pulled away from Ross. He tightened his hold on her for a brief moment. Their eyes met, and she lifted a hand to his cheek. He was worried about her.

"Be careful and don't go too far," he murmured.

"I will. Watch Ashure. He doesn't always fight fair," she warned.

Ross chuckled. "Neither do I," he replied.

She nodded and reluctantly turned away. They had less than an hour before darkness fell. She looked up at the sky. Both moons would be full the day after tomorrow. Time was running out. Throughout the day there had been minor tremors coming more frequently than before.

She unconsciously held her hands out to her sides and spread her fingers, trying to sense the changes. Nali walked silently beside her. Her expression grew troubled when she felt the rippling vibrations.

"How much longer?" Nali gently inquired.

"No more than two days," she guessed.

"We will be successful," Nali reassured her.

"What happened – to Magna and the alien?" Gem asked.

Nali walked over to one of the small bushes along the bank of the river. It was loaded with small, round purple berries. Gem waved her hand, and a bundle of nearby sticks and dried leaves wove together until a basket was created.

"Thank you, this will make it much easier to carry. We gathered on the Isle of Magic. Marina, the young witch who you met, and Mike, the human, were familiar with Magna and the alien's abilities and defenses, and so we came up with a battle plan that had a chance of success for the first time in centuries. By dividing its attention between us, we were able to weaken it enough for some to sneak into the palace. Mike, Marina, Orion, and Drago confronted Magna in the palace while the rest of us fought against the alien creature's overextended defenses. Magna was fighting to regain her free will and destroy the alien. In many ways, she was an ally that night. I believe it was her intention all along that we would focus our powers on her. Orion and Drago attacked Magna, Mike wounded her with a weapon he brought from his world, and the alien left her body through the wound to search for someone stronger. Magna ordered us to retreat and then released a powerful spell to destroy it. We thought Magna had been killed as well," Nali said.

Gem paused in the process of pulling a nut from a nearby tree. She thought of Magna appearing a split second before the alien creature had reached for her. Magna had turned her to stone—

*To keep the alien from taking over my body.* Gem was certain of this now in a way she had not been when everything was happening so quickly. It was a weight off her shoulders.

"She didn't die. Ross said that she is in his world," she murmured.

"Yes. Several of my monsters saw her return here. She undid the spells she had cast when she was under the alien's control. Our first confirmation of that was the return of the dragons," Nali explained.

Gem turned to look at Nali. "I saw her – here. She transformed me into stone before the alien could invade my body. I was trying to escape. My parents told me to find you and the others," she said.

"Magna did what she could. This alien is something our world has never seen before, and once it is destroyed, I hope we never see it again," Nali confessed.

"How did you know – to come here? How did you know that I – we – needed your help?" she asked.

"The Goddess's Mirror showed me the danger," Nali murmured.

Gem could tell that Nali didn't want to share any more. She placed the fist-sized nuts into the basket. Once the basket was full, she lifted it into her arms and began the short walk back to the camp. Perhaps Orion could supplement their meager meal with some fish from the lake. While she might not like to eat the meat of a living creature, she understood that others were not opposed to it and would prefer a heartier meal than tree nuts and fruit before entering battle.

"Tell me about Ross. He appears to be a very interesting man," Nali casually commented.

Gem looked at Nali. "He is… different," she replied.

"Your essence flows to him," Nali observed.

"Yes," Gem answered.

"Does he know?" Nali pressed.

Gem shook her head. "No. He sees it, but he doesn't understand the significance," she reluctantly admitted.

Nali laid her hand on Gem's arm. Gem turned toward the older woman and gazed into her concerned eyes. Unable to stand the sympathy reflected there, she looked away.

"Will you tell him?" Nali asked.

Gem shook her head again. "No. He wishes to leave after – after we find my parents and destroy the alien creature. I will not tie him to me if that is not his wish," she said.

She pulled her arm away from Nali and began walking again. She didn't want to think of what Ross would do once there was no longer a threat. Would he stay? He had called her his love and kissed her as if he felt something deeper than just a passing fancy.

She took a deep breath when she heard Ross's deep laughter. The men were sitting around a large fire. Orion had indeed gone fishing as indicated by the two large fish on a spit.

Ross looked up as they approached. His eyes met hers, and he gave her a smile that sent a wave of joy through her. His gaze was warm with a hint of another emotion that she was afraid to speculate about.

"He cares for you," Nali said, not feeling the same hesitation to decipher Ross's expression.

"I hope," she replied.

Nali chuckled when Ross broke away from the group and walked over to them. He reached for the basket. Pleasure coursed through Gem when he made sure that their hands touched.

"Good timing. Ashure said the fish will be done in about ten minutes," he said.

"We can throw the nuts onto the coals. They won't take long. I need to wash the berries," she murmured.

"I'll help you. Nali, you might want to help Ashure. Drago and Orion are skeptical about his cooking abilities," Ross suggested.

Nali laughed. "Out of the three, I trust Ashure the most when it comes to cooking. Let me take the nuts. I can add them to the fire while you two wash the berries," she said.

Ross held out the basket, and Nali picked out the six large nuts. Gem waited until Nali started toward the fire before she turned and began walking down to the edge of the lake. She tucked her hair behind her ear when the light breeze blew it across her face.

"They aren't so bad. I'm glad they came," Ross commented.

Gem looked at the group by the fire and nodded. "Yes, it will be nice to have them beside us when we reach the palace tomorrow," she replied with a sigh.

Ross placed the basket on the damp sand. "Are you worried about tomorrow?" he murmured.

"Yes."

He straightened up and looked at her. "We've done pretty well so far, I think, and now we have our own group of superheroes. Hell, if I can kill a piece of the alien with a cigarette lighter and some swamp gas, they can probably detonate a nuclear bomb up its ass with a snap of their fingers," he said in a teasing tone.

"I don't know what this nuclear bomb is, but I hope you are right," she said with a touch of humor before she looked out over the water in the direction of the palace. "What if I can't find my parents? The spell – my people vanished around me. What if they are gone for good and there is no saving my home?"

She leaned into Ross when he slid his arms around her. He pressed a light kiss to her brow and stared out across the water. This felt right.

"I know that it is hard to keep the doubts and negative feelings at bay, but you have to, Gem. Your parents are there. Ashure could see them – or at least shadows of them. We will defeat whatever we face and you'll have your home and family back again. I promise. We can do this – together," he vowed.

Her throat tightened at the sincerity in his voice. She turned and wrapped her arms around his waist so she could lay her cheek against his chest. He rubbed his chin against her hair.

"I believe you," she whispered.

"Hey, the food is done," Ashure yelled. "If you want any, you'd better hurry. Dragons don't like to share, and Drago is trying to hoard the lot."

Ross's chuckle blended with her smothered giggle. She pulled back and looked up at him. He brushed her hair back from her face.

"Thank you," she said.

"No problem. We sort of forgot to wash the fruit," he said with a rueful grin.

"I can wash them," she replied with a wave of her hand, sending a burst of water over the basket.

"That is still the coolest thing I've ever seen," he sighed.

Ross chuckled when he thought about the story Ashure had shared with them earlier about using Nali's sea monkeys to create havoc while he made off with some of the King of the Giants' finest brandy. The man had a good sense of humor, but there was an element of danger to him that made him fit right in with the rest of the badasses in the group.

Dinner had been a lively affair with stories from all the others. Ross had brushed aside their teasing when he refused to share any of his stories. That didn't stop Gem from sharing his encounter with the man-eating plant, though.

He was so lost in thought that he forgot what he was supposed to be concentrating on. It wasn't until he received a painful slap to the back of his hand that he pulled his mind back to what he was supposed to be doing – learning to fight with a sword.

"Ouch!" he said, shaking his hand.

Ashure put his hands on his hips and shook his head. "How do you expect me to teach you how to defend your fair maiden if you don't pay attention to the lesson?" the pirate asked in exasperation.

"Defend? I hate to tell you this, Ashure, but Gem can thoroughly kick my ass. She almost broke my nose and she kneed me hard enough to put my balls up into my throat. That woman is a fearsome adversary if I've ever met one," he dryly retorted.

"Ah, ouch. Still, you never know when you might need to defend her – not to mention yourself, but hey, she's more important, is she not?" Ashure asked as he lifted his sword and waved his hand at Ross to continue with the lesson again.

Ross tried to copy Ashure's movements. "Yeah. So, what's your story? I know Drago can change into a dragon, and the other guy – Gant – can change into a giant. Nali can do some kind of weird changes like those wings I saw on her back when you guys arrived, and Orion is like this fish guy who can breathe under water, but you seem almost normal, if I ignore the outfit," he mused, waving the end of his sword at Ashure's shirt, trousers, and knee-high, brown cuffed boots.

"Ah, but that is my power, young student. I appear normal and so am often underestimated," Ashure said, stepping forward in a classical fencer's pose.

"I'll try to remember that, Master Yoda," Ross chuckled.

They spent the next hour sparring. Ross was feeling pretty good by the time Ashure called a halt to their lesson. Of course, Gem and the darkness probably had more to do with the pirate calling it quits.

"Thanks, Ashure," Ross called out as the man bowed to Gem before walking back to the fire.

"You did well, human," Ashure responded.

Gem chuckled when Drago asked Ashure how Ross had done and the pirate replied, "Nali's sea monkeys could whip his ass."

"Ouch! That hurt," Ross muttered in a mock offended tone.

Gem laughed again. "Nali's sea monkeys can whip everyone's ass. They are cute as can be, but they have a devilish sense of humor and a fiendish knack for making mischief. Ashure has felt Nali's wrath more than once and had to deal with them," she replied.

"Ah, well, I don't feel so bad then," he chuckled.

Gem bit her lip and looked over at the others before she turned back at him. Ross tilted his head and returned her look with a questioning one of his own. If he wasn't mistaken, his Princess appeared to be a little nervous.

"You mentioned earlier that you would…" She cleared her throat before continuing, "…that you would like a little privacy…with me. I – there is a small private cove not far from here – if you would like to…?"

Ross placed a finger under Gem's chin, and gently lifted her head so that she was forced to look at him and he could see her eyes. He smiled and ran his thumb along her jaw. Her skin was glowing with the strange, wispy colors that he had noticed before.

She parted her soft lips. Before he took this any further, he wanted to be clear about how far she was willing to go, because he was pretty damn interested in exploring the feelings inside himself. For the first time in his life, he wanted more than a one-night stand.

"I want you, Gem, and I'm not talking about just a kiss. If you come with me to that cove, there is going to be a whole lot more than kissing going on. I want you to think about that, Princess," he warned.

She laughed nervously. "I wouldn't have suggested it if I wasn't hoping there would be more than a kiss," she admitted.

Ross briefly closed his eyes when a shaft of need, so unexpected that it was painful, shot through his body. His cock was now on full alert. Opening his eyes, he flashed her a heated look that conveyed his aroused thoughts.

"You – are dangerous, Princess, in more ways than one," he informed her in a slightly hoarse voice.

"You better believe it," she tartly responded.

Ross gripped her hand, and followed her as she led him away from the fire. He sure as hell hoped that the others did not worry about them. If they did, they might get an eyeful.

"Maybe I should…," he started to say, looking back over his shoulder.

"I told them that we were going to get cleaned up and would find a place nearby for the night," she informed him.

Ross made a pleased sound that resembled a growl. "You planned ahead. Got me right where you want me, seductress."

Gem sent him a heated glance laced with humor. "Not quite yet, but I will," she promised.

He grinned and tightened his grasp on her hand, looking around as they walked silently along the beach. The night was beautiful. He had seen some beautiful nights out on the water back home, but nothing like this.

The stars were so bright he felt like he could reach up and touch them even with the light of the double moons. He thought of the Milky Way back home that looked like a river of milk with all the stars running through it. Here, there were colorful bands of nebulosity that looked like a rainbow had been painted across the heavens.

The smooth, glass-like surface of the lake mirrored the sky. He stopped when Gem pulled away from him. She turned and smiled at him.

He stared at her hands as she gripped the bottom of his sweater that she was wearing. She slowly pulled it over her head. Beneath it, she wore a light green tunic over leggings.

He chuckled when she had to pause long enough to remove the assortment of knives hidden around her body. There was something hot about a woman with a weapons fetish. It wasn't until she pulled off her boots that he realized he was standing there gawking at her like some teenager.

He bent over, untied his boots, and toed them off. He crossed his arms and gripped the bottom of his T-shirt, pulling it over his head. He tossed it to the private pebbled beach and pulled off his socks. They joined the growing pile of clothes.

When he finally straightened up to remove his pants, Gem had already removed the rest of her clothes and was walking toward the water. He almost fell flat on his face in his haste to get his pants off. His eyes were glued on Gem as she waded into the water, naked.

"Hot damn," he hissed.

# CHAPTER TWENTY-ONE

Ross shook his head when his manhood bobbed in agreement. He'd been fifteen the last time he had a reaction like this. It had been his first sexual encounter with a girl on vacation from Portland. He had a feeling this was about to blow that memory right out of the water.

Deep down, he still found it hard to believe he was in a magical world about to make love to a Princess straight out of a fantasy. He rubbed his hands together and swallowed when she looked back over her shoulder at him. Okay, he would admit it – he was a bit nervous.

"Get a grip, Ross! Since when have you ever had trouble pleasing a woman? Hell, since when have you ever doubted that you could?" he muttered to himself.

He sauntered down to the water's edge. Gem turned and faced him. He waded into the water, surprised that the temperature was pleasant. It would have been very embarrassing if it was cold. The thought made him smile, and he couldn't resist looking down to make sure. He looked up when he heard the lilting sound of laughter.

"What?" he demanded with a grin.

"You are very impressive to look at Ross Galloway," she teased.

He wiggled his eyebrows and flexed his muscles. "You haven't seen anything yet, Princess," he humorously retorted.

"At the moment, I'm getting a very good eyeful," she responded.

Ross could feel his cheeks flush. Yes, she was getting a very good eyeful. She lifted her hand and blew a kiss before she turned and dove under the water. He knew in that instant that his heart was well and truly caught.

He leaned forward and dove into the water after her. It was refreshing and soothing against his aching muscles. The moons had risen and were almost full. They illuminated the water, and he was surprised to see the iridescent glow of assorted rocks under the shimmering surface.

He emerged in waist-deep water and turned around looking for Gem. He spun around when he felt a light tap on his shoulder. Gem looked up at him with a small, almost shy smile.

"You're beautiful, Gem," he murmured.

She leaned into him. He felt her sliding her hands up his arms to his shoulders and bent forward to meet her lips halfway, wrapping his arms around her waist and pulling her close. He groaned when the tip of his engorged cock brushed against her stomach. She tightened her arms around his neck in response and used the buoyancy of the water to lift her legs and wind them around his waist.

Their breathing became faster as the passion between them built. Ross wanted to take his time to discover every inch of her, but his body was demanding that he claim her hard and fast this time so that he could take his sweet time with her later. He slid his hands down from her waist and cupped her buttocks. In this position, all he had to do was enter her.

He swept his tongue across her upper teeth before he pulled back a little, sucking her bottom lip. Then he drew back and looked at her. They gazed at each other in silence. He wanted to watch her expression as he took her.

"Take me," she demanded, tightening her legs so that her heels dug into his buttocks.

"Over and over, love, over and over," he vowed.

He pressed the tip of his cock against her soft curls. She pushed down until he was between her soft folds at the tight entrance to her channel. He gritted his teeth together to keep from moaning when she slowly relaxed against him. The movement pushed him deeper.

There was no way he could control his reaction when she pressed her breasts against his chest and began moving up and down. He tilted his head back, and his eyelids drooped when she pressed small, hot kisses against his throat. All he could do was hold onto her and enjoy the way his cock was sinking deeper and deeper inside her with each stroke.

Ross bent his head and captured her mouth again. Gem parted her lips under his heated kiss. He pumped his hips as she rode his engorged shaft, and she tangled her fingers in his hair as their kissing grew rougher.

She tore her lips away from his and moaned. "Ross, this feels so good," she choked out.

"It's going to get even better, Princess," he promised.

She shook her head and leaned into his shoulder. "Right now I'm finding that hard to believe," she replied.

"Hold onto me," he instructed.

She tightened her legs. Ross could feel her heels pressing against his buttocks. He wanted to get his hands on her breasts. She leaned back when he slid his hands up her sides. Her low hiss told him that she realized what he was doing. He swore that if they weren't in the water at the moment he would have broken out into a sweat.

In her anticipation of what he was about to do, she instinctively tightened her muscles around his cock, and their lovemaking became even more frenzied. He cupped her breasts, lifted them high, and captured a taut nipple between his lips.

Gem uttered a muffled cry as he rolled the hard pebble between his lips before sucking it in deeply. She trembled in his arms as he worked her nipple until it was sensitive and swollen.

Ross released her throbbing nipple only to continue torturing her with his fingers while he worked on the other one. He kept up the assault of sensation on her breasts until he felt her channel pulsing in time with his suckling. Only then did he release the breast he was teasing with his fingers and move down to her clit. He found the hidden little nub and began rubbing it as he increased the rhythm of his thrusts.

She immediately began riding him harder and faster. Small waves welled in the water around them as their need to come washed over them. When they reached a crescendo, their loud cries rang out.

He thrust into her as she pushed down – both of them seeking to draw out their last moment of release. Their breath mingled when she captured his lips and held him like she would never let him go.

He hugged her tightly, holding them both upright as she melted in his arms. A final shudder ran through him as he felt the last bit of his hot semen emptying inside her. They remained locked together long after the final waves of their release.

Ross cradled Gem in his arms, his chin resting on her shoulder while her face was pressed against his throat. Their hammering hearts slowly returned to normal, yet neither of them was ready to pull away.

He looked out over the lake. The moons made the water look like a bed of brilliant diamonds glistening against black velvet. He studied the sky. The stars glowed like a million pinpoints of light. Somewhere out there was Earth, he imagined, yet he didn't care. The only thing he cared about was what he was holding in his arms.

He reluctantly released her when she lowered her legs. He held her waist and steadied her when she wobbled a little. She released a soft chuckle.

"What is it?" he asked, cupping her chin so that she was forced to look up at him.

"You were right – it did get much better," she confessed.

Ross shook his head and kissed her swollen lips. "If you think that was good, wait until I get you in a proper bed," he murmured.

"I can't wait," she replied.

Gem touched his cheek, and he turned his head, pressing a kiss to her fingers. He didn't want to think about what tomorrow might bring – or the days after that. He would take his time with her while he could because he knew that this moment couldn't last forever. A princess from any world didn't have long term relationships with a guy like him. If tonight was all that he would ever have with her, then he wasn't about to waste it on regrets.

"If you can make us a little pallet under the stars, Princess, you won't have to," he teased.

"I think I can manage that," she purred as she gripped his hand and began pulling him toward the shore.

Over an hour later, Gem sat up and looked out over the lake. Lightning flashed on the horizon. She could feel a drop in the barometric pressure. She looked down at Ross. He was lying on his back with one arm under his head, staring up at the stars.

"It is going to rain. We should find shelter," she suggested.

"Okay," he replied in a relaxed voice.

"What are you thinking about?" she asked, leaning over him.

He looked at her and smiled. "You, the universe, nothing," he replied, sitting up when she pulled back.

She grabbed his sweater and pulled it on. Bowing her head, she bit her bottom lip when she pulled the material over her tender breasts. Her whole body felt well and truly loved.

Ross had touched Gem in places where no man had ever touched her before and, oh, what he had done with his lips! Her body heated at just the thought of the places he had kissed her. She swore she could still feel the moist heat of his breath against her clit.

She stood up and surreptitiously watched as he pulled on his pants. Then she turned around and looked at a small cluster of trees near the bank. One of them would be perfect to stay the night in. There were enough vines to create a shelter, and the thick moss would make a comfortable bed.

"We can stay the night over there," she said, pointing to the trees.

"I'll follow you, Princess," he said.

He picked up the rest of their clothing before she could. Ross had suggested they wash and dry them while they had a chance. She had agreed, knowing he probably needed a short amount of time to recover before they made love again. She didn't mind. The short break had given her time to sort through what had transpired between them.

She'd had other lovers, but they were never serious. Tonight was different. Tonight, she had felt an emotional connection that terrified her on one level while making her feel invincible on another. This was the connection that the melding essences of their colors signified – soulmates. She had always doubted the possibility and was even skeptical when she saw her essence swirling around him, but their joining tonight had been – special.

She looked out across the lake in the direction of the palace. She wished that she could talk to her mother. There were so many things that she wanted to ask her.

*If all goes well, perhaps tomorrow I will be able to,* she thought with longing.

She turned when she heard Ross mumble a curse. He had dropped one of his boots. She grinned when he juggled the items of clothing in his hands as he walked barefooted across the uneven ground and stood next to her. She reached over and grabbed her boots off of the pile before she carefully rearranged several items that were teetering.

She kept her hand on top of the clothes and looked up at him. Staring into his warm brown eyes, she lost herself in the memories of their lovemaking. She wanted to kiss him, to feel his hands and lips on her body bringing her to intense pleasure again and again. She blinked several times to clear her vision when she heard his low chuckle. It was obvious that he knew what she was thinking. Her face flushed with pleasure.

"Thank you," he murmured.

"You're welcome," she replied.

"You know, I really like the way you fill out my sweater," he commented.

She laughed. "I believe you have mentioned that before," she remarked with a sassy grin.

They both looked out across the lake when a low rumble of thunder rolled across the sky. The clouds were getting darker, and they would soon see more lightning flashes on the horizon. A cool breeze was beginning to pick up.

"Looks like we washed and dried the clothes a bit too soon," Ross reflected with a rueful grimace.

"We will be fine," she reassured him.

He raised an eyebrow at her. "Don't tell me – you have a bungalow stashed somewhere around here," he dryly remarked.

She laughed again and shook her head. "No, but something almost as nice," she promised.

She walked over to the tree she had picked out for their shelter a few minutes earlier, and shot Ross a quick smile before she laid her hand against the trunk. Beneath her palm she could feel the life of the tree.

She murmured her request and felt the magic pass through her to the hearty fir. Several long vines lowered from the canopy above. Behind her, she could hear Ross's low whistle of appreciation.

"I can't tell you how cool it is to watch you do things like this," he commented.

Gem looked over her shoulder and smiled at him. "You make me realize that the things I take for granted are to be appreciated." She glanced at the horizon again. "Especially when there is a storm coming. We better hurry. It will be here in the next few minutes."

"What about the others?" he asked, stepping forward.

She chuckled. "They have their own skills for staying dry," she replied.

"Whoa, this is – strange," he muttered.

The vines wrapped around Ross's body since he didn't have any hands free to hold on and they began lifting him to the upper canopy. Gem gripped a thick vine with one hand and stepped into the loop it made. As she was lifted up, she slowly rotated around until she was facing out toward the lake. Through a break in the clouds, the moonlight revealed the silhouette of the palace towers in the distance.

Longing, mixed with apprehension, fear, and doubt, swept through her, making her catch her breath. She exhaled and relaxed her grip on the vine when Ross gripped her waist and pulled her onto a broad limb. She released the vine with a wave of her hand, and the vines began to weave together, forming a shelter for them.

She and Ross quickly moved inside the makeshift shelter as the first drops of rain began to fall. The branch was covered with a thick, spongy moss. She placed her boots next to Ross's.

"Perfect timing," he said as he sat down and leaned back against the tree trunk.

"Yes, it is," Gem murmured with a faint smile.

The sound of thunder rumbled through the sky, and the rain began to fall harder. She smiled her thanks when Ross shrugged out of his jacket and held it out to her. She took it while he pulled his T-shirt on.

She knew she should probably pull her leggings on, but she didn't feel like it. Crawling over to him, she twisted around, leaned back against his warm body, and used his jacket as a blanket.

He wrapped his arms around her when she shivered. She could feel him rubbing his chin against the top of her head. They sat like that for a long time, staring out at the falling rain.

"We should reach the palace tomorrow," she murmured.

"What's the plan?" he asked.

"We have to get across the lake first," she answered.

"So, we'll need a boat, unless we are going to try to swim it," he observed.

She nodded. "We can search the shore for a fisherman's boat. If we can't find one, we'll have to build a raft. We used to do that when I was a child," she replied with a deep sigh. "Every year there was a Spring Festival. Families would get together and build rafts out of anything they could find. It was such a fun time. Once my father and I built a raft out of an old tub and used mother's finest silk cloth as a sail."

"Did you win?" he asked.

She laughed and shook her head. "No. We forgot to put the plug in the tub. Mother was not amused when we returned the ruined cloth. To this day, father is still forbidden to go near Mother's private stash of material," she murmured. Leaning her head back against him, she released another deep sigh. "I miss them, Ross. What if we fail? What if they are gone for good? I'm so afraid that I will never see them or my people again."

Ross tightened his arms around Gem when he heard the longing in her voice. He could tell she was exhausted. Her vulnerability pulled at his heart, and he rested his cheek against her hair.

"You are the most powerful woman I have ever met. Hell, the first time I saw you, I could feel you were – amazing. If anyone can achieve this, it is you, Gem. You are an extraordinary woman," he said in a low, tender voice.

"Thank you, Ross. You are an extraordinary man," she murmured.

Ross continued to cradle her in his arms, and she finally fell into an exhausted sleep. He knew that using her powers must drain her, but she never complained. He pressed a kiss against her hair.

The last couple of days, he had done things he'd never thought he could, and it felt – good. Before this, there had always been an emotional distance between him and everything and everyone in his life, even with his mom. He'd realized that when his mom was dying. It had been a form of protection for both of them – caused by his father – but 'protecting' himself sure hadn't done him any favors.

Mostly his life had felt empty, and he had felt like a terrible, defective person. Here there was nothing to protect him, no barriers of his own making, not from the life-threatening dangers or from Gem. The first time he'd kissed her he'd felt like all his defenses were gone and he was really alive. His life here had been terrifying, but damn it felt good.

*It doesn't matter what I face as long as I do it with the woman I love.* He froze.

*I'm falling in love with her,* he thought in stunned disbelief. He closed his eyes as the truth of it swept through him. For the first time in his life, he felt an emotion that he had always avoided. *I am so totally screwed!*

Opening his eyes, he released the breath he had sucked in when the truth hit him. He gently rubbed Gem's arm. She murmured in her sleep and snuggled closer against him.

He gently lowered Gem onto the moss and settled down beside her, pulling his jacket securely over her legs. He moved her folded leggings under her head to use as a pillow. Wrapping his arm around her, he pulled her close, and stared out at the rain until the gentle rhythm lured him into a light sleep.

*I need to get to the palace, then I need to get out of here,* he thought drowsily. *That is what I need to do. Free her parents and run like hell. That's the best and noblest thing I can do for her. A princess has no business being with a man like me.*

# CHAPTER TWENTY-TWO

Ross woke up when Gem moved in his arms. He pulled her closer and kissed her shoulder before he opened his eyes. She rolled onto her back and gave him a crooked smile.

"Thank you," she murmured.

"For what?" he asked.

"For everything – for being you," she said.

Ross's stomach knotted at her response. "Yeah," he muttered.

She gave him a strange look. He knew she was about to ask him what was wrong, but thankfully, he was spared having to make up a lie – or worse, tell her that he wasn't what she thought – when a dragon's head suddenly appeared in the opening of their small shelter. The dragon grinned at them before shifting into human form. Ross muttered a curse and pulled his jacket firmly over Gem's legs.

"Do you mind?" he snapped.

Drago lifted an eyebrow. "Not at all. Ashure found a boat. Unless you want to swim, I suggest you get ready," he replied with a smirk.

"We will once you leave," Ross said, glaring at Drago.

Drago frowned and looked at Gem. "Does he always wake up this grouchy?" he asked.

Gem snorted and grinned. "I don't know," she honestly confessed.

"Drago, are they in there?" Ashure called from below.

Drago pulled his head out of the opening and looked down. "Yes. Ross is not a morning person," he answered.

"I wouldn't be either if I saw your ugly face first thing in the morning," Ashure replied.

"The last I heard, Ashure, pirates weren't fireproof. Would you like to call me ugly to my face?" Drago retorted.

Drago rose from where he was kneeling outside the opening to their shelter and jumped out of the tree. Ross was surprised that the ground didn't shake when the man landed – and that he didn't hear bones crunching and Ashure's loud scream of agony. Instead, there was the faint sound of laughter. He flopped back down and stared up at the woven ceiling.

"Those two would fit right in at my local bar back home," he marveled.

Gem twisted around and looked down at him with an amused expression. "The men in your world act like this too?" she inquired.

He chuckled. "Oh yeah – way more than we should," he admitted.

They both shook their heads when they heard Nali's shout a moment before there was a loud splash. Ross sat up when Gem giggled. He lifted his hand and caressed her cheek.

"I think Nali is having a difficult morning as well," she murmured.

"That tends to happen when you have a bunch of guys together," he said.

"Ross – about last night...," her voice dipped lower with emotion.

He shook his head. "Let's keep the memories where they belong. For now, we need to concentrate on getting across the lake and finding your parents," he said.

"You're right," she replied.

They dressed in silence, each lost in their own thoughts. Ross looked up when Gem waved her hands. The vines that had sheltered them last night unraveled, then wrapped around him. He gripped the vines to steady himself when they lifted him up off the branch and lowered him to the ground. Gem followed, but instead of using the vines, she turned into a mist and materialized next to him.

"Here," she said, holding out a small flower.

Ross took the small white flower from her and looked at it with a frown. "What am I supposed to do with this?" he asked.

"If you place it in your mouth, it will dissolve and clean your teeth," she explained, popping another small bloom into her mouth.

Ross held the bloom up and studied it before he popped it into his mouth. His eyes widened in surprise when he felt a slight fizz that tasted minty. It reminded him of the Fizzy/Pop Rocks candy he used to get when he was a kid. In fact, that was the first thing he had ever shoplifted.

Licking his lips, he ran his tongue over his front teeth. It felt like he had just been to the dentist for a cleaning. Once again, he was reminded that this world was far different from his own.

"You know, if you could package this stuff, you'd make a fortune back on my world," he said.

She laughed. "The blooms don't last long after they are picked so that might be a slight disadvantage," she remarked.

"Damn, there goes another brilliant idea," he joked.

A shout from the direction of the lake pulled them back to the reality of their situation. The thought of tooth-cleaning blooms faded with the gravity of what they were about to face. Ross looked out across the glassy surface of the lake and shivered.

"We'd better go," she said.

"Yeah, we better go," he absently replied, his eyes narrowing when he thought he saw something briefly break the surface.

"Are you sure this is big enough for all of us?" Nali asked with a skeptical expression.

"Of course. If it gets too cramped, we can throw Drago out," Ashure answered with a wave of his hand.

"Remember, no magic from here. Wayman – if he is still alive – will be able to sense the disturbance," Gem cautioned.

"We should be fine, Nali," Ross reassured. "I would say the boat is about eighteen feet. I haven't done much sailing, but I do know boats."

Nali sighed. "I am used to slightly larger vessels," she explained.

"Well, it is time to go," Drago said as he picked Nali up and placed her in the boat.

"Gem—" Ashure said with a smile.

"I'll help her," Ross muttered, slipping his arms around Gem and lifting her in his arms.

"Ah, a jealous suitor – more intrigue," Ashure said with a wicked grin.

"Ashure, you and Ross get in the boat. Drago and I will push it off," Orion instructed.

Ross nodded and climbed on board. He moved to the bow while Gem and Nali sat in the center on either side of the small mast. Ashure sat in the stern and gripped the ropes for the single sail. Ross gripped the gunwale to steady himself when the boat slid loose from the shore and rocked a bit. Drago jumped in on the starboard side while Orion entered on the opposite side to keep the boat from tipping over.

"Orion, you may want to take the bow. It never hurts to have another pair of eyes seeing where we are going. Drago, you can sit in the stern near me in case we need some hot air for the sails," Ashure said.

Ross chuckled when Drago muttered a dire threat to Ashure's health under his breath. Turning his back to the others, Ross looked out over the surface of the lake. He had an uneasy feeling in the pit of his stomach.

"Could you sense if there was something strange under the water?" he quietly asked Orion.

"Yes, I fear our trip across will not be all smooth sailing," Orion quietly answered.

"That's what I was afraid of," Ross replied.

He turned slightly to look back at Gem. She was talking to Nali. He studied her flushed face and delicate pink lips. Her hair blew away from her face as they picked up speed. She was still wearing his beige sweater. Her left hand was resting on her lap, and her fingers absently played with the hem.

He was aroused when he remembered how her fingers had caressed his skin last night, the way she had responded to his touch, the way she had felt wrapped around him. Making love to her under the stars had been – incredible. His mind skidded to an abrupt halt, and his warming flesh quickly cooled as a shiver ran through him. Last night – last night – he had….

*Shit!* he thought as a cold sweat broke out over him.

Ross looked up at Gem's face, then down to her stomach. He gripped the boat's gunwale tighter, tore his shocked eyes away from her, and stared blindly out at the lake.

Last night had been one of the most intense moments in his life. So intense, in fact, that he hadn't thought about anything but Gem, completely forgetting about using any type of protection.

The realization of what they had done – what he had done – hit him in the stomach like an Olympic boxer's fist. He had always been extremely careful. He was so paranoid about an accidental pregnancy that he had never let any woman even handle the condoms that he used. Luckily for him, most of the women he had dated felt the same way about kids. They were nice – when they belonged to someone else.

"Are you feeling unwell? You are not getting seasick, are you?" Orion asked.

Ross shook his head, unable to look the other man in the eye. "No, I – I'm good. I was just – thinking of some of the things that happened over the last few days, that's all," he muttered.

Orion nodded. "I remember well Jenny's feelings and her adjustment," he replied.

Ross looked at Orion with a surprised expression. "That's right, you and Jenny Ackerly got together. I forgot about that. How is she?" Ross asked.

"Beautiful, stubborn, perfect – I could go on and on," Orion chuckled.

Ross uttered a short, sharp laugh. "Yeah, that sounds like Jenny. After Carly disappeared, she was like a Bulldog searching for a bone. I'm glad things turned out well for her and Carly – and Mike. It would be interesting to see what people back home say when they realize that I'm missing now. I'm sure they will be thrilled," he said bitterly.

Orion was about to reply when Ross saw movement in his peripheral vision. He reacted instinctively, reaching out, grabbing the other man's arm, and yanking him back. They both stumbled backward as long, black tentacles emerged out of the water.

Ross lifted the sword Ashure had given him and swung at a tentacle. A three-foot section fell at his feet, dissolving into a black mist.

"It's a creation from the alien creature," Gem hissed with alarm.

"I don't think it matters now if your cousin knows we are coming," Orion grimly stated.

Ross swung around and reached out for Gem when the boat's stern was lifted out of the water. Drago shifted into his dragon form and flew off the boat when the creature lifted the boat higher.

Gem gripped Ross's arms while Nali wrapped her arms around the mast. Ross started to call out a warning when Ashure lost his grip. Drago saw what was happening and swooped down, grabbing Ashure when he began to fall.

"Look out!" Orion shouted.

Ross knew from the amount of water swirling around his feet that the boat would sink soon. Gem dove over the side first. He followed her, plunging into the warm water beside the craft. Orion cut through the water right beside him.

They struggled to evade the menacing creature that was visible in the clear water. Ross pulled Gem close when one of the creature's tentacles swept by them to grab the boat. The monster's head looked like something out of a Jules Verne tale. They all looked up when they heard the sound of splintering wood resonate through the water.

Pieces of the boat slowly sank in the water around them. Ross reached out and pulled Gem away when a piece of the rigging swirled dangerously near her. His grip on her arm tightened when Orion grabbed him by the back of his collar and yanked him, along with Gem, away from the sinking debris. Ross's lungs began to burn. He turned his head and looked at Orion. The other man understood his silent message and began swimming toward the surface.

The water swirled around them as they surfaced. Ross released his hold on Gem. He was still gripping the sword Ashure had given him with his other hand, thankful it was not heavy enough to act like a diving weight. He gaped in awe when he saw Nali. She once again had long, black wings, but now short horns curled upward from her head and her lithe body was covered in shimmering bluish-black scales. She swooped between the tentacles of the giant Kraken and spun around in an elongated twist when one of the long, black arms reached for her, maneuvering between two more as she headed for them.

"Raise your arms," Ross ordered Gem. "Nali can carry you a safe distance away if you show her that's what you want."

"I don't think so," Gem growled. "Let her take you, Ross."

"Son-of-a-bitch. Gem!" Ross yelled in aggravation when mist rose where Gem had been.

Gem soared upward. A shiver ran through her when she felt one of the tentacles pass through her. It was reaching for Nali. She twisted and materialized above the waving arm of the Kraken and drew her short sword. Her body dropped back toward the water without the support of her mist form.

Her arm swung out as she fell and the sword in her hand sliced through the tip of the Kraken's tentacle. Her feet slammed into the thicker part of the flailing arm and she buried her blade into it. She cut a long deep slice, opening the rest of the limb like a fisherman filleting his prize catch of the day as she slid down along the contours of the moving appendage.

She barely had time to dive off the limb before another of the creature's tentacles struck out at her. Nali soared down and grabbed her by her waist, catching her and carrying her out of harm's way.

"Thank you. I didn't see that limb," Nali commented.

Gem looked up at the other woman and nodded. "Do you see Ross? We have to get to him. He is still in the water," she said, looking around.

"I see him. I'll get him," Nali responded with a curt nod.

Gem nodded. She felt Nali release her arms. She shifted to mist again as she fell. On the other side of the Kraken, Drago breathed a long, intense stream of dragon fire. The creature snatched its tentacles back and suddenly disappeared under the water.

"Ross, look out," Orion shouted below her.

Gem turned at the same time as she heard Orion's shout of warning. Her eyes frantically searched for Ross. A silent cry of denial surged through her when she saw the shadow of the Kraken heading directly for him and Orion.

*Please, Goddess, let Orion or Nali get him out of there safely,* she thought.

Ross saw the wave from the submerging monster heading toward them. He drew in a deep breath, pulled his arms in, and stilled the motion of his feet. When he stopped treading water, the weight of his soaked clothing pulled him down. He rotated when he felt a ripple of movement. His eyes grew larger when he saw the Kraken reach out and wrap a tentacle around Orion's foot.

Orion twisted around and aimed his trident at the creature. Before he could fire the glowing staff, one of its other arms came up behind Orion and struck him on the head. Ross watched in horror as the merman went limp, the trident slipping from his relaxed hand and falling end over end downward to the bottom of the lake.

Ross swam back up to the surface and took in another gulp of air before he dove down. He kicked his feet as hard as he could. The lake wasn't as deep as he'd expected, approximately thirty feet. He'd done many free-dives deeper than this.

He grabbed the handle of the trident, which had become embedded into the rock strewn silt, and pulled himself until he was standing on the bottom. Then he gauged the movement of one of the Kraken's arms.

When it moved past him, he lifted his sword and plunged it into the monster's flesh. Ross gripped his sword and the trident firmly, the

Kraken yanked its tentacle away, and the movement pulled the trident out of the rocky lakebed.

Ross tightly held on to his weapons and ducked his head. The sword was stuck fast within the fleshy top layer of the tentacle and the Kraken was pulling him through the water like a speed boat pulling a skier. Ross focused on keeping his heart rate as slow as possible. The longest he had ever held his breath was a little more than five minutes – and that was while he was still smoking. Of course, he'd done that when he was free-diving, not when he was being pulled through the water by a monster and on an adrenaline rush.

Ross turned his head when he saw a movement out of the corner of his eye. Orion had regained consciousness and was struggling to break free. Ross waited until he was above Orion before he released his grip on the sword and swam down between the Kraken's flailing tentacles.

He spun around when another tentacle shot by him. Kicking as hard as he could, he hoped that Orion would sense his presence and look up. As if he could hear Ross's silent shout, Orion looked up at him. The merman's expression was grim until he saw Ross holding his trident.

Orion reached out, and Ross felt the trident lurching out of his grasp. He quickly released his grip on the staff. Using his arms and legs to keep himself steady, he watched as the trident sped through the water and into Orion's hand. The moment Orion grasped the shaft, the trident glowed with a brilliance that was almost blinding.

Ross nearly gulped in a mouth full of water when he saw what happened next. After a swift motion of Orion's hand, the tentacle binding the merman was severed from the Kraken and dissolved. Orion swam back a short distance, and the barbed point of light emanating from the end of the trident speared the Kraken and lifted it toward the surface.

Ross sped toward the surface, his lungs burning. Through the clear water, Ross could see the blurred image of Drago flying above them. He didn't know what Drago had done with Ashure. Ross was so focused on what was happening on the surface that he didn't see one of the long tentacles sweeping through the water. The black arm struck him in the back and pushed him down toward the bottom of the lake as if he'd been handed a ton of weight belts all at once.

He twisted a second before he hit the bottom. His head snapped back and hit a large rock just as the Kraken broke the surface above him. The powerful combination of dragon fire and electricity from the trident created a blinding light that matched the one exploding through his head. Ross's lips parted and a series of small bubbles floated toward the surface as darkness swept over him. His limp body drifted along the rocky bottom.

# CHAPTER TWENTY-THREE

Gem reached for Ross as the wave of water Orion had created to carry him to shore slowly receded under him. She turned him over. He was deathly pale with a slight tinge of blue around his lips. Her fingers trembled as she caressed his cold cheek.

"We have to get the water out of his lungs," she said in an urgent voice.

Her hands moved to the sides of his chest and she sent a gentle push against his lungs. A small, but steady stream of water slipped from his lips. Her throat tightened and she repeated the action over and over until she thought she had pushed all of the water from his lungs.

"Let me," Orion gently said when she brushed the back of her hand against her cheek.

Orion placed his hands over Ross's heart. Small electrical charges emitted from his hands and Ross's body bowed. Orion bent over Ross and placed his ear next to Ross's mouth. Gem watched with growing apprehension when Orion repeated the electrical charge again. He leaned forward and listened once more before sitting back and nodding at Gem with a half-smile.

"He breathes," Orion quietly stated.

Gem reached for Ross's hand. His lips were parted and they didn't appear to be blue anymore but he still wasn't moving. She laid her hand on his chest.

"He doesn't look like he is alive. Orion, are you sure he is breathing?" Drago's deep voice inquired.

"Yes. His heart is beating again," Orion replied.

"But he *was* dead. That means Nali's prediction came true and the rest of us don't have to worry," Ashure reasoned.

"Don't say that! He's not dead!" Gem hissed, glaring up at Ashure.

"I'd be careful, Ashure. I've heard Elementals can pull moisture right out of your body or even walk through you and take your organs with them," Drago warned.

Ashure looked at Drago with a startled expression. "Really? I had not heard that before," he commented with a wary look at Gem.

"We can do more than that when provoked," Gem angrily snapped.

If Ross's head didn't hurt so badly and he hadn't heard the tremor in Gem's voice, he would have laughed. As it was, besides the pain in his head, his chest hurt and his stomach was roiling with the desire to expel more lake water. He didn't want to think of all the Kraken crap he had probably swallowed.

"Ashure, might I suggest that now would not be a good time to bring up the possibility of death and dying – for your own safety," Nali calmly stated.

A slow, crooked grin curved his lips when Gem's fingers curled protectively over his heart. The grin turned to a grimace when his stomach finally heaved one too many times, and bile rose up in his throat. He turned his head and expelled the liquid, coughing and choking as he gasped for air.

Once it felt like he could breathe again without heaving, he fell onto his back and looked up at the ring of faces staring down at him. He slowly counted and breathed a sigh of relief when he realized that all of them were there. He hissed when Gem suddenly wrapped her arms around him, yanked him into a sitting position, and squeezed him tightly.

"I knew you weren't dead," she declared with a relieved laugh.

"That's good to know," he mumbled against her breasts.

He uttered a low moan when she carefully lowered him back to the ground. When she rested her hand on his heart again, he laced his fingers through hers. He noticed two things – one, that he was dry, and two, that Gem had tears in her eyes. He reached up, cupped her cheek, and caught a tear with his thumb.

She laughed self-consciously. "You are either the most stubborn man I have ever met or the luckiest," she softly informed him.

He gave her a crooked grin. "It is better than being the dumbest," he playfully retorted.

"So, Nali, does this count as one of us dying or not?" Ashure asked.

Ross looked up at Ashure with a frown. "What is it with you and someone having to die?" he demanded in a raspy tone.

Ashure grinned at him. "Nali told us that one of us would die on this adventure. Since I have no wish to be the one and you were technically not breathing and your heart had stopped when Orion brought you ashore, I hoped we were finished with that part of our journey," he explained.

Ross looked at each of the others before he shook his head. "Has anyone ever told you guys that you are just plain weird – don't get me wrong, I mean that in a good way – but you are still weird?" he replied before he shook his head and winced. "I could really use some pain medication."

"Perhaps I can be of assistance," Ashure suggested, leaning forward and holding his hand above Ross's forehead.

Ross crossed his eyes as he tried to focus on what the pirate was doing. Waves of color rose from his head to Ashure's hand. He blinked several times after Ashure pulled his hand away. He moved his head back and forth and gingerly sat up. Reaching up, he rubbed the back of his head and grinned at Ashure.

"Not bad for a pirate," he commented.

"I didn't know you could do that," Nali said with a raised eyebrow.

Ashure waved his hand. "A simple parlor spell taught to me by an old witch in exchange for a trinket," he nonchalantly dismissed.

"I'd like to talk to that old witch. It would come in handy when the kids tackle me or when Carly sees a mouse and hits me in my manhood with a broom," Drago muttered.

The others snickered, and Ross sympathized with the man. No one could really understand how dangerous Carly was if they hadn't met her, no one. He grasped Gem's hand when she held it out and stood up.

He saw that they were on the beach. He looked up at the tall shimmering white cliffs. They reminded him of the cliff he'd climbed the day he met Gem. It was hard to believe that it was only a few days ago.

"So, where are we?" he asked with curiosity.

"On the shore of the Crystal Cliffs. The northern edge of the palace is at the top. I hoped that we would be closer to the southern end – that is where the gardens are and where I left my parents," Gem answered.

Ross gently squeezed Gem's hand when he heard the anguish that she couldn't quite hide. He looked back at the towering cliffs. He hoped there was a set of stairs somewhere because he didn't relish trying to climb the cliff without any safety equipment.

"May I ask how we get to the top?" Ashure inquired, shading his eyes and carefully studying the top of the cliff.

"There is a hidden staircase. I will guide you," Gem said.

"I am sure the alien must be aware that we are here now. It may try to possess one of us," Nali warned with a pointed glance at Ashure.

Ashure frowned. "Here we go again. It warms my heart that you are so concerned, Nali, but really – I think we've been over this enough. I will take care now that I know of the threat," he grumbled.

"You should take heed of Marina's grandmother, Ladonna, who warned her to keep you away from it! Your possession is not a remote possibility among many, it has been seen. It is too late to keep you away now. You're here. We must simply guard you carefully," Nali told him.

"Ladonna Fae? I obtained the spell I used on Ross's headache from her. She is a looney old witch. Very strange, likes to talk in riddles, and has a cane that I once coveted until I realized it never shut up," Ashure replied with a dismissive wave of his hand.

"She's dead," Nali dryly retorted.

Ashure had the grace to look repentant. "Ah, yes, how remiss of me to forget that part," he remarked before looking at Gem. "You said there is a staircase, yes? I suggest that if Ross is up to it, we continue on. Of course I'd *prefer* a nice rest after our adventure on the lake, but since we need to confront the alien *and* prevent the Isle from crashing to the ocean below, I guess we should continue."

"I concur with Ashure. It will be difficult enough dealing with the alien during the day. I would prefer to fight when it cannot hide in the shadows of the night," Orion agreed.

"Follow me," Gem instructed.

She started to turn when a violent quake struck the Isle. Ross reached out, wrapped his arms around Gem's waist, and pulled her tightly against his chest. Normally the tremors lasted only a few seconds. This time, the shaking continued far longer.

The ground shook, almost knocking them all off their feet. Rock crystals started breaking off the cliffs; the sound reverberated through the air like the simultaneous cracking of hundreds of whips. One large crystal shelf suddenly broke like an iceberg calving, sliding down with a rumble before hitting the water.

A loud curse broke from Ashure's lips. "We need to get out of here," he said, looking at Gem.

"There is a narrow cut in the cliff that leads to a cave and the staircase," Gem said, pointing to a dark crevice barely visible from where they were standing.

Ross looked up with a grim expression. There was a broad ledge not far above the entrance. At the moment, it was holding, but he wouldn't bet on it remaining in place for very long.

He started forward when Gem pulled out of his arms and grabbed his hand. Running across the swaying ground and keeping their balance wasn't easy. Rocks large enough to kill rained down like hail. Ross regretted losing his wooden shield after a rock struck him in the shoulder with enough force to leave a nice bruise, but they were at the entrance to the cave now, so hopefully any falling rocks wouldn't be coming from the same height as the ones sloughing off the cliff face – though they could still be large enough to cause injury or numerous enough to bury the group alive. Ross tried not to think about that as Gem released his hand, and slid through the narrow entrance, disappearing into the darkness.

He turned sideways and followed. Up close, he could see lines of colorful sediment embedded in the smooth, crystal wall. The narrow passage extended for ten feet. He looked up to make sure there were no rocks that would fall and crush him. Fortunately, the top of the passage made a triangular peak, so there were no large slabs to worry about – at least not at the moment.

Ross continued to shuffle through the cave. He could hear Ashure muttering curses behind him. He placed a hand on the wall beside him when another intense quake shook the Isle. He winced when he heard a loud rumble, and then all light from the entrance disappeared.

"Goddess, I should have stayed on the beach with the others," Ashure groaned.

"The others didn't make it?" Ross asked.

"Nay," Ashure tersely replied.

The shaking stopped and Ross deeply sighed in relief, focusing on remaining calm. Gem was somewhere up ahead. Hopefully, the quake hadn't destroyed the stairs – or their exit above.

*On a good note, if we are stuck in here, at least Drago, Orion, and Nali know where we are and can help dig us out,* he thought.

"Ross, are you alright?" Gem called.

Ross turned his head when he saw a glowing light. He smiled. His Princess had struck again.

"Thank you, Goddess," Ashure mumbled.

Ross looked at Ashure. He was surprised to see a thin film of sweat beading on the man's brow. Ashure's eyes were focused on the light in Gem's hand.

"What's the matter? Are you afraid of the dark?" Ross asked.

Ashure shook his head. "The dark is fine. The dark combined with a very, very small place is not so good," he confessed.

"Ross…?" Gem called again.

"Yeah, we're good," he answered.

"Thank the Goddess. The passage opens into a large cavern," she informed them.

"You can move a bit faster – I think she misses you. It is just an observation," Ashure said, nodding his head at Ross.

Ross snorted in laughter. How he could find amusement at a time like this amazed him. Was it because he was lucky that he was still alive or that he knew the damn pirate wanted to get out of the narrow passage? Whatever the case, he would go with the flow.

He stepped out of the passage with relief and looked around. Behind him, he could hear Ashure murmur his own amazement. The light in Gem's hand reflected off the crystals in the cavern, causing a prism of color to dance along the walls and ceiling. On the opposite side, Ross could see a staircase winding along the wall before disappearing through an opening.

"Here, open your palm," she instructed.

He held his hand out, and she rolled the ball of light onto his palm. He blinked in surprise when he realized that it was not one of her creations, after all, but a light that was sealed inside a crystal sphere.

Ross looked up when Gem stepped over to a large pillar. It was covered with the round light globes. She pulled one free and shook it. He grinned when the light swirled inside like a glow stick.

"This is for you, Ashure," she said, holding the sphere out. "If the light begins to dim, all you have to do is shake it again."

Ashure took the orb. He shook it and the light became brighter. Ross chuckled when Ashure held the orb up and studied it with a thoughtful expression.

"You know, I could probably sell these for a good profit," he murmured.

Gem shook her head. "I'm sure you could," she replied.

"What about the others?" Ross asked, looking back at the dark entrance.

"They will have to use their magic to reach the top," Ashure stated.

Gem nodded. "It won't make much difference now. They had to use it to reach the shore. Wayman and the alien will know that we are here now," she responded.

"Well, if the bad guys already know we're coming, I guess there's no need to tread lightly. I really wish I hadn't lost the sword you gave me, Ashure. I'd feel a hell of a lot better if I had some type of weapon," Ross said.

"A good pirate always carries a spare – or three," Ashure chuckled.

Ross blinked in surprise when Ashure lifted his empty hand and held out a jewel-encrusted sword. Ross moved the glowing sphere to his other hand and took the sword. He stepped back and lifted it.

"Nice! Where you hide these damn things, I don't want to know, but I'm glad you've got them," Ross exclaimed.

Ashure dropped his voice to a loud, conspiratorial whisper, "Some secrets are best left to the imagination."

Ross laughed when Ashure winked and patted the crotch of his form-fitting pants, as if insinuating that he hid his weaponry there. Shaking his head, he patted Ashure on the shoulder.

"I agree," he said with an answering grin.

"We had best be going. I can feel a change in the Isle. I have a feeling that our time has just about run out," Gem said, looking at them grimly before she turned and began walking toward the staircase.

# CHAPTER TWENTY-FOUR

Gem kept her eyes on Ross as she climbed the staircase behind him. Once again, he had insisted that he go first. She paused when he stopped to kick some loose pebbles off the steps.

"You care deeply for this one, yes?" Ashure murmured behind her.

Gem flashed Ashure a startled look before she turned back around and focused on the steps in front of her. "What I feel is none of your business, Pirate," she haughtily stated.

Ashure chuckled. "These humans in our world intrigue me. They are amazed at the things we take for granted, yet are surprisingly resourceful without having the ability to do magic or shapeshift," he observed.

"He doesn't need to do any of these things," she replied.

"I saw another human," he suddenly confessed.

Gem stopped, twisted around, and looked at Ashure with a frown. "There is Carly, Jenny, and the man who was with Marina," she said.

Ashure shook his head. "No, another woman," he murmured.

"Where did you see her?" Gem asked in surprise.

Ashure looked over her shoulder at Ross. "I don't know. The mirror – I see only confusing glimpses. She is tied to Ross in some way. I saw her with him," he said.

Gem swallowed and gave him a sharp nod before she turned away. She looked at Ross. He stopped when he realized that she and Ashure had paused. He was gazing down at her with a curious expression. She closed the distance between them.

"Is everything alright?" he asked.

She nodded. "Yes, we only have one more level to go before we reach the top," she explained.

"Okay, if you need to stop, let me know," he murmured.

She fought the urge to close her eyes when he tenderly caressed her cheek. Instead, she looked deep into his eyes. He gazed down at her with concern, warmth, and a question in his eyes.

"Ross – when this is over—" her throat tightened, and she couldn't continue.

"When this is over, Princess, you'll have your kingdom and your people back to normal," he promised.

She nodded. "Do you want me to take the lead?" she asked.

He shook his head. "No. I've got this," he replied, looking over her shoulder at Ashure.

"Are you doing okay, Ashure?" he asked.

"Well, if you want the truth—" Ashure started to say before Gem glared at him. He shrugged. "I've never been better," he finished in a dry tone.

Gem turned back to Ross.

"Okay, next stop is the top," Ross said.

Gem took a deep breath and gently shook the orb in her hand. In silence, they finished the journey to the top of the staircase. Ahead of them, a heavy, wrought-iron gate protected the entrance. She and Ashure stood back when Ross signaled them to wait. He carefully lifted the metal latch, pulled the gate open, and stepped out.

She watched him as he moved along the rock wall to the outer area. The narrow passage was strewn with smaller rocks that had broken free from the tremors shaking the Isle. Gem slid the orb into her tunic pocket under Ross's sweater. She pressed her palm over her heart. It was pounding so hard that she was afraid it would be heard.

"Clear," Ross quietly called out with a wave of his hand.

Gem moved forward on silent feet with Ashure behind her. She slipped through the open gate and hurried over to Ross. He was still scanning the area.

"Do you see the others?" she asked.

"Not yet," he murmured.

"They are still here," Ashure said, walking around them as if pulled by an invisible force.

"Ashure – who are still here?" Gem started to protest before she paused in bewilderment.

Ashure stepped out into the open. Gem looked at Ross with concern before they both cautiously followed him. She walked over to the Pirate King and touched his arm.

"What do you see, Ashure?" she quietly asked in concern.

"Your people," he exclaimed in awe. "This magic is – beautiful. I've never seen anything like it."

Gem looked around her, then at Ross. He shrugged. Neither of them saw anyone. At the top of the staircase, the entrance opened into a vast courtyard that was used as a public park. The staircase had been built a thousand years ago by the first King as a gift for his wife who loved going down to the lake for a swim. The vast park was added later so that families could enjoy the wonders of the cavern on their way to the lake.

"Tell us what you see?" she murmured.

Ashure slowly turned to her. He opened his mouth to explain when a shadow passed over them. They all looked up. Ashure grinned when he saw Drago landing a short distance away.

Drago shifted back to human form and scowled at them. Gem frowned when she didn't see Orion or Nali with him. She looked back at Drago.

"Where are Nali and Orion?" she asked with concern.

"They are not far. We encountered another taste of the alien's reception when we flew over the palace," Drago said.

"What happened?" Ross asked, coming to stand next to them.

Drago turned to him. "Gem was correct when she said the alien knew we were coming. An Elemental's shadow appeared out of thin air and attacked Nali," he explained.

"Nali! Did the alien survive?" Ashure asked with a raised eyebrow.

"Ashure," she hissed in admonishment.

"Is Nali okay?" Ross asked.

Drago nodded. "Yes, she shifted into a Gargoyle. The alien could not penetrate her skin, but it did drag her out of the sky. She was not happy about that. She hit the ground pretty hard," he replied.

"We went after him but he disappeared. Unfortunately for the creature, it didn't stay gone," Drago growled in satisfaction.

"Did you destroy it?" Gem asked.

"No. Nali wants to see if she can get some information out of it. It is obvious that the creature we caught is nothing more than a fragment of what is here," Drago replied.

Gem nodded and looked at Ashure. "Ashure, you said you can see my people, correct?" she said, gripping his arm.

"That is true," Ashure reluctantly agreed.

"Can you share your gift with me – so that I can know for sure that my parents survived? The alien is bound to be near them and I don't want to endanger them if it is," Gem requested.

Ashure vehemently shook his head in denial. "Never, Princess Gem. You do not know what you are even suggesting," he responded in an uncharacteristically hard voice.

"Gem, I think it would be better to join Orion and Nali. Drago said that Nali was trying to get information out of the alien fragment. Maybe they will know," Ross suggested.

Gem bit her bottom lip and nodded in agreement. "You are right," she said.

"I'll lead the way. I noticed what looked suspiciously like the round mud traps that I saw back in the forest when I was searching for you. We will need to proceed with caution. Not all of the traps were easy to see from the air. They will be even more difficult from the ground," Drago said.

Gem nodded. She was thankful that Drago's keen eye had spotted the traps. The last thing they needed to do right now was deal with falling in a trap in addition to dealing with the alien. She felt like an idiot for forgetting the very real possibility of there being more of her father's traps so close to the palace. She had been too preoccupied with the alien to think about it.

She stepped forward, following Drago and Ashure as they moved ahead of her and Ross. She started when Ross gently grasped her hand. A glance at his face told her that he knew she was troubled.

"What is it? I know you've got a plan forming in that beautiful brain of yours," he gently inquired.

She shot him a rueful smile. "You sound like Samuel," she said, her voice breaking on the guard's name.

Grief struck her at the thought of the old guard who had meant so much to her. Even though he'd died almost three years ago, to her, it was like it had just happened. Ross stroked her hand with his thumb. She looked down at their linked hands.

Samuel had been there for her all her life, and yet somehow, Ross had also become extremely important to her. It was a very different feeling what she felt for Ross, but if she lost him too.... How could she feel so strongly about someone she had only known a short time? It was more than a physical need; the connection was all-encompassing – mind, body, and soul – and she desperately needed that right now. Ross was the constant keeping her grounded right now, after everyone she ever cared about had been ripped away.

"What happened to him?" Ross asked in a gentle tone.

Gem took a deep, shuddering breath and blinked the tears away. Her grief would have to wait until after they defeated the alien. She refused to believe there could be any other outcome.

She lifted a hand and brushed her hair behind her ear. "He was killed protecting my parents and me. The alien took over my cousin – Wayman's – body. It targeted my father when my parents tried to stop it. Samuel was the King's Personal Guard, but he was more than that to me. He was my mentor and my friend. He taught me how to ride and fight. He helped me deal with the frustrations that came from being the only child and next in line for the throne when all I wanted to do was fly away and go on adventures. I never expected to be on an adventure like this, though," she shared in a somber voice.

"It's hard losing someone close to you unexpectedly," he said.

She looked at him. "You lost someone as well?" she asked.

Ross nodded, staring straight ahead. "Yeah, my mom. She died a few months back from cancer. She knew she had it but didn't tell me. I never realized how much she had done – or given up – to protect me.

She left me a little money – enough for a fresh start somewhere else." He snorted and shook his head. "She even made me promise to quit smoking," he said with a sigh.

"I'm sorry for your loss, Ross. I – What will you do when you go back to your world?" she hesitantly inquired.

He gazed down at her in surprise before turning his head and looking around in bemusement as he thought of her question. She felt a moment of loss when he pulled his hand free from hers and rubbed his face. He grimaced when he felt the rough whiskers on his jaw.

"I need to shave – but, to answer your question, I don't know. I honestly haven't thought about it the last few days with everything that's happened," he admitted.

"But surely you did before you came here. You mentioned going to this Hawaii. Do you still wish to go there?" she asked.

"Yeah, I guess so. I don't know. Things seem – different now. Almost dying a few times a day gives you a different perspective on the things you once thought were important," he said.

Gem wanted to ask him if he had further considered staying, because he'd said he might, but she bit her tongue. Their night together may have meant something different to him than it did to her.

Other things made her hesitate. The first was his comment about almost dying a few times a day. That alone was not something that would exactly say 'stay'.

She looked around her, trying to see the place she had always known through his eyes. Even with the damage from the quakes, there was a beauty to it that she had never fully appreciated. Did he see it the way she did?

The second reason she didn't ask was because she was afraid of the answer. Ashure said that he had seen Ross with a woman from his world. What if he wanted to return to her?

"Yes, almost dying does give you a different perspective," she agreed.

"Careful, there are three traps here. You can see the first two, but the third is well hidden," Drago cautioned.

"Good eye, old man," Ashure said in an impressed tone.

"There are two more up ahead. You may want to leave the love talk until we get past them," Drago added, glancing over his shoulder to look at them with a grin.

"Have you no couth, Drago? Hasn't your lovely Carly taught you anything? We could die today and you are eavesdropping on a very intimate moment. One or both of them could die today! Surely you could give them a little privacy as they share their deepest sorrows," Ashure admonished.

"Shut up, Ashure," Ross, Gem, and Drago all said at the same time.

Gem grimaced and shot Ross a wary expression. "I forgot that dragons have a very keen sense of hearing – and so do pirates, apparently," she said.

"Pirates use our exceptional hearing to gather information about things that may be of use to us later – like which merchant has a ship-ment worth stealing or who might not want their lovely spouse to know they are cheating on them. It's all business, of course. We never meddle in other people's business for malicious purposes," Ashure hastily added.

"You are not helping your or my cause, Ashure," Drago growled.

"I see Nali. She does look a bit upset," Ross remarked.

Gem nodded. Nali looked more pissed than upset. She wasn't sure that she'd ever seen the Empress angry before. She hurried forward when Nali and Orion turned in their direction. Nali's right arm was dark gray with a marble-like texture. Gem's eyes focused on the squirming black mass held tightly in the palm of her claw-shaped hand.

"Is that—?" she started to ask, looking at Nali with concern.

Nali nodded. "Yes, this is a piece of the alien creature that was not as fortunate as the rest when it escaped," she said.

The alien tried to wiggle free from Nali's grasp, but every time it attempted to change shape, Orion waved his trident over it. Small arcs of bluish electrical charges surrounded the alien. The alien stiffened before reforming into a black, tar-like blob.

"You should have killed it," Gem warned, looking at the creature with an expression of disgust.

"I wanted to see if we could learn anything from it," Nali replied.

"How are you going to learn anything from that – thing?" Ross asked with a look of distaste.

Drago slapped Ashure's shoulder. "We thought Ashure might be able to help with that," he said.

"You and Orion thought it. I voted against it," Nali retorted.

"You worry too much, Nali. Of course I will do what I can to help. I'm sure that we can do this safely," the Pirate King softly reassured her.

Gem frowned when she heard Ashure's voice change. There was a rumbling to it that had an oddly dangerous edge. She watched as Ashure adjusted the cuffs of his shirt, which were sticking out from under the sleeves of his jacket. She wasn't quite sure she understood what Ashure, Nali, and Drago were talking about. Scanning their faces, she couldn't help but wonder if it had anything to do with Ashure's ability to see her people when no one else could.

Ashure pursed his lips and nodded to Nali. "Whatever you do, my darling Empress, please don't let it go. I would hate for Ladonna's prediction to come true," he instructed.

Nali's stern expression softened with concern. "I won't," she promised.

Ashure motioned for her to hold her hand up so that he could see the squirming creature better. The black blob stretched as far as Nali and Orion would allow. Nali was forced to shapeshift until her entire body was made of the stone-like material of the Gargoyle so that she could keep a solid grip on the alien when its fight to escape intensified. She gripped it with both hands as she strained to hold it.

Six-inch-long jagged black tentacles greedily reached for Ashure. Gem was shocked when they stopped less than an inch from Ashure's face as if they had hit an invisible barrier. Ross leaned closer to her.

"What's up with Ashure?" Ross whispered near her ear.

Gem concentrated on Ashure's magic as he focused on the creature in front of him, calling for the living thing's essence to reveal itself... commanding its *soul* to unveil its secrets. Gem gasped. She had only heard of one being who could do this. "He is the Keeper of Souls! I – I've heard of them but always thought they were a myth," she replied in a hushed voice.

"Myth – this whole place is made up of one big myth," Ross responded.

Ashure began to speak, and Gem swayed as the seductive sound of Ashure's voice washed through her. His magic was hypnotic. There was no way she could have resisted him if he had been looking at her.

"They seek out worlds, take them over, and drain them before moving on to another," Ashure explained. "This creature searches for the other three who were on the spaceship. Their vessel broke apart when they arrived."

"It took the combined power of Magna's magic, Orion's, and my powers to destroy the alien on the Isle of Magic. Why is this one weaker? Is it truly weaker – or is this a trap to lure us into a false confidence that it will be easy to defeat?" Drago impatiently demanded.

Ashure silently stared at the alien fighting desperately to escape Nali. The alien's desire to reach Ashure grew more frantic, and Gem could see Nali and Orion were struggling to contain it between them. The powerful charges from Orion's trident seemed to have little effect on the black blob as it became more desperate to reach Ashure. Nali hissed an urgent warning when the alien suddenly broke free – leaping at Ashure. The alien hit the barrier that Ashure had erected and bounced back, but immediately it struck again.

Rage built inside Gem at the intense evil contained within this species and the harm they had unleashed against so many worlds – including hers. She raised her hands as a surge of power swept through her that she had never felt before. She stepped in front of Ashure, her body glowing with a brilliant white light.

The power flowed out of her hands, forming a sphere that captured the alien. At the same time, Orion pointed his trident at the creature and released a powerful burst of energy while Drago, who had shifted to his dragon form, released a torrent of dragon fire.

The sphere glowed as brightly as a star for a fraction of a second before it exploded. Gem felt the shockwave of the blast ripple through her before it faded. She blinked several times to clear her vision and looked around. The blast had thrown the others several feet away.

She watched as they each slowly rose to their feet and stared at her as if they had never seen her before. Lowering her hands, she looked at them in confusion. Drago shifted back to his two-legged form and walked toward her. Ashure had a huge grin on his face. Nali was looking at her with a sudden understanding. Orion briefly bowed his head in a sign of deep respect.

Out of everyone there, it was Ross's expression that captured her attention the most. He gazed at her with a mixture of awe and uncertainty. Gem forced her attention back to Ashure when he finally spoke.

"To kill the alien requires the Gem of Power – a source as powerful and bright as a star," Ashure calmly explained. "You, Princess Gem, control the gift that the Goddess gave to your people."

# CHAPTER TWENTY-FIVE

The small group moved cautiously through the palace grounds. Ross noticed that Nali, Orion, and Drago had formed a semi-circle around Ashure while he and Gem took up the rear. For once the pirate didn't object. If anything, this was the first time since he'd met Ashure that the pirate appeared to be completely serious and somewhat wary.

He also didn't miss the tentative glances and the worried look haunting the depths of Gem's eyes whenever she looked at him. He looked down at his sword. Deep down he was still trying to process what he'd seen. Over the last few days, he had begun to think that he might actually be able to hold his own in this crazy magical world.

It wasn't so much seeing what Gem could do, he already knew she was amazing – it was seeing the others' reactions to her. Their reverence toward Gem had shaken him, especially since each of them held their own unique positions of power and prominence within this world. He'd been delusional to think that a lowly fisherman from a poor family could ever fit into this realm – much less into the life of a princess.

"Ross," she started to say, a slight tremor in her voice.

He looked at her for a moment before focusing on the others, but he reached out and grasped her hand. It was clear that what happened earlier had shaken her as well.

"Everything will be alright, Gem," he reassured her.

She tightened her grip on his hand. "Thank you. I needed to hear that," she confessed.

He saw her lift a hand to her cheek and wipe it. "What's wrong, love?" he gently asked.

She released a choked laugh and sniffed. "I don't know. I think it is because I am back home and seeing everything like it used to be, except now it is empty of people. What if this is all that it will ever be? I don't know how Drago survived for so long when he lost his people. The silence is overwhelming," she said in a voice filled with emotion.

Ross looked at Drago. The man was scanning the grounds with a sharp eye. Even from the back, there was no way to miss the power radiating from him.

"Your Isle won't be empty forever. If nothing else, Magna can reverse the spell, just like she did with the dragons, but I bet you'll be the one to save the day," he said.

She sniffed and laughed. "Magna did reverse her spell on the dragons, but it was not Magna who put the spell on my people. It was my parents. If we cannot find them…," her voice faded.

"We will. Look how far we've come, and now we have a kick-ass Princess with superpowers gifted by a Goddess. How can we *not* win? We've got all the odds in our favor," he stressed, pulling her close and kissing her brow.

She tilted her head and looked up at him. "You're a good man, Ross," she murmured.

He chuckled. "Just do me a favor and don't tell anyone else, I have a reputation of being a badass that I'm trying to maintain," he told her with a wink.

She nodded. "I promise to keep your secret, Ross, always," she vowed with a small smile.

"I can't think of anyone I'd rather trust it with," he tenderly replied.

She parted her lips and gave him a look that made him clear his throat and nod in the direction they were traveling. He could see the tall hedges that made up the entrance to the maze. His stomach knotted, and he fervently wished he had a good old-fashioned tank. He would give anything just to be able to plough a path through it.

It wasn't that he was afraid of what could be hiding in the thick hedges – okay, maybe there was a little fear there, but it was more for Gem than it was for himself. He loved her, and because of that love, he would do anything to keep her safe – including eventually letting her go for her own good.

"Gem," he started to say before his attention was caught by a figure that emerged from the maze.

Gem turned to follow his gaze. She released a long hissing breath. It was her cousin or what was left of him. Scenes from all the zombie movies that he had ever watched scrolled through his mind. Ross wondered if perhaps some unwary screenwriter or producer had at one time encountered the alien creature that now inhabited Wayman's body.

"Wayman," Gem breathed out in a scornful tone, confirming his assumption.

"Ashure, get behind Gem and Ross," Nali ordered.

Wayman's insane laugh stopped Ashure in his tracks. Ross gripped Gem's arm and moved closer to Nali and the others. He and Gem turned when they saw dark shadows rising up out of the ground behind them.

"Behind you," Ross warned the others.

"Gem, we knew that you would eventually return," Wayman chuckled.

"Gem, don't—" Ross protested.

He reached for her arm but she shrugged off his hand and pushed through the group. A frustrated curse slipped from his lips when he saw the others move aside for her to step to the front. So much for him – or the others – protecting her! He could almost feel the waves of anger rolling off her as she confronted her cousin.

"I don't want to speak to you, Wayman. I don't even want to speak to the alien that was stupid enough to inhabit your weak and feeble body," Gem stated.

"Then what do you want, Princess?" Wayman sneered.

"To kill you," Gem coldly replied.

"Well, that was real subtle," Ross muttered.

"I'm impressed, no yap-yap-yapping," Ashure mumbled with an approving nod of his head.

Ross shot a glare at the pirate. Nali signaled Ashure to move back to the center of the group. Ross moved next to him.

"The alien will want Ashure. With his voice, he could ensnare an entire world," she murmured.

Ross looked at Ashure. The man was now rubbing his hands together as if he anticipated picking out a new toy. The guy was enjoying this far more than Ross thought he should.

"Are you sure about this?" he asked under his breath.

Nali nodded at Ashure. "About using Ashure as bait? Most definitely, about destroying the alien – we can only wait and see," she murmured.

Gem flexed her fingers and pushed all distractions aside. Drago and Orion stepped away from the group. Drago shifted into his dragon form and blew a stream of blue fire in a semi-circle around them while

Orion closed the circle by releasing a steady current of bluish-white electrical charges from his trident.

Her focus was on the shell of the man that used to be her cousin. Today would be the end of the terror that had begun three years before. She ignored the screech of the dark shadows. They quickly retreated from the combination of Dragon and Mer magic.

This alien was not as large or as strong as the one that had taken over Magna. The shadows merged back into Wayman. His body jerked with a sickening motion, and Gem's stomach roiled when she thought she heard the sound of shifting and snapping bones.

She knew she hadn't imagined the sound when Wayman's body contorted and began to change. His knees snapped before popping backward like the knees of an insect or bird. His chest swelled as the alien moved through his body.

Disgust filled her when his hands rose, and his fingers twisted and split. The knuckles grew larger while the tips of his fingers became long and claw-like. It was his face, though, that horrified her the most. In that instant, Gem knew that her cousin was dead. He had probably died shortly after the alien took over his body.

Wayman's skull expanded and became more sphere-shaped. His jaw protruded outward, and his mouth widened, stretching the gray paper-thin texture of his skin until parts of it cracked. His eyes were solid black and sunken into their sockets.

"Where are the others of my kind?" the alien demanded in a hissing voice.

Gem lifted her chin. "Dead, just as you shall be," she replied.

The alien leaned forward and roared in rage. Gem stood her ground. The alien took a step forward. Gem curled her fingers to keep from reacting too early.

"You lie. Your species is weak. I have been inside them. I can give you power," the alien said.

"Ashure," Gem called in a low voice.

Ashure stepped up next to Gem. "I have seen your power and what it does to the worlds you take over. We do not need your power here. We have our own that is much stronger," he said in a soothing voice.

"You are strong," the alien almost singsong purred.

Gem stepped to the side, putting a small amount of space between herself and Ashure. The pirate was using a hypnotic voice to draw the alien close enough so that she could capture it. A fear that she might not be able to do it again surged inside her. What if she was only able to create that sphere once? What if the others were wrong, and she wasn't the Gem of Power? Surely her parents would have told her if she was.

The alien must have sensed her uncertainty because it suddenly stopped and turned its attention to her. Gem could see her image reflected in the solid black eyes staring at her. Her head began to shake back and forth even as she took a step forward, drawn to the creature like a bug to a light.

"Gem, stop," Ashure warned.

She felt Ashure's hand on her arm. With a flick of her hand, Ashure was thrown away from her. He landed on the ground near Orion's feet.

"Gem, you must resist whatever the creature is doing to you," Nali anxiously said, reaching out to grab Gem's upper arms from behind. Nali fell forward when she went through Gem's now transparent body as there was nothing for her to hold on to.

Deep in the creature's eyes, Gem could see another being trapped there. A long, golden arm reached for her, begging for her help. That is what drew her forward.

"Goddess," she murmured.

She lifted her hand in response. Someone's fingers wrapped around her wrist and slowly pushed her hand down. A face appeared before her, blocking her view and breaking the hypnotic image in the alien's eyes.

"I can't let you do this, Gem," Ross said, standing in front of her.

"Ross?" she breathed, blinking to clear her vision.

"It's time to finish this, love. It's time to find your parents," he murmured.

"My parents – I have to find my parents. I have to save my people," she replied, coming to her senses.

"That's right. It's time to kick some ass, warrior Princess," he added.

"I – Ross!" Gem cried out when Ross suddenly stiffened in shock.

He stumbled back several feet. Gem cried out again and reached for Ross's hand when he lifted it. His face contorted with agony when he was lifted off the ground. A long, black shaft pierced him from behind and exited his chest.

"Kill – it," he brokenly ordered.

"Ross! No! No!"

"I – love – you, Princess," he gasped. "You – have – to – kill – it, Gem. Now."

Her screams shattered the air. Grief unlike anything she had ever felt before rose up inside her. She began to shake uncontrollably as the alien hoisted Ross higher in the air. Ross cried out in agony. He arched backward on the long spear of blackness.

"You will come to me," the alien demand.

This time when Gem looked into the creature's eyes, all she saw was death. Agony welled inside her. She saw all the countless worlds that had died because of these aliens. She saw her mother and father. The frantic pleas of her people for help. She saw Ross holding her as they made love.

A cry of unimaginable agony was torn from her throat, and she began to glow. The brightness expanded outward. She was vaguely aware of Orion helping Ashure to his feet and pulling him back. She saw Nali stumble over to Drago out of her peripheral vision, but the sphere of light did not touch them. The light was for the alien – and for Ross. Tears blinded her as she tried to focus on Ross's beloved face. The light in his eyes was fading. She shook her head in denial even as she released the full power of her gift.

"I love you," she whispered as a wave of blinding light sent a shock-wave that rolled over the Isle.

The seconds ticked by into minutes. Gem remained still long after the light had faded. Orion lowered his glowing trident. It was no longer needed to protect himself and Ashure. Drago raised his still steaming wing and lifted his head while Nali rose from where she had been sheltering next to Drago.

There was nothing left of the alien. The power of her love and grief had been strong enough to kill the alien without the help of Orion and Drago. Ross had been right; they could have done it without the help of the others.

Her shoulders began to shake as she cried for Ross. He was gone. The sound of her wounded soul was torn from her throat. Nali grabbed her around the waist when her legs gave out. Her shattering heart was too much to contain.

"No! Ross, no! Oh, Goddess, please – no, please," she sobbed.

"Gem, I'm so sorry," Nali murmured, turning Gem around and holding her close. "Oh, love, I'm so sorry. "

Nali calling her 'love' only enflamed the pain inside her. Ross had called her that. He had told her he loved her. He loved her – and he was gone.

"I can't... I can't... Nali, it hurts. Oh, Goddess, please," she brokenly whispered. "I loved him. I loved him. "

"I know, Gem," Nali said in a soothing voice.

"Nali – Gem," Ashure quietly called.

"Gem, the spell over the Isle—" Nali breathed.

Gem forced her head up. Still blinded by her tears, she could barely see at first. It was the sound of hushed voices filled with awe that made her lift her hands and wipe the tears from her eyes.

"Gem? Darling!" the sound of her mother's voice made her throat tighten.

Through blurry eyes, she saw her parents emerge from the maze – her mother's dress torn and bloodstained, but her body healed. Her mother pulled free of her father's arms and ran toward her. Nali released her into the warm, familiar comfort of her mother's arms. Soon her father wrapped his arms around them both.

"He's gone. I loved him, and he is gone," Gem sobbed against her mother's shoulder.

"Who's gone, sweetheart?" Adrina asked in a puzzled voice.

Gem lifted her head, her voice thick with sorrow and her face wet with tears. As happy as she was that her parents and her people were back and safe, her heart felt like it had been ripped from her chest and she was slowly dying.

"Ross," she replied.

"Who is Ross?" Ruger inquired, looking over Gem and his wife's heads at Drago, Nali, Ashure, and Orion.

Nali lifted a hand and gently rested it on Gem's upper back. "Ross is the man who saved your kingdom, Ruger," she explained.

"He saved all of us as well as the Seven Kingdoms," Ashure corrected.

"What Isle was he from?" Adrina softly inquired. "I would like to show our gratitude. "

"He was not from our world. His name was Ross Galloway; he was King of Yachats – or at least of the fishing boat he owned, and he was the man who I fell in love with," Gem answered before she buried her face back against her mother's shoulder and began to cry uncontrollably.

# CHAPTER TWENTY-SIX

**Yachats, Oregon**

"Hey, Ross! Where've you been? Do you need a tow?" Nathan Grumby yelled.

Ross jolted up into a sitting position. The sudden movement sent a wave of dizziness through his head. He groaned and leaned forward, pulling his legs up so he could rest his forehead against his knees. The familiar sound of a motor shifting gears, the smell of diesel, and the uneven rocking told him that he was on a boat.

He lifted his head when he heard someone's boots hitting the deck. Lifting a trembling hand, he wiped his face. He was surprised when he felt dampness on his cheeks that had nothing to do with the mist surrounding them.

"You look like shit. What'd you do? Slip or get drunk?" Hannibal Grumby said, holding out a hand.

Ross reached up and gripped Hannibal's beefy palm. He didn't care

much for Hannibal, but he needed some answers. He looked at Nathan
– Hannibal's cousin and the nicer, if dumber, of the two.

"He don't drink, Hannibal. At least not like us," Nathan answered
for him.

Ross ignored Nathan. "What day – what day is it? How long have I
been gone?" Ross demanded in a raspy, dry voice.

"Don't drink, my ass. You don't know what day it is?" Hannibal
demanded.

"Just tell me the fucking day, and how long I've been gone," Ross
growled, reaching up and fisting the front of Hannibal's plaid shirt.

"Damn, Ross, now I know you must've hit your head," Nathan
snorted.

"Shut up, Nathan," Ross and Hannibal both snapped.

"It's Thursday. You've been gone over a week," Hannibal answered.

"Yeah. The folks in town have a bet going. Some say that you took off
and was going to fake your own death to hide the disappearance of
more people while others was saying you'd moved to Hawaii on your
mom's inheritance. I said it didn't make no sense to take your boat.
That you was either out fishing or had taken the boat up to Seattle to
have some work done," Nathan rattled on.

"Shut up, Nathan," he and Hannibal both snapped again.

"I don't know why I work for either of you. Neither one of you treats
me right. I could go get a job…," Nathan's voice faded when he went
below deck on Hannibal's large trawler.

"Sit down," Hannibal ordered.

Ross ignored Hannibal and turned on his heel. He stumbled and
reached out for some of the rigging to steady himself. For a second, he
had a flashback of another rocking surface. Pain lanced through him
sharper than a surgeon's scalpel, and he took a deep breath.

"Where you going?" Hannibal demanded from behind him.

"To get a fucking drink," Ross replied.

"Finally, something that makes sense," Hannibal grumbled.

Ross ignored the heavy-footed thumping as Hannibal followed him down the short set of stairs to the galley. Ross pulled open one of the two storage cabinets mounted to the hull. The first was empty save for some fishing line, extra hooks, and a vinyl repair kit. He opened the second one. Inside was a plastic container with a few staples.

He pulled the container out and set it on the narrow counter. He turned around and scanned the galley. Everything looked familiar – yet, different. With a new perspective, he studied the obvious age and familiar wear and tear of the old fishing boat, and smiled a little at how neat and organized it was. Perhaps he'd inherited a little more from his mom than he'd given himself credit for.

"So, are you going to tell me what's going on?" Hannibal said, leaning against the opening.

Ross raised an eyebrow before he bent over and tugged a small ice chest out from under the table. He opened it and pulled out a couple of bottles of water. Closing the lid, he pushed the ice chest back under the table with his foot.

"Where have you been? I know you haven't been out here fishing. I've spent every day for the last week coming out here with Nathan. No man should ever have to do that, by the way. My cousin never shuts the fuck up. You weren't on your boat," Hannibal stated.

Ross lit the small single-burner propane stove and placed the kettle filled with the bottled water on top of the flame. He reached back into the cabinet and pulled out a tin cup. A minute later, he was pouring the steaming water over a tea bag that he had placed in the cup.

"Tea? You're drinking fucking tea?" Hannibal asked in a voice laced with disbelief.

Ross scowled at the man. "I didn't ask if you wanted any so don't act so outraged," he retorted.

"Nathan!" Hannibal yelled.

"I brought some beers for us, Hannibal," Nathan said behind him.

Hannibal took two beers from Nathan and walked over to the bench seat. He slid onto it and twisted off the beer bottle's cap. Ross's jaw hurt from clenching it, but he sighed and slid onto the seat across from Hannibal.

"Nathan, keep an eye on my boat," Hannibal ordered, not looking at his younger cousin.

"One of these days, Hannibal," Nathan muttered under his breath before he turned and stomped back up to the deck.

Ross watched the younger man and realized that he'd never treated Nathan much better. Shame and remorse washed through him. Nathan was a good guy. He was just trying to make ends meet, which was hard to do when you came from a shitty home life.

"You should be nicer to him," Ross said.

Hannibal paused for a second with his beer bottle halfway to his mouth. Then the man took a slow, deep drink before he lowered the bottle back to the table. Ross dipped the tea bag in his cup and waited.

"What happened to you?" Hannibal asked in a surprisingly soft voice.

Ross lifted his cup and blew on the tea. He took a sip before he lowered it back to the table and looked up at Hannibal with a troubled expression. Hannibal was the last man on the planet that he would ever think to confide in, yet – he was seriously contemplating it. He shook his head.

"Nothing," he replied instead.

"Don't give me that bullshit answer. What the fuck happened to you?" Hannibal said, leaning forward.

Ross raised an eyebrow at the other man's tone. "Why do you want to know?" he demanded.

Hannibal shook his head and wiped his mouth. Ross watched as the man's hand dropped to his lap and he sat back. They stared at each other for several minutes, each assessing the other.

"I've been coming out to your boat every day for the past week. Every day it was empty – until today," Hannibal replied.

Ross shrugged and looked down. "So? That doesn't mean anything," he replied.

"Don't fucking blow me off, Ross. Your Goddamn boat has been here – in this same place – for a week with no anchor out and no one on board. I know because I tried to tow it in and it wouldn't move, no matter how hard I tried to tow it," Hannibal bluntly informed him.

Ross looked back up at Hannibal, registering the anger and confusion in the man's eyes. He could understand that – after all, he'd been like that once. Angry at the world, fighting back, willing to hurt others before they could hurt you. He, Hannibal, and Nathan had grown up with the same type of fathers and the same type of poverty.

The difference was that Ross had learned from his father's mistakes, Hannibal was destined to repeat them, and Nathan would always be a victim of it. He lifted his drink and drained the contents. He needed someone to talk to, but that person wasn't Hannibal.

"Get off my boat, Hannibal," Ross said, rising from his seat.

"Where are you going?" Hannibal asked, sliding off the bench and rising to his feet.

"Back to the docks. I have a few things to take care of," Ross calmly stated.

Ross was surprised when Hannibal didn't argue with him. The big man quietly exited the galley. Ross walked across the deck, feeling more at ease with the familiar motion of the waves. He waited while Hannibal climbed back onto his boat.

"Answer me one question," Hannibal suddenly demanded, holding on to the gunwale of Ross's boat to keep his from floating away.

Ross stiffened. "What do you want to know?" he asked.

"Were you abducted by aliens?" Hannibal asked.

Ross blinked at the unexpected question. This was the last thing he had expected Hannibal to ask. He thought about it for a second before he answered.

"No, I wasn't abducted by aliens," he replied. He saw the look of disappointment wash across Hannibal's unexpectedly expressive face. He reached out and grabbed Hannibal's wrist when the other man released his boat. He gave Hannibal a grim smile. "But I was killed by one," he truthfully answered before he let go of Hannibal's wrist.

Ross saw the stunned expression that swept over Hannibal's face before he nodded his head and turned away. Climbing the ladder to the helm, he turned the key in the ignition. The twin-diesel engines roared to life. Pressing the throttle forward, he made a wide arc and headed back to the marina.

*I've got a Sea Witch to visit,* he thought with determination.

Two days later, Ross sat in the front seat of his pickup truck and pulled a comb through his damp hair. When he'd done what he could with his newly, professionally cut hair, he slid the comb back into the duffle bag on the seat next to him. He drummed the steering wheel while he debated how long he should wait.

He had been busy the last couple of days, putting his affairs in order. He just hoped that it wasn't all for naught. He had cleaned out the money in his accounts and changed it to a different type of asset – gold and jewels. He didn't know anything about currency or economics in a magical world. The only thing that might be of value were those two things.

Last night, he had visited Nathan. The younger man had been shocked and puzzled when he had asked if they could talk privately. He didn't tell Nathan anything about what had happened to him – or that he hoped he would be leaving soon.

What they had talked about was life – and dreams. Ross thought about his apology to Nathan for how he had treated him over the years. Nathan had stutteringly told him it was no big deal. Ross felt even more like a heel when Nathan told him about how he had met a girl a year ago and that she was expecting a baby. Nathan was working hard to earn some extra cash because he wanted to buy a house and settle down.

"I want to be the kind of dad I never had. I'm not ever going to yell and hit my wife or my kid. I want – I want to go to ballgames or dances. I want my kid to remember me with love, not as an abusive drunk or worse," Nathan had shared.

Nathan had broken the cycle and he'd known what he wanted long before Ross had realized what was important in life. Ross had known at that moment what he was going to do with his trawler and truck. He had found the truck and boat's title and signed them over to Nathan.

"You can use the trawler, or you can sell it and use the money for a down payment on a house. Fishing is a hard life. If I were you, I'd sell it and start fresh. Same thing goes for the truck," he had advised.

The stunned look on Nathan's face and the sudden tears in the other man's eyes had been all the thanks that Ross had needed. Ross had left the tavern feeling lighter in spirit. He had nothing left to keep him here. The one person that he had been surprised to see was the reporter. He had ducked out of sight when he saw her leaving the pub through the back patio. Dorothy had said the woman was staying at Mike Hallbrook's house.

"Everyone thought you might have killed her too when she disappeared a couple of days ago and her car was found at the State Park," Dorothy had said.

When he had asked what happened, Dorothy had shrugged and shook her head. "No one knows. She showed up again a few days later, walking along the beach. She was found by one of the park rangers. She claims she hit her head and has amnesia, but that doesn't explain how she got a letter from Mike Hallbrook stating that she can stay in his house here as long as she wants. If you ask me, something mighty fishy is going on around here, what with all the disappearances and then the 'oh, everything is just fine'," Dorothy grumbled.

Ross had quickly excused himself after that. He froze when he saw the flash of headlights coming up the drive. The SUV slowed as it pulled by him. He could see Kane Field's deep frown when the man recognized who he was.

He waited until the car had pulled up in front of the garage before he opened the door of his truck and slid out. He shut the door, slid his hands into the pockets of his dark brown leather jacket, and waited as the occupants of the car exited the vehicle. Kane slid out of the front passenger seat and turned to open the back door.

Ross stood straighter when Gabe Lightcloud walked around from the driver's side. He looked down to Gabe's hand when he saw the glint of metal in the glow of the headlights from his truck. He breathed a sigh of relief when he saw that Gabe was carrying a flashlight.

"What do you want?" Gabe demanded, walking over to stand in front of him.

"Gabe," Magna's soft, chiding voice called out from behind Gabe.

Ross looked over Gabe's shoulder before he returned his focus to Gabe's face. "I need to speak with Magna," he politely requested.

"No," Gabe immediately replied.

"Gabe, quit being a Neanderthal," Kane admonished.

Ross turned his attention to Magna when she walked over to thread her arm through Gabe's. She returned his steady gaze with a worried one. Her expression softened, and he wondered if she could sense his growing desperation.

"Come inside," she instructed, gently pulling Gabe to the side.

"Thank you," he replied.

They stepped up the walkway, unlocked and opened the door, and Ross followed them into the entryway.

"Jacket," Gabe gruffly said and pointed to the coat rack.

Ross shook his head. He bent over and scratched the two dogs that had greeted them at the door when they stepped inside. He hoped there wouldn't be any reason to take his jacket off.

"Damn it, Buck, you need to tell Wilson that chew toys don't mean destroy toys. These damn things are expensive," Gabe growled when he stepped on a squeaker that had been ripped out of a fluffy, mangled duck.

Ross chuckled and followed Kane and Magna through the kitchen to the living room while Gabe cleaned up Wilson's homecoming present. It was funny to see such a big, gruff guy playfully chiding the happy Husky. He hoped Gabe would be in a better mood when he rejoined them.

"I thought you had left. I heard in town that you hadn't been seen for the last week and that your boat was missing," Kane commented.

"I did leave – thanks to the magic shell that Magna gave me," he replied.

Ross could sense Magna studying him. He pulled his hands out of his pockets and sat down across from the couch she was sitting on. A shiver ran through him when she waved her hand and the fireplace came to life.

"Tell me what happened," she requested.

Ross opened his mouth and took a shuddering breath when a wave of pain at the memory of Gem's tortured cries suddenly hit him. Tears burned his eyes, and he looked down at his hands. He rubbed them together as he fought to regain control of his emotions.

"I died – but I'm still alive. I don't know how, but I think I know why," he began.

"Oh Ross, I never meant for you to be hurt," Magna murmured, sitting forward.

Ross looked up when Gabe entered. He held out a beer. Ross took the beer with a nod of gratitude.

"I have to go back. I love her, Magna. I have to go back," he said in a voice filled with emotion.

"Where do you need to go?" Magna gently inquired.

"It'd probably make more sense if I tell you what happened. I need to know – I need to know that I wasn't dreaming, that this – if – everything was real," he added in a low, urgent voice.

"Take your time," Kane said.

"This should be good. Do you want me to make some popcorn?" Gabe dryly added.

Ross chuckled and gave Gabe a rueful grin. "That may not be a half-bad idea," he said.

He leaned back and took a long swig of the cold beer. The stress and worry from the last two days eased, and he began to relax. He looked at Magna. Her curious but compassionate expression gave him hope that she would use her magic to help him.

"Her name is Gem Aurora LaBreeze. She is a princess from the Isle of the Elementals," he began.

"I turned her into stone," Magna added.

"To save her and her people," Ross said.

"Yes," Magna replied, a single tear coursing down her cheek.

"Thank you," he said.

Magna nodded and sniffed. "Please go on," she encouraged.

Over the next several hours, Ross shared everything – well, almost everything – that had happened. All three asked him questions. Magna's concern focused on the alien creature and her fear that it may not have been killed. Kane was interested in Ashure while Gabe wanted to know more about the traps and how he and Gem had escaped them.

"So there are two more alien creatures left," Magna said.

"Yes, at least, that is what they think," Ross replied.

Magna nodded and looked down at her hands. "The one that took over my body was a General. The others are lesser soldiers. They were dispensable in battle. They do not have the same power as a General, but that does not make them any less dangerous. In the right situation, with the right body, they can be just as deadly," she explained.

Kane and Gabe wrapped their arms around her, and Ross felt a pang of loss. He really understood now what it meant to love someone. This couldn't be the end for himself and Gem.

"What is it that you want from Magna?" Gabe asked.

Ross turned his attention to Magna. "I think you already know," he said.

"Yes," she replied, turning her hand over and showing him the glowing blue shell in the center of her palm.

# EPILOGUE

**Isle of the Elementals**

"Gem," Adrina greeted.

Gem looked up when she heard her name, then turned her face away from her mother's searching gaze. Her bottom lip trembled, and she closed her eyes to keep from crying. She knew she wasn't successful when she felt the tear coursing down her cheek.

"I'd like to be alone," she requested in a thick voice.

She should have known it was not likely to happen. Either her mother, her father, Nali, or one of the servants had practically been a constant companion over the last two days. She wanted to be alone so that she could grieve. She didn't understand how her heart could hurt when she felt like it had been ripped from her body.

"There is a celebration tonight," her mother said.

Gem looked at her mother and scowled. "A celebration? What for? I have no desire to celebrate," she replied in a sharp tone before she looked down at her hands in shame at taking her hurt out on her mother.

Her mother walked over and sat down on the bench beside her. She'd thought hiding in the maze would shield her from all of the worried stares. She had returned to the garden where everything had started. Yet even here, she could find no peace. The ghost of Samuel haunted her here, and the spirit of Ross haunted her outside of the maze.

A choked sob rose in her throat, and she buried her face in her hands. Her mother held her, and she snuggled closer. They remained that way while she cried, her mother softly singing an old song that she used to sing when Gem was a child.

*Softly do the roses grow,*
*They sing the song of love,*
*For in their soft red petals,*
*My sweet love's blood does flow.*

*Cry no more, my lady,*
*Cry no more, my love,*
*For on the moonlight's rays,*
*My love, he will always come.*

*On the sweet breeze, I will hear*
*The words of my love to me*
*Cry no more for me, my sweet Princess,*
*For my love for you still grows.*

*I will come to you, my love,*
*I will come to you, I swear,*
*For softly on the waves that rock*
*It will carry me home to you*

Gem's crying slowly eased with the gentle rocking and soothing ballad. She pulled the image of Ross close to her heart. Memories of their days together flowed through her mind – his crooked smile, the teasing light in his eyes, the touch of his fingers as he caressed her cheek, and the love reflected in the way he looked at her.

"It felt like I knew him forever, yet we had just met," Gem murmured against her mother's shoulder.

"When you find your soul mate, that is the way it feels. Your father and I have been together for hundreds of years – yet every day feels like we just met. I never tire of his smile or his touch. Your grandmother said that it is because our souls already know one another from a previous life," her mother explained.

"Will it always hurt this much?" Gem asked, her voice catching on a sob.

Her mother shook her head. "Not always, but sometimes. When it does, remembering the good times with him will help ease the pain. As long as he is in your heart, he is never gone. He will always be with you as long as you remember him," her mother said.

"What if I forget?" Gem asked, sitting back and holding her mother's hand in hers.

Her mother shook her head and gently cupped Gem's hand in hers. Gem frowned in confusion when her mother guided her hand down to her abdomen and firmly pressed it so that her palm lay flat against her belly.

"How can you forget when you carry his child?" her mother asked.

Gem frowned. "His child? How can... We only... It is too early to know," she faltered.

Adrina chuckled and shook her head. "I'm your mother, Gem. Your colors gave it away. The power of the Goddess's Gem is not only in you, but in your child. You carry in your womb a new future for the Elementals – one that will make us stronger. The Gem of Power is the Goddess's love. It has the power to heal our kingdom, our people, and you if you give it a chance. The power of love is the most powerful emotion in the universe. Though you unleashed it in grief, it saved our world," her mother explained as she caressed her face.

"But – it couldn't save Ross," she softly said.

"Didn't it?" her mother asked.

Gem rested her cheek against her mother's hand for a moment, afraid to think about what Adrina had just suggested. After all, if Ross was alive, where was he? She kept her hand protectively against her stomach. They both turned when they heard the sound of curses and dire threats coming from outside the wall.

"It would appear that a pirate has become lost in the maze," Adrina chuckled.

"I'll go help him," Gem murmured, rising to her feet.

She took a couple of steps before she stopped and turned around. Retracing her steps, she brushed a kiss across her mother's cheek. She moved her hand back to her stomach.

"Thank you," she whispered.

"I love you, Gem," her mother replied.

Gem nodded and hurried out of the garden. She didn't know if what her mother had said was true, but for the first time in two days, she had hope that she would survive. It wouldn't be easy, but as long as she held Ross in her heart, he would be with her.

Later that evening, Gem stood on the cliffs overlooking the lake. Far below, Nali's ship could be seen. Every once in a while, the Thunderbirds would raise their wings and the crackle and pop of the electricity they emitted could be heard along with the explosions of fireworks high in the sky.

Her people were celebrating being alive and safe. The sound of laughter and the squeals of young children running through the gardens warmed her heart a little. Yet, everything felt different. She felt different.

"The occasion is far too joyous to be so sad, my Lady," Ashure said from behind her.

Gem sighed and looked at Ashure with a raised eyebrow. "Are you leaving?" she asked.

Ashure nodded. "Yes. My ship has arrived," he explained.

She looked at him in surprise. "Surely there is nothing so pressing that it can't wait until morning. Besides, I thought you always enjoyed a party. There has to be at least one Elemental female who would be excited to share her celebration with you," she teased.

"Ah, yes, but there is only one that intrigues me enough to be tempted. Alas, her heart is already taken by a man from another world," he replied.

Pain rippled through her. She turned and looked back out at the lake, waiting for the pain to pass. One night – they'd only had one night together. She pressed her hand to her stomach and pushed the pain away.

*At least we had that,* she thought.

"I suspect that may not have been the best thing for you to say, Ashure," she responded in a strained voice.

"Perhaps, but…," he started to say.

She looked at him from under her eyelashes. "But?" she repeated.

He opened his jacket and reached inside. She curiously watched him pull out a mirror. He held it up and moodily stared at it.

"I have a magic mirror that shows what your heart desires the most," he said in a distracted voice.

She turned and faced him. "And what do you see when you look into it – jewels, gold, the finest liquor?" she asked.

He looked at her. "I see the woman who can fill the darkest part of my soul with light," he replied. He held the mirror out to her. "Is there something you would like to ask it before I leave?"

Gem stared at the mirror in his hand. Her heart pounded with fear and a small measure of hope. Dare she ask for something that she knew no longer existed? Her hand trembled when she reached for the mirror and took it from him.

"What – what do I say?" she asked.

"Oh, magical mirror, grant my wish, and tell it what you want the most from the bottom of your heart," Ashure said.

She nodded in understanding. She was thankful when he politely turned around and looked at the lake. She knew he was doing it to give her some privacy.

"Oh, magical mirror, grant my wish – where is the love of my life?" she whispered.

Gem couldn't contain her gasp of surprise. The mirror tilted in her hand. She almost dropped it when the swirling colors parted, and she saw Ross walking toward her. She held the mirror closer, devouring the image of him.

She was so focused on him that it took a few seconds for the background of fireworks and the silhouette of a palace to register. By the time it did, the image began to fade.

"No! How do I bring it back? I – Oh magical mirror, grant my wish—" her faltering voice suddenly faded as she looked up and saw Ross – Ross! – standing in front of her – in real life!

"Careful," Ashure exclaimed in an urgent tone.

He caught the mirror when it slipped from her suddenly numb fingers. Her eyes blurred for a moment, and she swayed. Firm, familiar hands grabbed her waist and steadied her.

Gem stared up into the soft, warm eyes of the man she'd thought she would never see again. She parted her lips on a hushed plea, and Ross captured them in a deep kiss that left her dizzy. He reluctantly pulled away and stared deep into her eyes.

"You're alive. Oh, Ross, you're alive," she whispered in a voice filled with disbelief. "But, I saw you die. "

"Yeah, well, I guess destiny – or this Golden Goddess of yours – had a different plan for me," he tenderly replied.

"Golden Goddess?" she whispered, remembering the figure she'd briefly seen reflected in the alien's eyes.

She shook her head and wrapped her arms around his neck. She softly sighed when she felt him tremble. He tightened his arms around her, and she reveled in the feeling that he would never let her go.

"I love you, Gem. I love you. I know it sounds crazy. I'm just a fisherman, or I was until I gave my boat away. I don't have a hell of a lot, but if this crazy, mixed-up magical world accepts gold and a few jewels, then I might have enough to get us started. I'm pretty handy, and I've been told I have a cute ass. I swear if you give me a chance...." He stopped talking when she placed her fingers on his lips.

"I love you, Ross, King of Yachats – or at least King of the fishing boat before you gave it away. I love you for you – and your cute ass," she murmured.

Gem laughed when Ross suddenly picked her up and swung her around in a circle. She leaned forward and captured his lips. He slowly placed her feet on the ground, but his arms never left her.

"You have to tell me what happened after – well, after shit hit the fan," he said.

Gem slid her hand from his shoulder down to her stomach. "I have a lot to tell you," she acknowledged. "But first, I would like to introduce you to my parents. "

Ross tightened his grip on the handle of his duffle bag. Everything he owned was inside it. The only reassuring thing about the bag was the weight – it was heavy.

As they walked across the park, he felt a little overwhelmed by the number of residents who turned and stared at him. He gripped Gem's hand tighter when several children ran up to them. He expected them to greet Gem with adoration, not him.

"Would you mind telling me what the hell is going on?" he muttered when a young girl held out a bouquet of flowers to him. "Ah, thanks. They are very pretty. "

The girl giggled and ran back to her parents. He shook his head and warily looked at the blooms. He wanted to make sure that they weren't going to grab him, eat him, or do some other weird thing like singing or dancing.

"You are a legend among our people. Ashure has spent the last two days regaling the kingdom with your heroic deeds – how you carried all of us from certain death, fought a monstrous Kraken that made the great King of the Sea Serpent tremble in fear, survived the magnificent Yeti of the Canyon, were swallowed by the carnivorous Butterwort plant, and even saved his beloved hat from the Field of Fire," she explained.

He stopped and looked at her. "Wait a minute, how did Ashure know about – oh yeah, you told him when we were sharing stories," he said with a shake of his head.

"Gem, is it true? Is your…?"

They both turned and looked at an older couple who hurried toward them – or should he say floated toward them. He swallowed and set his bag on the ground. Gem held her hands out to them.

"Mother, Father, we were coming to see you," she said.

Ross stood as straight as he could when the man stopped and looked him over. He looked down at the bouquet when he felt one of the flower's fragile stems bend. He cleared his throat and looked up. This was a first for him. He had never met a woman's parents before. He was the kind of guy that most girls would avoid introducing to their parents.

"You must be Ross," the man said.

"Yes, sir. Ross Galloway. I'm from… a long way from here," he awkwardly greeted.

Unsure of what the protocol was for meeting royalty, he held out the flowers to Gem's mother who was standing silently by her husband. She smiled at him before taking them with a murmur of thanks. He nodded to them both before taking a step back. He looked down when Gem threaded her arm through his.

"I am Ruger and this is my wife, Adrina. We would like to welcome you to our home," Ruger greeted.

Adrina stepped forward and kissed both of his cheeks. She squeezed his arms. Ross shot Gem an uncertain look when he saw the tears glittering in her mother's eyes.

"We owe you a great debt for all you have done for our people and our daughter," Adrina said before she laughed. "Thank you for the flowers. "

"Let us return to the palace. Tonight, there is truly a reason to celebrate!" Ruger declared.

Ross picked up his bag. He looked down at Gem and smiled when she threaded her fingers through his. He absently answered the King and the Queen's questions as they walked, but his mind was on the woman holding his hand and the magic all around him.

*This is way better than living on the beach in Hawaii,* he thought as the sky lit up with a brilliant display of fireworks.

It was nearly two in the morning before the festivities quieted down. Gem had murmured an excuse for them to depart the main banquet area half an hour before, and since then they had silently walked along the corridors to Gem's living quarters. He held her hand as they walked.

"I can't stop touching you," he said.

Gem smiled. "Have you heard me complain?" she asked.

He chuckled and shook his head. "It's hard to believe that all of this was right in front of us the whole time, just hidden," he commented.

"The Elders' spell froze everything and hid it so that the alien could not harm them," she said with a nod.

"Gem – are you sure about this – about me?" Ross suddenly asked.

She paused outside a set of double doors. His heart pounded in his chest when she smiled at him, opened one of the doors, and pulled him inside. He had no sooner closed the door than she was in his arms kissing him.

He groaned when she pushed his jacket from his shoulders. He grasped the ties on the back of her sky blue tunic and loosened the ribbon, pushing the material off her shoulders.

"I want to make love to you in a bed this time. I want to explore every inch of you," he murmured between kisses.

"Down… the hall to the right," she breathlessly instructed.

They left a line of clothing from her apartment door to the bedroom. By the time they reached her bed, there were no more barriers between them. Ross fell back across the bed, pulling Gem with him. He gazed up at her.

"I love you, Princess. The first time I saw you, I thought you were the most beautiful woman I had ever seen," he murmured, lifting his hand and caressing her cheek.

"When you touched me, you asked me about the colors. You tried to brush them away. Do you remember that?" she asked.

"Yeah, I remember. I see it every time you are near me. It feels natural –
like it should be there," he reflected.

She leaned down over him until her lips were a breath away from his
before she answered. "It is the essence that binds us together. You are
my other half, Ross. You are my soulmate," she explained.

"I can handle that. Mine to love, Princess. Mine to protect," he said.

"Mine to save your ass," she countered with a smile.

Ross buried his hands in her hair, pulled her down, and kissed her. A
shudder ran through him when she began rubbing against him. He
loved the feel of her breasts against his hairy chest. Her legs were
parted as she straddled him, and his cock brushed back and forth
against the soft curls covering her mound.

He slid his hands down her arms to her waist. Without breaking their
kiss, he gently rolled her over until he was on top. He reached down
between her legs, slid one finger through the curls, and began to stroke
her. Her soft moan filled the air, and she rocked her hips.

"Ross," she breathed.

Ross pulled away and kissed her shoulder. He pressed against her
while she rocked, and he continued exploring her body with his
mouth. He paused at her taut nipples. They were too succulent to
resist.

He rolled the tip of his tongue over her nipple, moved his head in a
circular motion, and continued to tease her until she reached up and
threaded her hands through his hair. She thrust her breast against his
mouth, and he sucked deeply on the sensitive pebble.

"More, oh yes, more, Ross," she begged.

He released her nipple and did the same to the other. She raised her
restless legs as an invitation to enter her. He knew that he wouldn't last
long once they came together. He could already feel pre-cum beading
on the head of his cock.

Sliding down her body, he gripped her thighs and pulled her legs open. Her moan of desire told him that this was probably something that she really enjoyed. He wickedly smiled in delight. He was going to be merciless.

Ross gently parted her labia and exposed Gem's clit to his view. Bending forward, he blew a warm breath over the sensitive nub before he buried his face against her. Her loud cry drove him on. He tightened his hold on her thighs when she began to thrash in an attempt to escape the intense pleasure he was creating with his tongue and teeth. He continued to caress the sensitive nub of her womanhood until he felt her shaking with uncontrollable need.

She arched backward and stiffened when he drove her over the precipice. She came hard, her gasping breaths mixed with her sobs, and she twisted her fingers in the fabric of the bedspread. The warm liquid of her orgasm washed over his tongue.

He timed it perfectly, waiting until she was over the most intense part of her orgasm but not too sensitive to come again. Rising up over her, he grabbed his throbbing cock and entered her pulsing depths. Gritting his teeth, he pushed deeper.

She released the covers and grabbed his forearms when he buried himself as deep as he could. He gave her a few seconds to adjust before he began moving. She was tight. The heat and moisture from her orgasm wrapped around his cock, coating it.

Sweat beaded on his brow as he fought to maintain control. He wanted to bring her to another release, but he wasn't sure he could hold out. He pumped his hips faster and deeper until it felt like he was touching her womb.

"Oh, Goddess!" she gasped, digging her fingers into his arms as she came again.

The clenching muscles from her orgasm gripped his engorged cock, resisting his attempts to pull out, and it drove him over the edge. He threw his head back, and a hoarse, guttural cry ripped from his throat as he came. The muscles in his neck and shoulders bulged at the intense pleasure igniting his blood, and his seed pulsed deep inside her.

Ross's arms trembled. His breathing was harsh, a reflection of the intensity of his release. He carefully lowered himself over Gem and slid his arms under her. Pressing his lips against her damp shoulder, he closed his eyes and embraced the feelings coursing through his body. His cock continued to react to her pulsing core.

A silent groan swept through his mind when he realized something else. He was buried balls deep inside her, had just had the most amazing orgasm, and he wasn't wearing any protection, again. He didn't know if Gem was on some kind of magical birth control, but if she wasn't, then he needed to reassure her that he was there for whatever happened. He was there for the long term.

"Ross," she started to say.

"Gem," he said at the same time.

"You first," she replied, kissing his shoulder.

He leaned up on his elbows and looked down into her eyes. He wanted her to know that he was serious – that they were together forever as far as he was concerned.

"I... We didn't use any type of contraceptive – this time or the last. I don't know if you are on anything," he said.

"I'm not," she softly replied.

"I want you to know that if anything happens – if you – if we – if there is a baby.... I want you to know that I'll be there, every step of the way. I love you and I'll love our baby," he promised.

Tears filled her eyes, and she chuckled. She wrapped her arms around his neck and pulled him down. He held her tightly, feeling her shake as she cried. Hell if he didn't make a mess of things even when he was trying to do the right thing.

"Ross," she sniffed.

"Yes, love," he murmured, kissing her neck.

"I'm glad you feel that way because you are going to be a wonderful husband and father," she whispered.

It took a second for her meaning to sink in. It was only when she took one of his hands and guided it to her stomach that he realized what she meant. He rolled off of her and sat up. He looked down at their joined hands as they covered her stomach before he gazed at her flushed, tear-stained face.

"Yes – I will be," he promised, bending over and capturing her lips.

To Be Continued... **A Pirate's Wish**
Seven Kingdoms Tale 7

When the magic mirror shows his true heart's desire, Ashure Waves, the King of the Pirates, will do anything to find her – including traveling to another world. What Ashure never expects is that the human woman – Investigative Reporter, Tonya Maitland – can see the shadows hidden in his soul. Can a pirate capture the heart of a woman who has a few secrets of her own?

Find the full book at your favorite distributor with the link below!
books2read.com/apirateswish

# HISTORY OF THE SEVEN KINGDOMS

## The Legend

It is believed the realm of the Seven Kingdoms was created after a fight between the Goddess and her mate. She divided the world into two realms, and now she rules over one while her mate rules over the other.

The Goddess first created the elements of earth, wind, fire, water, and sky. Then she created the Elementals to control these fundamental forces and the Isle of the Elementals to be their home and stronghold, for she was not nearly done creating the people of this world. To her first race, the Goddess gave the Gem of Power, a physical representation of creation itself.

The Dragons were next, born of her fiery love for all her creatures. She gifted them the Dragon's Heart, a red diamond containing a piece of her heart. It holds the dual essence of the dragons that allows them to shift.

Then the Sea People were created, and they were given the Eyes of the Sea Serpent, so that a single ruler could hold dominion over the realm's entire ocean.

This was how the people of this world were created, and one by one, each was given a powerful gift. The Orb of Eternal Light was given to Isle of Magic. The Giants were given the Tree of Life. The Cauldron of Spirits was given to the Pirates. The Monsters were given the Goddess' Mirror.

Each gift contains a piece of the Goddess. She gave so much of herself to the realm of the Seven Kingdoms that whoever controls all the gifts could then control the Goddess, and if one piece were to be destroyed, it would be a mortal wound to the Goddess, which it would mean the death of their world.

So says the legend: the Kingdoms will continue in peace and harmony as long as the Goddess' gifts are never used against each other. Should they ever do so, the Seven Kingdoms will cease to exist.

## The Seven Kingdoms Details
*Story Bible Contributions by Christel*

### Isle of the Elementals – created first
*King Ruger and Queen Adrina*
• Can control earth, wind, fire, water, and sky. Their power diminishes slightly when they are off their isle.
• Goddess' Gift: The Gem of Power.

### Isle of the Dragons – created second
*King Drago*
• Controls the dragons.
• Goddess' Gift: Dragon's Heart.

### Isle of the Sea Serpent – created third
*King Orion*
• Can control the Oceans and Sea Creatures.
• Goddess' Gift: Eyes of the Sea Serpent.

### Isle of Magic – created fourth
*King Oray and Queen Magika*

- Their magic is extremely powerful but diminishes slightly when they are off their island.
- Goddess' Gift: The Orb of Eternal Light.

**Isle of the Monsters** – created fifth for those too dangerous or rare to stay on the other Isles
*Empress Nali* can see the future.
- Goddess' Gift: The Goddess' Mirror.

**Isle of the Giants** – created sixth
*King Koorgan*
- Giants can grow to massive sizes when threatened – but only if they are off their isle.
- Goddess' Gift: The Tree of Life.

**Isle of the Pirates** – created last for outcasts from the other Isles
*The Pirate King Ashure Waves, Keeper of Lost Souls*
- Collectors of all things fine. Fierce and smart, pirates roam the Isles trading, bargaining, and occasionally helping themselves to items of interest.
- Goddess' Gift: The Cauldron of Spirits.

**Notable Quotes**
"It is how we deal with what we are given that defines who we are and who we are to become."

~King Ashure Waves~

# ADDITIONAL BOOKS

If you loved this story by me (S.E. Smith) please leave a review! You can discover additional books at: http://sesmithfl.com and http://sesmithya.com or find your favorite way to keep in touch here: https://sesmithfl.com/contact-me/ Be sure to sign up for my newsletter to hear about new releases!

**Recommended Reading Order Lists:**

http://sesmithfl.com/reading-list-by-events/

http://sesmithfl.com/reading-list-by-series/

**The Series**

**Science Fiction / Romance**

Dragon Lords of Valdier Series

*It all started with a king who crashed on Earth, desperately hurt. He inadvertently discovered a species that would save his own.*

Curizan Warrior Series

*The Curizans have a secret, kept even from their closest allies, but even they are not immune to the draw of a little known species from an isolated planet called Earth.*

Marastin Dow Warriors Series

*The Marastin Dow are reviled and feared for their ruthlessness, but not all want to live a life of murder. Some wait for just the right time to escape....*

Sarafin Warriors Series

*A hilariously ridiculous human family who happen to be quite formidable... and a secret hidden on Earth. The origin of the Sarafin species is more than it seems. Those cat-shifting aliens won't know what hit them!*

Dragonlings of Valdier Novellas

*The Valdier, Sarafin, and Curizan Lords had children who just cannot stop getting into trouble! There is nothing as cute or funny as magical, shapeshifting kids, and nothing as heartwarming as family.*

## Cosmos' Gateway Series

*Cosmos created a portal between his lab and the warriors of Prime. Discover new worlds, new species, and outrageous adventures as secrets are unravelled and bridges are crossed.*

## The Alliance Series

*When Earth received its first visitors from space, the planet was thrown into a panicked chaos. The Trivators came to bring Earth into the Alliance of Star Systems, but now they must take control to prevent the humans from destroying themselves. No one was prepared for how the humans will affect the Trivators, though, starting with a family of three sisters….*

## Lords of Kassis Series

*It began with a random abduction and a stowaway, and yet, somehow, the Kassisans knew the humans were coming long before now. The fate of more than one world hangs in the balance, and time is not always linear….*

## Zion Warriors Series

*Time travel, epic heroics, and love beyond measure. Sci-fi adventures with heart and soul, laughter, and awe-inspiring discovery…*

## **Paranormal / Fantasy / Romance**

## Magic, New Mexico Series

*Within New Mexico is a small town named Magic, an… unusual town, to say the least. With no beginning and no end, spanning genres, authors, and universes, hilarity and drama combine to keep you on the edge of your seat!*

## Spirit Pass Series

*There is a physical connection between two times. Follow the stories of those who travel back and forth. These westerns are as wild as they come!*

## Second Chance Series

*Stand-alone worlds featuring a woman who remembers her own death. Fiery and mysterious, these books will steal your heart.*

## More Than Human Series

*Long ago there was a war on Earth between shifters and humans. Humans lost, and today they know they will become extinct if something is not done....*

## The Fairy Tale Series

*A twist on your favorite fairy tales!*

## A Seven Kingdoms Tale

*Long ago, a strange entity came to the Seven Kingdoms to conquer and feed on their life force. It found a host, and she battled it within her body for centuries while destruction and devastation surrounded her. Our story begins when the end is near, and a portal is opened....*

## Epic Science Fiction / Action Adventure

### Project Gliese 581G Series

*An international team leave Earth to investigate a mysterious object in our solar system that was clearly made by someone, someone who isn't from Earth. Discover new worlds and conflicts in a sci-fi adventure sure to become your favorite!*

## New Adult / Young Adult

### Breaking Free Series

*A journey that will challenge everything she has ever believed about herself as danger reveals itself in sudden, heart-stopping moments.*

### The Dust Series

*Fragments of a comet hit Earth, and Dust wakes to discover the world as he knew it is gone. It isn't the only thing that has changed, though, so has Dust...*

# ABOUT THE AUTHOR

S. E. Smith is a *New York Times, USA TODAY, International, and Award-Winning* Bestselling author of science fiction, romance, fantasy, paranormal, and contemporary works for adults, young adults, and children. She enjoys writing a wide variety of genres that pull her readers into worlds that take them away.

Printed in Great Britain
by Amazon